What others have said about
The 31st of February:

"Nobody has painted a more gruesome picture
of the advertising business since Dorothy Sayers
. . . and very few people have written a more
entertaining or dramatic mystery story."
—*New Yorker*

"Sharpened by satire, this is cold, precise and
pitiless."   —*Kirkus*

"English advertising men and women are por-
trayed in a tale that suavely blends subtle wit,
bitterness and abject torment."
—*Chicago Sunday Tribune*

JULIAN SYMONS
THE 31st OF FEBRUARY

Carroll & Graf Publishers, Inc.
New York

To Kathleen

Copyright © 1950 by Julian Gustave Symons
Copyright © renewed 1978 by Julian Gustave Symons

Reprinted by arrangement with Harper & Row Publishers, Inc.

First Carroll & Graf edition 1987

Carroll & Graf Publishers, Inc.
260 Fifth Avenue
New York, NY 10001

ISBN: 0-88184-317-2

Manufactured in the United States of America

THE 4th OF FEBRUARY

On Monday, February the fourth, in one of the years following the second of our great wars, the wife of a man named Anderson died. Her life ended at the comparatively early age of twenty-eight; and the circumstances of her death, as recounted at the inquest, were curious without being remarkable. She had been preparing dinner in their flat when she suggested (her husband told the coroner) that they should drink a bottle of wine with the meal. They debated which wine they should drink with the fillets of sole she was preparing, and decided on a bottle of Chablis. The Andersons kept their modest stock of wine in a cellar below their ground-floor flat; and Mrs. Anderson had left the sitting room, where her husband was reading the evening paper, to go down and fetch the bottle. He sat reading for a few minutes, until it occurred to him that his wife was a long time in the cellar. He got up (Anderson told the coroner), went to the head of the cellar stairs and found, to his surprise, that although the outside switch which gave illumination to the dark twisting stairway was switched on, the cellar was in darkness. He turned the switch on and off, as a man will do in such a case, but no light appeared. (It was found afterward that the fuse had blown.) He called his wife, but there was no answer. Anderson, now a little alarmed, went back to the sitting room for a box of matches, and with their aid groped his way down the steep, narrow stairs. At the bottom he found his wife, dead. She was, in fact, quite decisively dead, for she had sustained a fractured skull and a broken neck. Anderson made sure that there was no hope of her revival, and then went upstairs and telephoned doctor and police. He made a favourable impression at the inquest by giving this evidence in a composed manner, but with a subdued voice.

Why did Mrs. Anderson fall? A box of matches lay near her body, so that when going down the stairs, she had presumably, like her husband, the benefit of their light. Perhaps her match

5

had blown out and she had not troubled to strike another; perhaps she had slipped on one of the steps, which was very uneven. One conjecture seemed as idle as another, after the event. The only awkward question that Anderson was asked came from a little juryman, wearing a stiff collar and a made-up bow tie. "Whose suggestion was it that you should drink this bottle of Shablees?" the juryman asked.

"My wife's," Anderson said in a low voice.

"And she made it while she was cooking supper?"

"Yes."

"And then—while *she* was doing the cooking—*she* went down to the cellar to get the Shablees?"

"Yes."

The little juryman cocked an eye up to the ceiling. "Did she ask you p'raps to keep an eye on things while she was gone?"

"No."

Tugging at his stiff collar, the juryman pounced. "Why didn't *you* go down to the cellar, if she was busy with the supper?"

The look of absent-minded resignation on Anderson's face did not change. "My wife always liked to choose herself the particular bottle of wine we drank. It was one of—it was something she liked doing."

The little juryman cast a look of triumph round the court and sat down. The coroner expressed sympathy with Anderson. The verdict was "Accidental death."

After the funeral, Anderson went back to his job as an advertising executive. During the following weeks the quality of his work, and his ability to concentrate, were poor; but that was not surprising, since they had been poor for some time before his wife's death.

THE 25th OF FEBRUARY

At a quarter to ten on Monday morning a small regiment of black Homburg hats marched down Bezyl Street. Beneath the hats advertising men were to be found, respectably overcoated, equipped with briefcases, wearing highly polished shoes: the younger faces among them alert, with pushing doglike noses, the maturer ones lined and yellow or red and sagging like overripe tomatoes. These older faces wore, beneath their outward cynicisim or bursting good humour, a look like that of men hurrying for a train. Then the hats shot into offices, right and left, and in five minutes Bezyl Street was clear of them.

One of the hats, concealing a face that had graduated from dogginess to a lined and yellow maturity, turned into a corner building. Above the first floor of this building was a sign that ran round the corner into Vale Street and said VINCENT ADVERTISING VINCENT ADVERTISING VINCENT ADVERTISING VINCENT ADVERTISING. The word VINCENT was on the corner, so that if approached from Vale Street the sign read ADVERTISING VINCENT ADVERTISING VINCENT ADVERTISING. The Homburg hat tilted upward, looked at the sign and above it at the watery grey February sky, and disappeared inside the building.

The swing doors closed with a faint hiss. In the reception hall the air was warm and slightly sweet. A body as soft as a cushion moved behind the reception desk.

" A cold morning, Mr. Anderson.

" But seasonable, Miss Detranter."

Framed advertisements reviving the glories of past campaigns lined the corridor. Anderson walked slowly between them, came to a small square landing with three doors set into it, turned right down another corridor and opened a door. Within it were the apparatus of a life—kneehole desk, revolving chair, hatstand, oak cupboard, green carpet. He took off his dark overcoat and put it on a hanger, hung above it his black

7

Homburg hat and sat down in the revolving chair. The watch on his wrist said eleven minutes to ten.

A typewritten note was propped against his desk calendar. It said: " 9:20 Mr. Bagseed rang. Please ring him back. J.L." underneath it was another typewritten note: " VV has called a conference at 10:30. He would like you to be there. J.L." He turned the pieces of paper face downward, and looked at the morning's mail. A letter from Artifex Products about next year's advertising for Quickies, the lightening pick-me-up; some proofs of new advertisement for Crunchy-Munch, the tasty chocolate-covered mixture of toffee and biscuit. He picked up one of the telephones and said: " Mr. Bagseed of Kiddy Modes, please."

The switchboard girl's name was Miss Vine, and she had a clinging voice. " Mr. Bagseed's ringing you, Mr. Anderson. He's on the line now."

" Put him on."

Bagseed came on, as always, with a rush, as though he had been talking for some time and was taking up a point made in the middle of a conversation. " I say, you know, this won't do, Mr. Anderson; we can't let this appear."

" What won't do, Mr. Bagseed?"

" I've been on to you once already." The voice was nasal, querulous, accusing. " We must stop this advertisement at once; it just won't do."

" Which advertisement, Mr. Bagseed?"

Impatiently the voice said: " Why, the one for tomorrow's *Gazette*. Just look at it yourself. Are you with me, Mr. Anderson? Are you there? Have you got a proof of the advertisement there? Are you with me?"

He held the telephone between left ear and shoulder and flicked over the contents of a folder marked *Kiddy Modes Proofs*. He stopped at an advertisement showing a little girl wearing a Kiddy Modes frock and looking rather anxiously up at her mother.

" I'm with you, Mr. Bagseed."

" Well." The voice laughed nasally. " Do you know what Mr. Arthur said when he saw the proof this morning? He said —I can't repeat his exact words, because they're not polite—

8

but the gist was that he said the little girl looks as if she's asking to go to stool."

" But Mr Bagseed——" He picked up a pencil and began to draw on his blotter.

" Mr. Arthur asked if we were trying to make Kiddy Modes a laughingstock. I said of course not; I said it's only if you look at it in a certain way. But he said—" Anderson put the telephone down on the desk and drew a man's head with a wide-open mouth. Occasionally words came out from the receiver: " But I said—but he said—and I had to admit——"

The pencil point snapped. Anderson threw it across the room, picked up the receiver again and spoke in a deliberately gentle voice.

- " This advertisement has already been approved by you, Mr. Bagseed, as Kiddy Modes' advertising manager. Isn't that so? And we agreed then that the drawing was excellent? Isn't that so?" The door opened and a face followed a pipe round the opening. " Just to keep the record straight," Anderson said amiably.

The nasal voice changed to a whine. " I know, I know. The fact is sometimes Mr. Arthur's simply—unpredictable. It makes life difficult."

" It makes life difficult." Anderson raised a hand in greeting, pointed to the telephone and turned down the corners of his mouth. The newcomer sat in the visitors' chair, placed one leg over another, and looked at his beautifully polished black shoe. " But now that we've got it straight, let's see what we can do to help you. I've got two advertisements that we can substitute —the one with the teddy bear and the one with the doll's pram. The paper won't be pleased, but to hell with the paper. Which do you want? The teddy bear?"

Whining apologetically, the voice said: " The teddy bear will be fine. You can't imagine, Mr. Anderson, what a weight that is off my mind. You've no idea——"

" Not a bit, Mr. Bagseed. I'll make that substitution right away. 'Bye." Anderson dialled a number on the house telephone. " Production. This is Anderson. Kiddy Modes. Scrap B18 for the *Gazette* tomorrow and give them E21 instead." There were protesting noises. " Yes, I know it's late. Complain, hell—let them complain. Who pays for the bloody advertisement anyway?" He put down the house telephone and sighed.

"Swear words so early on a Monday morning," said the man with the pipe. He was a big man with a square face, in his early forties, who looked both friendly and dependable. His name was Reverton, and he was one of the three directors of Vincent Advertising, who were housed in the three rooms facing the square landing. "What's the matter with the Bagwash?"

Anderson mimicked the nasal voice. "Mr. Arthur's looked at one of our advertisements and Mr. Arthur wants it changed."

Reverton puffed at the pipe. "We could do without that account. Can't have important executives getting hot under the collar over penny numbers. What's it worth—thirty thousand a year?"

"Twenty-five."

"They get more than that in service." He looked reflectively at his black shoe. "How's it going? Getting you down at all?"

"No. Why?" Anderson found it difficult to meet Reverton's straight, inquiring gaze, and stared at the desk. But there was something wrong with the desk, although he could not have said just what, and his gaze shifted to the broken-pointed pencil lying on the carpet. He saw that Reverton was also looking curiously at the pencil, while his square nailed fingers tamped down tobacco in the pipe. Reverton picked up the pencil and put it on the desk. The match flame flickered above his pipe.

"The best thing to take a chap's mind off worry is work. Like to handle a new account? Something big?"

Anderson put both arms on the desk and stared keenly at the wall. "Try me."

"This is really something, Andy. I wanted you to have it. I told VV as much."

After keenness, gratitude. "That's damned nice of you, Rev."

"Nonsense. We've all got our plates full. Besides, it's just up your street." Anderson's eyes followed blue smoke on its way up to the ceiling. "Appeal to your sense of humour, too."

"Sense of humour?"

"It's something rather—" puff puff went the pipe —" special. VV's absolutely sold on it. You know the way he gets. That's what the conference is all about." Reverton rose, a square head and thick neck running into a stiff white collar, belching smoke like an engine. "Thought I'd put you in the picture."

"And you are sold on it?"

Reverton paused at the door and grinned, man to man, not director to executive. "Not necessary. If VV's sold on it we're all sold on it." The door closed. His steps faded along the corridor.

What was wrong with the desk? Blotter, letters, engagement pad, calendar, he thought, calendar. The calendar was made of brass, and you turned the small and inconvenient knobs at the back of it to alter the day of the week, the date, and the month. Anderson stared at the calendar and then looked at his morning paper. The paper said Monday, February 25, 1949. The top slot in the calendar said Monday, the slot to the right said February. The slot to the left said 4. It was simple enough.

The calendar was showing a wrong date. But Monday, February 4, was a very special wrong date. It was the date on which Anderson's wife had died.

The house telephone rang. A plummy voice said: "This is Mr. Pile. Can you—h'm—spare me a few minutes?"

"Right away, Mr. Pile." Mr. Pile was another director.

He sat staring at the calendar, then picked it up and turned the knob so that it showed a correct date. Then he got up and walked further down the corridor, away from the directors' offices, to a large room where half a dozen girls sat in front of typewriters. He stopped before one of them. Her name was Jean Lightley, and she was Anderson's secretary. She was a plain girl of about nineteen, who wore horn-rimmed spectacles and had a great fund of embarrassment. She said with a slight gasp: "Oh, Mr. Anderson, did you get the messages?"

"Yes, thanks." He said casually: "Jean, did you change my calendar this morning?"

"Why, I always do, Mr. Anderson."

"And what's the date today?"

"Today, Mr. Anderson?" She gasped again. "Monday the twenty-fifth."

"Quite sure that's what you changed it to this morning?" She nodded, beyond speech, and he turned away, out of the room and back along the corridor to the square landing where the three doors bore the names of the three directors. Anderson knocked on the door which said in gold letters L . E . G . PILE and opened it without waiting for a reply. He said "Good morning" to a small man in his early sixties who sat behind an enormous desk.

Mr. Pile wore a plain dark gray suit of an old-fashioned cut, a decorous striped tie and rimless pince-nez. He was looking at some papers and said "Good morning" without raising his head. Anderson remained standing in front of the desk. In Reverton's room he would have sat down without being asked. In Vincent's the chairs would have been covered with magazines, which Vincent would have thrown on the floor. But Pile was one of the elder statesmen of advertising, a man who believed in emphasizing social and administrative distinctions. However important an executive might be, he was less important than a director. In Mr. Pile's room an executive stood up until he was told to sit down, and it was perhaps thirty seconds before Mr. Pile looked up from his extensive study of the papers on his desk and said in a surprised tone: "Sit down, Anderson." Then Anderson sat down. Mr. Pile stared at him, a little wizened old man with small, hard eyes behind the rimless pince-nez. Below the hard shell of his exterior was a layer of soft, warm shyness and embarrassment. And below the shyness, Anderson guessed, was solid rock. Now he seemed to have difficulty in forming his words.

"Did you—have a pleasant week end, Anderson?"

"Quite, thank you."

"Did you—spend any time in the garden?"

"My flat is in town," Anderson said. He had conducted this conversation many times, in half a dozen variations. Which would it be this time, he wondered—the Beauty of Getting Away from It All or Town Mouse and Country Mouse? As Pile talked behind the immense desk in the sombre room the electric desk lamp flashed ever so often upon his rimless spectacles, so that the eyes behind them were almost invisible.

". . . so that in some ways," he was saying, "the country cousin, ignorant and foolish as he may be in the way of the world, has an advantage over the—ah—more sophisticated town mouse. But I mustn't push my little joke too far. All we advertising men are town mice, are we not?" Anderson covertly looked at his watch. "Are you an admirer of the immortal Walt? I refer," Mr. Pile said with a slight cough, "to Disney, not Whitman."

Wasn't this preamble more than usually lengthy? Was there a slight uneasiness behind the pince-nez? "I admire the early films very much," Anderson said, and added: "I'm due for a conference with Mr. Vincent in a few minutes."

Mr. Pile regarded him, apparently sightlessly. "You know of—ah—Sir Malcolm Buntz?" Anderson nodded. Sir Malcolm Buntz was a director of South Eastern Laboratories, one of the firm's largest accounts. "Sir Malcolm has a nephew who contemplates—" Mr. Pile coughed—"a career in advertising." Anderson said nothing. "He is, I am sure, an amiable young man, but amiability is not, as I remarked to Sir Malcolm, the sole, or perhaps the chief, requisite for a successful career in advertising. Sir Malcolm, however, has been insistent." He sighed to indicate the degree of Sir Malcolm's insistence. "And it is difficult to refuse him. In short, the young man is coming here to serve a brief apprenticeship. I have agreed with Mr. Vincent and Mr. Reverton that he shall begin it under your watchful eye in the Copy Department."

"We're very busy."

"So much the better. It will be a baptism of—ah—fire for him. Let me have a report on him, and do not," Mr. Pile smiled with wintry shyness, "spare Sir Malcolm's feelings."

"When does he begin?"

"He begins this—ah—morning," Mr. Pile said. Light shone on his pince-nez. "His name is Greatorex."

2

Reverton and Anderson sat in armchairs in VV's room. Wyvern, head of the Art Department, a thin dyspeptic man who wore a sports jacket and dirty gray trousers, sat staring out of the window into the street. The time was twenty to eleven. Wyvern said suddenly: "Here he is."

There was a commotion outside, and then a little man rushed into the room. "Boys, boys, I'm sorry," he said. "But wait a minute. This'll kill you. Just wait a minute, that's all I ask." He flung on to the floor a briefcase stuffed with magazines and papers, whisked off hat scarf and overcoat, and darted out of the room again. There was the sound of a lavatory flushing, and then he was back. "Well," he said. "Well. What's all this on my desk? Books, magazines, papers, nothing but junk." He threw a handful of art magazines to the floor and beamed round at them. His hair stood on end and his thick eyebrows stuck out. "I suppose Rev's told you two boys what this is all about?"

Placidly puffing at his pipe, Reverton said: "Only hints, VV. I thought you'd like to explain."

"Well," said VV, delighted. He uttered an indistinct exclamation, and darted at a bell push. A girl appeared. VV smacked his hand on the desk. "My hot milk and my tablets, Miss Jones." The girl vanished. VV sat back in his chair and looked round at them as though they were an audience of three hundred, instead of three. "There's one thing," he said, "that every one of us has done this morning. Do you know what it is? Not only every one of us in this room, but every man in these offices." His hands fluttered, his triangular gnomelike face shone with pleasure. "It's not what you're thinking, Jack my boy," he said, pointing at Wyvern, whose face gave no indication that he was thinking anything. "We don't do *that* every morning—not even the biggest rams among us."

Reverton took his pipe out of his mouth. "There are no statistics on that, VV."

"Statistics? We've got the whole history of the human race." He rocked with laughter. "And we don't all evacuate every morning either, unfortunately. What do we *do*, then?" Miss Jones returned with a glass of milk and three green tablets which she placed at his side. He waved them away impatiently. When she had gone out he repeated: "What *do* we do?" His voice dropped to a whisper. "I'll tell you, gentlemen. We *shave*."

Reverton went on blowing smoke from his pipe. Wyvern continued to look out of the window. Anderson sat forward, looking, he hoped, keenly interested. In his mind he saw the calendar which said MONDAY, 4 FEBRUARY. What did it mean? VV jumped up and began to walk up and down the room among the piles of *Scope, Verve, Vogue* and *Printers' Ink* on the floor.

"Every morning homo sapiens crawls out of his warm bed, stretches, faces a mirror and assaults his face with cold steel for anything from five to thirty-five minutes. He cuts and scrapes and hacks away, fighting the unending battle against the growth of Nature. Every morning he gains a victory—but at what a price. Bits of sticking plaster, after-shave lotion, cooling powder—he calls them all into play; he has a row with his wife and catches the eight-fifteen feeling very much the worse for wear." VV's voice, which had risen to a pitch of histrionic excitement, changed suddenly to a mellifluous cooing. "Now supposing we had a means of eliminating this daily torture, supposing we could say 'Hey Presto' and find ourselves shaved—wouldn't that be the greatest boon ever brought to twentieth-century man?" He stood for a moment with one hand stretched before him, and then slowly lowered it. "Boys," he said solemnly, "this is something big. Really big. This is something more than just another advertising account. It's a national benefit." He sat down, put one of the green pills on his tongue, and sipped the milk.

Wyvern shifted in his chair. Anderson looked down at his legs. He had for the moment the extraordinary impression that the lower part of his body was separated from the upper half. Suppose that was really so? Suppose that the foot, the whole leg, failed to obey the instructions telegraphed from the brain. Suppose that one telegraphed such a message now, and —suddenly his right foot flickered on the carpet as though moved by a tic. He watched its performance dispassionately.

"Better get down to cases," said Reverton. "I've got it all down here in outline, VV. Shall I give it to them?" Drinking his milk, swallowing his tablets, glancing from one to the other

15

of them, VV nodded. " All right then. This is a new product, absolutely unmarketed. It's extracted from the tgojumba tree which grows in Central Africa, refined and specially processed."

" The what?" said Wyvern.

" The tgojumba tree."

" Any relation to the miraculous yam-yam you find on the shores of Coromandel?"

" I know, I know," said Reverton. " It's funny. Maybe it isn't the tgojumba tree; maybe it's simply a laboratory product. We'll have to know that—they mustn't think they can do any wool-pulling with their advertising agents. But the important thing is that it works. You use it almost exactly as you use a brushless shaving cream—except that it's razorless as well as brushless. Smear it on your face, leave it on for a minute, wipe it off, and your face is perfectly smooth and stays smooth the whole day."

" No five-o'clock shadow?" said Wyvern.

" No five-o'clock shadow," Reverton said solemnly. " That's the product. Now, here's the set-up as far as this agency is concerned. Manufacture is beginning in South Africa and it's planned to market the product simultaneously here and over there. Negotiations are going on now in the States and on the Continent. Our first job is to suggest a name for the product. At present it's just called Preparation Number One, but the name the manufacturing company suggests is Nu-Shave. Both VV and I think that stinks. Next, we've got to think how we're going to handle a campaign, which may start by the end of this year. The sky's the limit for the South African company, Multi-African Products, who're making the stuff. We've got to decide where we're going to pack our biggest punch. Press, cinema, posters—we've got a revolutionary product to advertise, and if we can find revolutionary means so much the better." Reverton stuck his pipe back in his mouth, and then took it out again. " One more thing, Andy and J. W., VV's called this preliminary conference to start you thinking. He'll handle the account from the creative side. I shall deal with administration. You'll be responsible for copy ideas, Andy, and you, and J. W. for what comes out of the studio. Your boys are bound to know about it. Enthuse them, but tell them to keep it under their hats." Reverton stuck his pipe back, apparently for good. VV swallowed the last of the green pills, got up and stood with his hands behind his back, staring at Anderson and Wyvern. "Any ideas, boys? How does it seem?"

Sucking his pipe, Reverton said delightedly: "Hold on now, VV; give the boys a chance to think."

Anderson thought it was time he said something. "The end of this year means it's not all that urgent."

VV wheeled and confronted him, genial but admonitory. "It *is* urgent. I want it treated as urgent. I want the sparks to fly. I want creation, boys, and no damned nine months' gestation, either." Like a little dynamo he moved between the three seated figures.

Wyvern said in a discontented croak: "Does the stuff exist?"

Like a conjurer, Reverton produced from his pocket a small brownish jar, and passed it round. I label said PREPAR-ATION NUMBER 1; the top screwed off to reveal a white paste. Wyvern and Anderson looked at it curiously, and then Anderson said: "Has anyone tried it?"

"This very morning." Reverton tilted a perfectly smooth face for inspection. "Worked like a charm. On, off, beard gone."

"Nu-Shave," Anderson said thoughtfully. "You know, there could be worse names."

"Or Razorless," Wyvern suggested. "Might be something in Razorless:

Pa and grandpa both bless
The day they changed to Razorless."

VV's fist struck the desk. We're in for it now, Anderson thought; he's got a scheme hatched out already. The little figure behind the desk was bristling with annoyance, but when he spoke he was not annoyed, but histrionically grieved, humorously disappointed. "You're not thinking right, boys." The fist unclenched and cupped his chin. "This isn't a product for humour. You don't sell a revolution with humour."

It's foolish to contradict, it's foolish to question, Anderson thought, as his foot moved to make circles and crosses in the air. But he wants just a little opposition perhaps. He said,

17

with the right mixture of protest and conciliation: " But other shaving devices have been sold on humour, VV. We don't need to talk about tossing our razors over the windmill, but surely there's a case for being lighthearted. After all, it's an occasion for celebration."

VV's fine hands fluttered in the air, his voice beat like an incantation, his eyes stared straight ahead of him, like the eyes of a man in a trance. " This is the way I see it, boys. Shaving is one of the acts which bind us to a world of ritual, the world that each of us secretly detests. The alarm clock, the tooth-brush, the razor, the railway timetable—they're all part of the pattern that makes up the mechanical life of modern man. Take a thousand jigsaw pieces, fit them together every day— and our lives are the result. But what we are doing is to take away one of those pieces. There's a hole in the jigsaw, the pattern's not complete. Through that hole modern man can catch a glimpse of freedom. It may be a small thing in itself, but my word, it's a wonderful symbol.

" Now, I want you to think in those terms, boys. Forget that you're advertising men and remember that you're human beings. We don't want humour here; we want humanity. I can see one headline that says just FREEDOM FROM SHAVING. That's the essential, simple human story." VV's voice had dropped to a low, reverent note. " The whole day's changed—no more family quarrels now Dad's in a good temper every morning. I can see another heading that says I THREW AWAY MY RAZOR—and the story there is the symbolism of it; that it's the finest thing he ever did. I can see a sweet little girlie writing in her diary HAPPY DAYS BEGAN LAST FRIDAY. I can see a little boy saying DADDY HAS TIME TO SAY 'GOOD MORNING' NOW.

VV's voice changed again. Reverence disappeared, and an easy conversational tone took it's place. " I'm just thinking aloud, you know. This is general direction, nothing more. I don't want to interfere with you boys. Think it out for yourselves. There's always another way of doing it. But don't miss the wood for the trees. There's a great human story here. Don't miss it through trying to be clever or scientific or funny. And don't get bogged in detail. The great thing is the tone. Once we've got that the details will arrange themselves." He had talked himself into a good temper. He stood up and beamed at Wyvern. "And don't try to find out about the tgojumba tree, J. W., so that you can draw it. Look for the secrets of the human heart instead. Go to it, boys."

The audience was over.

Outside the door Wyvern said: "Now we know it all. God has spoken. I need a drink at lunch. You?" Anderson nodded. "See you in the Stag," Wyvern said and shambled away down the corridor. His gait was equally unsteady, whether he was sober or (as was often the case) drunk. Anderson started to walk after him and then turned back and re-entered the room he had just left. The effect of his entrance seemed to him extraordinary. Reverton was bending over VV's desk, the heads of two men were close together, almost touching. As he came in they almost sprang—it seemed to Anderson— apart. More than that, it was Anderson's impression that the two heads close together had worn expressions that were perfectly serious, and even sombre; but now, when they looked up, Reverton's face was set in his characteristic self-deprecatory grin, and VV looked eagerly amiable. Was the change, then, nothing more than a trick of light, or had their expressions been adjusted deliberately to receive him? He stood for a moment, while both men looked at him inquiringly.

"It's about Greatorex." VV looked mystified. Anderson said with a kind of exaggerated self-conscious humour: "The nephew of Sir Malcolm Buntz, you know."

Reverton's mouth had clamped hard on his pipe. He took it out to say: "Lad who fancies he wants to be an advertising man. You remember L.E.G. wanted to put him through the mill here and it was agreed he should start in Copy."

"Oh ah," said V. He took no interest in such matters. "What about him?"

"I understand he's started this morning. I think, as head of the Copy Department, I might have been told before today."

Reverton said: "Andy, old boy, I must plead guilty. We've been working like stink on this new account. Tried to stave off L.E.G., but you know what he's like when a client like Sir Malcolm asks him a favour—never lets go. He asked me to let you know on Friday and I forgot. We've all been blowing our tops here the last couple of weeks." His smile was an apology.

"Can't he start in another department? Lessing and I have got enough to do."

Reverton looked unhappy. "L.E.G. particularly wanted him to start in the Copy. Brains of the place, you know."

There was silence. Anderson said sulkily: "If that's the way it's got to be, then."

"Now now," VV said. "Don't take this too seriously, Andy. How long's this boy supposed to stay in Copy? A fortnight. All right then, let's make it a week. Give him an idea how the wheels go round, see if there's anything in him; toss him out after a week if he's no good. How's that?"

"All right." On the way back to his room Anderson thought that he should have been firmer; he should have said *No*. But it was not easy to say *No* to VV.

Charlie Lessing was waiting in the room when he got back. He was a donnish, soft-spoken, thirtyish young man with a small mouth and large horn-rimmed spectacles. "Six pieces of Crunchy-Munch copy are on your desk. I have consumed a great deal of that nutritious and delicious sweetmeat to put me in the mood. I feel a little sick. What was the conference?"

"Somebody's found a way to end razoritis. VV's discovered the fifth freedom," he explained. Lessing's small mouth made an O of surprise.

"Are you sure the End of the World League didn't dream this one up in the night?"

"That's what Wyvern thinks, but VV won't have any of it. He says it's all genuine. He's given a directive," Lessing groaned. "Humour is out. Science is out. Humanity is in. Regard this as a great human problem and you'll be thinking the way the boss thinks."

"That's the way I always want to think," Lessing said seriously. "Life began for me today—it's a different man who says 'Hallo' in the morning—is that the line?"

"That's about it. And don't forget how wonderful it is for the kiddies that Daddy can spare a minute to clip them over the ear after he has breakfast. There it is. You may as well ask Research to get out a competitive file on shaving, although I can't see that we shall need it. And a little bit of historical research won't do any harm."

"What about the tgojumba tree?" Lessing squinted down his snub nose. "I long to say something about that. We don't need any research. The sap's extracted by the natives and they anoint themselves with it—that's why they've been the cleanest-shaven tribe in Central Africa for so many years. But for the sensitive white skin the original treacly sap has been refined by our laboratory chemists and combined with an unguent derived from powdered hippopotamus testicles to produce a shaving preparation of a kind hitherto unknown."

"I forgot to tell you," Anderson said. "That won't do."

"Won't do, sir?" Lessing looked comically offended.

"Shaving. This is antishaving, not shaving. We need a name, and it mustn't be comic or smart. *Nu-shave* and *Razorless* have received heavy frowns."

"Depilo?"

"Too scientific."

Lessing laughed. His laugh was surprising, a high-pitched scholar's giggle. "You know, I can't believe this. Somebody's having a little joke."

"Rev's tried it and he says it works." Anderson dismissed the question, and Lessing with it. When the copywriter was at the door he called him back. "I say, have you got a mother's only son in there? Nephew of Sir Malcolm Buntz, answers to the name of Greatorex?" Lessing nodded. "What's he like?"

"Nondescript but harmless. I kept him happy looking at our old ads in the guard books." Lessing giggled again. "He kind of thought he'd like to do something creative. Do you want him?"

"Not now. I'll see him this afternoon. But get him to work making out a list of names, will you, Charlie? He can't break anything while he does that. And forage about a bit yourself."

With a parody of VV's most cooingly persuasive tone, Lessing said: "And don't be inhibited by anything I've said. Think for yourself." He went out.

Anderson sat down to look at the new Crunchy-Munch scheme. The telephone rang and the switchboard girl said:

" Oh, Mr. Anderson, Mr. Bagseed's been asking for you. He said it was important."

" Get him for me, will you?" He was frowning at the headline CRUNCHY-MUNCH SAVES SECRETARY'S JOB when Bagseed came through, nasal and anxious.

" Look here, Mr. Arthur's on my back about those drawings. You know, the ones for our summer campaign."

" Ah yes." Anderson unhooked the house telephone and dialled Jean Lightley's number. " Jean," he said, " drawings for Kiddy Modes that should have come in last week from Crashaw Studios. Find out what's happened. Quick." Bagseed had been talking about a check. " Yes," Anderson said. " Yes. Yes."

" I simply must have those drawings for Mr. Arthur this afternoon."

" I'm right behind those drawings, Mr. Bagseed." He improvised. " You'll have them today."

Nasal complaint became nasal friendliness. " Grand, Mr. Anderson, grand."

" Not a bit." He improved the situation with a little invention. " As a matter of fact, these drawings are a bit late because I asked the artist to make sure they were right. And you can't hurry an artist. You know what artists are, Mr. Bagseed."

" I do indeed, Mr. Anderson. I'm sorry to have bothered you."

" It's what we're here for." They both said ha ha. Anderson put down the receiver. He saw that Lessing's scheme was a series of strip movies, each containing four little pictures. In CRUNCHY-MUNCH SAVES SECRETARY'S JOB, Picture 1 showed a crestfallen secretary being reprimanded for carelessness by her employer. " You're all right in the morning, Miss Jones, but every afternoon you make these silly mistakes." In Picture 2, Miss Jones talks to her friend. " The fact is, Sheila, I get hungry and we don't have time for a tea break." Sheila replies: " A Crunchy-Munch keeps you going. Tastes good, too." Picture 3: Miss Jones, with typewriter in front of her, letters at side, is eating a Crunchy-Munch bar and thinking: " Yum-yum, it *does* taste good." Picture 4:

Employer says: "These letters are perfectly typed. Congratulations on snapping out of the depression, Miss Jones." Miss Jones (thinks): *Congratulations to Crunchy-Munch, you mean.* Underneath the story was a slogan: CRUNCHY-MUNCH THE VITAMIN-PACKED CHOC-COVERED BAR OF ENERGY. The other pieces of copy exploited the same theme in strip form. The Art Department had made rough layouts that looked very neat and clean.

Anderson sighed, shook his head, and scribbled headings on a sheet of paper. After ten minutes he looked at them:

AFTER LUNCH COMES CRUNCHY-MUNCH

CRUNCHY-MUNCH ROUNDS OFF YOUR
    LUNCH

LUNCH TIME'S ALWAYS CRUNCHY-MUNCH
    TIME

ALL THE BUNCH EAT CRUNCHY-MUNCH

He sighed again. Jean Lightley coughed. "Oh, Mr. Anderson, Crashaw Studios say they can't have those drawings until tomorrow. The artist's away ill and somebody else is finishing them off."

"Hell!" Anderson sat looking at the desk. "Did you employ all your feminine charms?" Jean Lightley went red. "Did you speak to Crashaw himself?"

"To his secretary, but I don't think——"

"All right, all right. You go to lunch. If Bagseed rings up again I'm in conference." He talked to Crashaw and by a mixture of wheedling and threats obtained a promise that the drawings would be sent that afternoon. He was about to go out to lunch when he noticed the calendar. It read MONDAY, 4th FEBRUARY.

Anderson sat down and stared at the calendar. Somebody had turned it back again to the three-weeks'-old date. Why? But as he continued to stare at the neat "4" he felt an obscure uneasiness. Was he quite certain that he had made the alteration back to "25"? Was it not possible that he had forgotten? He said aloud: "You know perfectly well that you altered it," and the spoken words seemed to give small reassurance. He put on his Homburg hat and dark overcoat, and went out.

Wyvern said: "What I like about you, Molly, is the way you pour it down. It might be the kitchen sink instead of your throat."

"Pour it down fast and you don't taste it. Only way to drink beer." Molly O'Rouke's hair was bunched in tight curls on her head and her long nose looked as if it was made of chalk. She had once read sociology at the London School of Economics and now ran the Research Department of the firm. "So I said to him you can take it or leave it. So he said if that's the way you feel I'll leave it. So I said all right, but don't come crying back for more tomorrow. That's original and good. It's not good, he said, but you've certainly got something about it being original. Original, I said, you don't know what originality means. If I——"

The Stag was crowded. Somebody dug Anderson violently in the ribs and he lost the end of Molly's story, as he had lost the beginning. "So that was the end of a perfect romance." She turned to Anderson. "You seem a bit low, pet. What's up?"

"Nothing. Have another drink."

"Thanks, another beer, beautiful chemical beer—how I love it. Wouldn't recognize real beer if I met it nowadays." They were standing at the counter, and the rising and falling swell of people pushed their bodies against each other and then gently ebbed away from them. The glass behind the bar reflected back at Anderson a yellow face, deeply lined and folded, with melancholy bloodshot eyes and thinning hair. He ordered drinks.

"Let the man alone," Wyvern said in his deep croak. "He's got every right not to be cheerful."

"Because of his wife."

"Partly because of his wife."

Molly stuck her long nose forward. "So what? I never thought you were tied up all that tight to Valerie, pet."

Anderson pushed over the beer. "It's only three weeks." He

was annoyed that his voice sounded apologetic. "February the fourth. Three weeks today."

"You ought to snap out of it," Molly said. "In my time—if I may let my back hair down for your benefit—I've lost three husbands. Not to mention all those I mislaid before the ceremony. The first time I was young and innocent and went into it neck first. He used to beat me, but I didn't mind that. It was when he wanted me to beat him in front of his girl friend that I stepped out. He was what you might call sophisticated."

"You make it different each time," Wyvern said admiringly. "And I will say you make it better. What happened then?"

Molly gulped her beer. "Then? Then I got a divorce and married again. This time he was young and innocent, looking for his mother. You wouldn't think I was the mother type, would you? But that's the way he used to think of me, and perhaps he wasn't so far wrong in a way. He was sweet, always bringing presents—nothing valuable, you know, cigarette cases, powder puffs, silk stockings, everything you can think of. Then the police picked him up in a store. Turned out to be a kleptomaniac. That was the end of another romance."

"What about the third?"

"Oh, the third was a bastard. But what I want to show you, Andy pet, is that you've got to keep your chin up. Life's nothing but a succession of kicks in the jaw, anyway."

Anderson joggled the beer in his glass. "What else have I got to worry about?" he asked Wyvern.

"Eh?"

"You said partly my wife. What's the other part of my worry?"

Wyvern bent his narrow head forward until Anderson saw, fascinated, the small pockmarks and blemishes in the sallow skin "Somebody's whispering things in the office. Somebody's saying you're slipping and need a rest."

"Who's saying that?" Anderson was surprised by the sharpness of his own voice.

"A little birdie told me." Wyvern put his head to one side. "I'd look out on this shave-me-quick account if I were you."

"Rev suggested I should handle it."

"Good old Rev, dear old Rev." Wyvern's smile was lop-sided. "Know what he said to me the other day, with his pipe sticking out of his mouth. 'Andy's a good scout—puff puff —but he doesn't quite—puff puff—believe in his work.' When Rev says you're not believing in your work, boy, that's the time to look out."

"But how can you believe in your work?" Molly asked. "You can only do it. Don't tell me VV and Rev believe the stuff that goes in their own advertisements."

"I know what they mean," Anderson said. He remembered Rev's head by the side of VV's, the sombre faces quickly changing to false geniality.

"You not only know what they mean; you know they're right." Wyvern tapped a nicotine-stained finger on the dirty knee of his trousers. "You want to be a successful advertising man. All right. You've got to be able to draw or write a bit. But that's not much. You've got to be intelligent, so that you see it's parasitic, you see it's a bloody fleecing of the public. All right. But that's not all. In fact, that's not much. Because then you've got to believe it all while you're working on it. You've got to believe that Crunchy-Munch is the most nutritious and delicious chocolate bar ever made, that Kiddy Modes really make the best baby clothes. That some stinking patent medicine which can be made for a penny a bottle is really a remedy for physical states that should be treated by a doctor, that this bloody little device for avoiding shaving in the morning is something that can revolutionise people's lives. And it's because he can see through advertising and be deceived by it at the same time that VV's a bloody perfect advertising man." He ordered more beer.

"What about you?" Anderson said. "I've never noticed you showing much belief in blessings of advertising."

"Don't talk about me," Wyvern cried in a passion of de-lighted frustration. "I'm no advertising man. I'm just a painter who took to commercial hack work because he had to keep his mother. And Molly is just doing a job. We don't have to believe; we aren't inside the charmed circle. I can afford a bit of irresponsibility, a few drinks too many, dirty trousers and an old jacket. But you're different, Andy boy, you're *it*.

You're the next best thing to a director. You talk to clients and soothe them down. You're a big boy, not just a technician like Molly and me. You're all set for your directorship if Rev doesn't trip you up before you get it. You've got to wear that black hat, you've got to be serious. I can stay silent in a conference if I want to, but you've got to have an opinion of everything. In short," Wyvern croaked happily, " if you want to be saved you've got to believe."

Anderson drank his beer, ordered another round, and argued it out as he was expected to argue it out. The same discussion, he reflected, was going on between hundreds of advertising men over lunch-time drinks. Dozens of commercial artists were blaming the mothers or wives or children who had made them take the road to commercialism instead of the road to high art, a herd of copywriters were busy biting the hands that fed them when they should be regretting their own lack of talent or toughness. But he had got beyond all that himself; he was reconciled to advertising, he was prepared to take it as seriously as anything else. The pub got more and more crowded. They ate sandwiches. Wyvern began to talk to a commercial artist named Harvey Nicols, Anderson found himself standing thigh to thigh with Molly O'Rourke, who was telling him about her third husband. People all round them were talking so loudly that he heard only snatches of what she said, mixed with other fragments of conversation.

"—Left Rayson, Jones and Johnson and went to Palefox, Wiggins and Grass——"

"—One of these schemes stinks, they said, and it's not your competitor's——"

"—He gave me a black eye." That was Molly.

"—A new slogan, he said, so I told him——"

"—There's absolutely nothing down *that* alley——"

"—So she said, really I'm too Jung to be a Freud——"

"—Ask for a thousand and he'll offer eight fifty. Ask for twelve hundred and he'll offer——"

"—And we Adler good time together. Like it?"

"—So I gave him a black eye." That was Molly again.

He had heard it all before. Wearily, he said he must go away and work. Molly went to talk to Wyvern and Harvey

Nicols. When Anderson got outside, his head was slightly fuzzy with beer.

4

After lunch Anderson interviewed Sir Malcolm's nephew Greatorex. He was fair-headed, wore a neat brown suit, and was perhaps in his middle or late thirties. Anderson was surprised both by his age, and by the fact that he was not obviously a booby. Greatorex talked about himself readily enough, and with a pleasant absence of bumptiousness or embarrassment. He had travelled a good deal, and had been farmer, shorthand typist, journalist, factory worker, and a dozen other things.

" And now you want to be an advertising man. Why?"

" During the war I edited our regimental wall newspaper. That was fun." For the first time Greatorex showed a trace of embarrassment. " When I came out I took a course in advertising. I thought it would give me some background, but Mr. Pile said advertising people don't think you learn much from courses."

Anderson played with an ivory paper knife. " Why advertising? Why not journalism? After all, you've got some experience there. By the way, what paper did you work for?"

Greatorex coughed apologetically. " *The Herts and West Essex Reporter*. Dull. In advertising you're dealing with real products. I think that's a bit more worth while. The army gives you different ideas about things like that."

" I wouldn't know—I wasn't in it. But you must talk to Mr. Wyvern about advertising being worth while." Greatorex looked puzzled, and Anderson regretted the remark. He explained something about the new account, and the list of names that was required. Greatorex listened with almost pathetic eagerness. When he had left the room Anderson grimaced, said " Idealist," and forgot him. But he began to think about what Wyvern had said in the pub. Was it true that he was slipping?

He recorded mentally the mistakes of the day. Bagseed's first telephone call had been handled well enough, but he

28

should never have made that promise about delivery of the drawings on the second call. For that matter, he should not have forgotten the drawings. Then it had been a tactical error to adopt an even faintly critical tone to VV about the new account in face of his obvious enthusiasm. It had been foolish to make that remark to Greatorex reflecting on the sanctity of advertising. Above all, it had been foolish to ask Jean Lightley about the calendar.

Was any of this important? Anderson asked himself, and answered No. It was not important, but it was disturbing. A successful advertising executive should possess above all things the kind of mind that enabled him to know when to be judiciously angry, when to blurt out his thoughts with calculated ingenuousness and when to keep to himself. Anderson had always regarded his own ability to judge the likely reactions of other people to any remark as his most valuable stock in trade. If he could no longer trust——

But it was foolish to meander on in this way. With determination Anderson brought back his mind to the new account. VV's instructions were always sketchy, but this time they had been more than usually inadequate. How was it possible to talk about this stuff at all without knowing something about its ingredients and history? Anderson decided that he had better talk to Reverton; and talking to Reverton, he reflected, might enable him to discover how he was regarded. He had always assumed that it would be only a matter of time, and a comparatively short time, before he was offered a place on the board. If Reverton had really made that remark to Wyvern (although Wyvern, who was malicious, was quite capable of inventing it), then he must be very careful in future.

Reverton's office was slickly modern, with bleached furniture and two abstract paintings on the walls; it offered a sharp contrast to the gloom of Pile's office and the disorder of VV's. Reverton sat behind his pipe at the desk and listened while Anderson talked in jerks, ticking off points on his fingers. One, before doing anything serious, they must have some dope about the secret process, not necessarily for use in the advertising, but for their own information and satisfaction. Two, they must think in terms of an educative campaign, as well

29

as of the announcement of a modern miracle. They must remember that miracles were always greeted with incredulity. Three, they must test the product throughout the firm. Four, they must know the approximate price at which it would be marked. Reverton nodded again and again.

" I absolutely agree, Andy. I'm damned glad you've brought all this up. Between you and me, the trouble with VV is that he rushes into these things half-cocked." He became suddenly solemn. " VV's a great man. But when it comes down to practicalities he can be a bit of an ass, too." Anderson said nothing. That was the kind of remark that it was dangerous to answer. " Now, point one. We're fighting it out with people in South Africa about the process. They're very cagey about ingredients and processing, but we'll get it out of them in the end. Meanwhile just for the present we must go ahead on the assumption that we'll have a story to tell on the manu-facturing side, without making it the principal story.

" Point two, education. I agree entirely. We advertising men have a duty to the public. I know all the smart boys think that's funny, but it happens to be true. We've got a responsibility to society." Puff puff. " We've got power—and we have to be careful not to misuse it." Puff puff. " Think of this as an educative project, Andy, and you'll have me with you."

Anderson still said nothing. Reverton took the small jar out of his desk. " Point three. This is the only sample of Number One that we've got at the moment. So we can't test it out throughout the firm. I used it this morning, of course, but my beard's not much." He looked at Anderson's blue chin.

" I'd like to take it home and try it out this week. Then I'll pass it on to Lessing."

" Good old Andy. Getting right down to brass tacks. Glad there's another practical man in this organisation." Reverton tamped down tobacco, looked at the small pot in Anderson's hand and grinned. " Chin chin, Andy. Let me know how the old white magic works."

Back in his room again Anderson took off the cap and looked at the white paste again, then smelt it. There was an odour which faintly resembled eucalyptus. Anderson turned down his mouth in distaste and called in Lessing. Lessing sniffed, and shook his head.

"They'll have to find a way of getting rid of that smell. By the way, do you like the Crunchy-Munch scheme?"

Anderson hesitated and then said: "Well, to be frank, I don't. It's too farfetched."

"Farfetched, hell. There really are vitamins in that stuff."

"And I don't think we ought to try to sell a chocolate biscuit by a strip scheme. With rationing, it sells itself anyway. I roughed out some headings myself." Anderson read them. "What do you think?"

"Not much. I don't think we want to be comic about the stuff. It's not a joke; it's got serious food value." They argued for nearly half an hour. Lessing repeated the same points unwearyingly, his eyes mild behind the large round spectacles. Anderson had difficulty in keeping the conversation on the friendly plane that generally existed between them. Suddenly Lessing broke off. "Your calendar's wrong. It says the fourth. Today's the twenty-fifth." Deftly he twirled the little knob and altered the date. Anderson stared at him, and at the calendar.

"You want to scrap this strip scheme, then?" Lessing held out his hand for the copy and layouts.

"No," Anderson said with an effort. "No, I'll present it to VV tomorrow morning and I'll put up my own headings and copy as an alternative. Both anonymously, of course. Okay?"

Lessing grinned. "Whatever you say. Let's go out and have a cup of tea on it."

They went out and had a cup of tea and a piece of cake. Lessing told Anderson about the new words spoken by his two-year-old child, who said "Eyeoo" when she wanted her right shoe and "Effoo" when she wanted her left shoe. When they came back Jean Lightley met them in the corridor and gasped: "Oh, Mr. Anderson, Mr. Crashaw says he can't let you have these drawings this afternoon after all."

Molly O'Rourke opened the door of her room, marked RESEARCH. "Thought I heard you. Bagwash is on the line, and he won't take 'Out' for an answer. I think Mr. Arthur's in the eighth month of an idea and he wants you to act as midwife."

31

Pile's secretary came out of the typing pool. "There you are, Mr. Anderson. Can you spare Mr. Pile a moment?"

Anderson telephoned Bagseed, apologized for the delay in delivering the drawings and listened to complaints that Mr. Arthur was right on Bagseed's back. Mr. Arthur wanted to see the drawings now. Mr. Arthur thought they were not getting good enough service. Confidentially, Mr. Arthur had said to him——

A pulse was beating in Anderson's forehead. He interrupted. "Mr. Bagseed, you're getting as much service from us as any other three clients put together."

"Well, really——" Mr. Bagseed's nasal voice almost expired.

"And the moment your drawings arrive they'll be sent up to you. Now, there are six people on my back, and I'm going to try to shake some of them off. Good-bye." He told the telephone girl that he was out to any further calls from Kiddy Modes. He talked to Crashaw, who was apologetic. The artist who had started work on the drawings was eager to finish them himself, and they thought that would be a good thing after all. The drawings were going to the artist that night, and would be delivered tomorrow morning. Anderson saw Mr. Pile, who wanted to know how Greatorex was getting on. "I may meet Sir Malcolm at the club tonight and he will be taking a—h'm—avuncular interest, you know." Anderson said that Greatorex seemed rather old to be starting a career in advertising, and Mr. Pile looked embarrassed.

"To make a clean breast of it, he has—tried several occupations without complete success." Did the eyes twinkle behind the rimless pince-nez? "But can I—report back—to Sir Malcolm in a satisfactory sense on his first day?"

"He seems a bright enough chap," Anderson said wearily. "And eager. That's a great thing. He's been with Lessing most of the time."

Mr. Pile talked for another ten minutes. Back in his room once more, Anderson stared at the green carpet. He headed one sheet of paper with the words C R U N C H Y - M U N C H and another with the words P R E P A R A T I O N N U M B E R O N E and stared at them. What a way to spend a life, he thought: Crunchy-Munch, the shaving revolution, and Sir Malcolm

Buntz's nephew. And for how many years now had that been his life. His triumphs had been a toothpaste, a chilblain ointment and a patent medicine, his disasters a breakfast food and a motor car. Could a life be more meaningless?

He pulled up his thoughts again. That was the way Wyvern would think; those were not the thoughts of an executive who was looking for a place on the board and believed it to be almost within his grasp. There was a job to be done and you did it—well or badly. To give the job itself a moral value was a lot of nonsense.

And then he noticed the desk calendar. The date it showed was the fourth of February. He felt suddenly very angry at the idea that somebody was playing this kind of vulgar and unpleasant joke on him. But there was a simple way to stop it. He pressed the buzzer for Jean Lightley and kept his finger on it, so that she came running into the room. He asked her questions. Gasping, she reiterated that she had not touched the calendar since she put it to the right date that morning. She did not know who had been in the room. " But nobody would alter your calendar, Mr. Anderson." She looked as if she thought he was mad.

" Somebody has." He said it very gently. " It's been altered three times today, Jean. Unless there's a magic spell on it."

" A magic spell!"

He articulated clearly, as one would to a child. " Now I want you to take this calendar outside, and keep it in your room for the rest of the week. Then we shall see if the spell works when it's on your desk as it does when it's on mine. Do you understand?" She nodded. " That's good, then. Off you go." She retreated, her eyes flickering from his face to the brass calendar. When she was outside the door Anderson sighed with relief and regret. Relief that the calendar was out of the room, and regret that again he had acted foolishly. It remained to be considered who would want to worry him—and who would choose exactly that way to do it.

That remained to be considered. In the meantime, it was certain that he would do no work that afternoon on Crunchy-Munch or Preparation Number One. He put on his hat and overcoat and left the office. On the way out he passed Mr.

Pile, who looked at him sharply, but said nothing. Mr. Pile did not approve of staff leaving before the office closed at five-thirty, not even men who had a place on the board almost within their grasp.

5

It is well known that, in our carboniferous era, managers and administrators frequently find their lives separated into two distinct parts which involve a division of the personality. Fiction and film have familiarised us with the capitalist who is a tyrant to his employees, but an emotional slave to his wife and children; with the gangster whose eyes well with tears at thought of the old folk while he is treating the young ones with summary brutality; or with the theme ingeniously reversed, of the executive unendingly patient in his office, but brusquely unpleasant outside it. The case of Anderson resembled this classic businessman's schizophrenia. In his capacity as advertising executive he had developed through years of training an incisive intelligence, and the ability to make quick and generally correct decisions about the people and problems confronting him; as a private citizen he was erratic, irresponsible and quite incapable of assessing the motives from which people act, or of maintaining a viewpoint for any length of time. This double nature was the cause of most of his misfortunes. A man of strong personality who wishes to achieve practical success in life will no doubt do so; a man of weak personality who recognizes his own limitations may batten very well off the strong or the rich; but Anderson's personality combined strength and weakness in ways of which he was quite unaware. Such a combination is dangerous both to its possessor and to those who come into contact with him. Anderson, who was not by nature inclined to investigation of his own character, had become vaguely aware of this fact in the past few weeks.

Anderson was the only child of a bank manager; and soon after his birth in 1909 his father and mother moved from a small terrace house in Wood Green to a new and more commodious establishment in Ealing. This house, in which the child

34

grew up, was built in a modern Tudor style of architecture.
It had an oak door with studs, imitation Tudor external beams
and plaster, and leaded light windows. The fireplaces were
modern with coloured tiles, except the fireplace in the lounge,
which again was an imitation Tudor open fireplace in bright
red brick. There was a wooden fence in front of the house
protecting a neat small lawn, which Anderson's father mowed
on week ends during the summer. At the back of the house
was another small lawn with flower beds. The house was
called " Tudor Vista," and it was situated in a road of similar
houses, each of which, however, differed from the others in
some small architectural details. Tudor Vista fulfilled the
ambitions of Anderson's parents. It gave his father a garden,
modern plumbing and a touch of the picturesque, all of which
had been lacking in the house at Wood Green. His mother was
happy to move into such a really nice neighbourhood, with
really nice people in it. The importance of this achievement
could be understood only in terms of the background from
which Anderson's father and mother had escaped : on his
father's side the family had been small, unsuccessful tradesmen
struggling with a grocer's business ; on his mother's they had
been, even more humiliatingly, in service. Anderson's parents
never spoke of these things ; he learned of them through his
maternal grandmother, who came to live with them when
her husband died. When she talked to the child of the family
in which she had been for many years second housemaid he
was puzzled, and asked her why she worked for other people.
" To make my living, silly," she said, and told him of the great
house near Wimbledon Common, the six servants that were
kept, and the two gardeners—her husband had been one of
them. " Like a park—" she said to Anderson—" the garden
was like a park," sniffing contemptuously at the little patches
of lawn tended so carefully by Anderson's father. In the child's
mind the garden was like Richmond Park, where he had once
been taken for a picnic ; great pies were eaten from spotless
white cloths laid on the grass, fluid was poured from strange
bottles into little metal cups, everyone always wore their
best clothes, deer flickered in and out of the shade. He could
see the park, but he could not visualize the great house she
35

described with its wide stairway and splendid gallery nor understand his grandmother's contempt for the small rooms and funny windows of Tudor Vista, and for the dainty teas provided by his mother for the ladies of the neighbourhood. Sometimes his grandmother appeared at these teas, and at the social evenings when a near-by husband and wife came round for a game of whist or auction bridge, interrupted after a couple of rubbers by a long pause for refreshments, neat little sandwiches or fragments of sardine placed upon fingers of toast. Hers was an awkward presence upon these social occasions, however, for she would not sit quietly nodding in the inglenook. " I think I'll be clearing away now," she would say, or " I'll just be washing up while you play your hand of cards." Mrs. Anderson would say quite sharply, " Sit down, mother, do," and would say that she had made the necessary arrangements for the daily woman, Kitty or Mary or Bessie, to come in that evening. There was not the slightest necessity for anybody to stir. But somehow Anderson's grandmother would find her way out to the kitchen, and there could be heard among the rattle of plates, talking altogether too familiarly to Bessie or Mary or Kitty. It was a relief to his mother, Anderson thought years later, that Granny died peacefully in her bed when he was nine years old.

That was in 1918, just before the end of the war. His father had been upset when he was rejected for service because of his flat feet. A quiet little grey man with an inoffensive moustache, he said little, but after his rejection mowed and trimmed the front and back lawns with fanatical care. His mother was upset also; but his parents' distress seemed to Anderson, when he looked back on it, to have been more social than patriotic. It was the right thing to go to the war, the thing other people were doing, and it was an unpleasantly individual mark to be separated from service by flat feet. The flatness of his father's feet had always been a joke, but after his rejection for national service it was treated very seriously. " He suffers from a disability in a manner of speaking," his mother would say to visitors, adding with a sigh, " It kept him out of the army."

The war went on, there were shortages, Bessie was replaced by Elsie, Anderson went to a local high school. And then the war was over, the cost of living was high, and there were thousands of people who kept it high by deliberately refusing to work. Anderson's father spoke about them with a passionate anger, an anger the more noticeable and impressive because he was usually so quiet. " If they can't work let them starve," he would say. " It's not can't work, it's won't work. There's work for everybody to do that wants work. Those miners." And words would fail him to describe the treason of the miners, whose positive refusal to hew coal for the nation he compared with his own readiness to serve his country.

But the treachery of the miners was not sufficient to wreck the financial stability of Tudor Vista, although Mr. Anderson pulled his small moustache upon occasion with more than customary vigour. When Anderson was twelve years old, an event occurred of some importance in his life. He won a scholarship, but did not take it up. Acceptance of the scholarship would have meant attendance at a public school as a boarder, and a certain financial strain upon his parents. It was, therefore, superficially surprising that his father was anxious to take the scholarship, while his mother's influence was thrown, in the end decisively, against it. Why had she not wanted him to take the scholarship? Anderson wondered afterward, and decided that the incident provided a clear indication of the extent and limits of her snobbery. The limit of her ambition had been reached with occupation of Tudor Vista, dainty teas and people in for auction bridge. She understood the social scale represented by attendance at the local grammar school, and membership of the tennis club; public school and university, however, meant nothing to her but an alien world whose inhabitants had queer aspirations beyond anything she could conceive. Mrs. Anderson divided people into three social classes: " Stuck up," " a nice class of person," and " rather common." It is probable that she disliked those who were stuck up even more than those who were rather common.

It was beside the imitation Tudor fireplace and within the leaded light windows that Anderson grew up, a curly-haired boy with an easy smile, exceptionally intelligent and reasonably good at games. His parents were, it may seem, exceptionally snobbish, exceptionally unimaginative in regard to any way of life except their own. But is such complacency really exceptional? Mr. and Mrs. Anderson had moved into the lower reaches of the middle class, and were effectively able to conceal their comparatively humble origin; such worldly success may be thought adequate for one lifetime. In the morally ambiguous but practically distinct division between satisfied sheep and unsatisfied goats, they belonged to the sheep. Sociologists have remarked that such satisfaction carries with it an illusion of security within their class by observing approvingly certain institutions outside their reach (Mrs. Anderson had an encyclopediatic knowledge of the genealogy of the English royal family) and regarding with uncomprehending disapproval the behaviour of dissatisfied goatish figures (like those treasonable miners) well below them in the social scale.

When it had been decided that Anderson should not take up the scholarship, his parents planned their child's career in a simple and satisfactory way. Grammar school would be succeeded by bank or insurance office, at first in a junior and later in a managerial position: such a course appeared to them not only desirable but almost inevitable. They were baffled, therefore, as well as distressed, by their son's deviations from their own way of life. The first of these deviations might, indeed have upset any parents; for Anderson was expelled from his grammar school for theft. The affair was altogether discreditable and disturbing; he was found in the changing room engaged in transferring five shillings from the pocket of another boy's trousers to his own. His parents were most injured, perhaps, by the social disgrace to themselves that attended his expulsion. As far as their son was concerned personally, they were pained equally by the fact that there was no possibility of belief in his innocence, and by their inability to induce in him knowledge of moral wrongdoing.

It would clearly, have been rash to expose such a boy to the monetary temptations of a bank; Anderson became office boy in a firm of shipping merchants. Here his conduct was for a time exemplary. He was promoted after a year to the position of junior clerk, wore striped trousers and a black jacket and carried a carefully rolled umbrella to work every day. At the age of seventeen, however, when he was earning thirty shillings a week, Anderson showed an extraordinary inability to produce the pound which his mother deducted for his board and lodgings. Mrs. Anderson kept careful watch upon her son, and discovered that he was constantly in receipt of letters addressed in a backward sloping hand upon salmon-pink envelopes. It was a short step from realization that the backward hand was a woman's to execution of a parental duty in steaming open the letters; and another disturbing and discreditable affair was disclosed. Anderson had become mixed up (the phrase was his mother's) with a girl named Ethel Smith, a shop assistant whose father was a railway brakeman. The missing weekly pound had been spent upon Ethel, and the process of mixing had gone so far that she was expecting a baby. What was particularly distasteful to Anderson's parents in the affair was the revelation of their son's taste for low society. "How could you?" Mrs. Anderson asked him. "With a girl of that class?" But the time was one not only for reproaches, but also for swift and decisive action. Mrs. Anderson saw Ethel, Mr. Anderson saw the railway brakeman. Hard words were exchanged ; but money was exchanged also. One more letter came in a salmon-pink envelope, to tell Anderson that Ethel had taken a job in Bradford; and that was the end of the affair. When Mr. and Mrs. Anderson talked the affair over in later years they agreed that their son had narrowly escaped a shameful marriage through their promptness; but at the same time they were able to convince themselves, by a curious feat of mental legerdemain, that the whole of Ethel's mixing-up story was false. "That girl certainly pulled the wool over our eyes," Mr. Anderson, who had now retired, would say to his wife; and this instance of duplicity in the lower orders of society afforded them a satisfaction which was at least some compensation for the money laid out on their son's behalf.

And what of Anderson himself? The central figure in this small drama appeared hardly interested in the fate of this carefully cultivated and costly relationship. His only comment when his parents tried to discover a reason for his actions seemed to be ridiculous. " Why don't you find some nice girl of our own kind?" his mother said. "I can't think what you could see in a common girl like that." Anderson said then, as though the remark had some relevance: "She always had dirty fingernails." He added after a moment's reflection: "She was rather dirty altogether. Her feet were never clean." His mother was triumphant. "There you are," she said. "Disgusting. I don't suppose she took a bath once a month." Anderson said nothing more, and since his father and mother never spoke of disagreeable subjects if they could be avoided, the affair was dropped.

It is perhaps instructive that the fact that a letter addressed to him had been opened never became a subject of argument between Anderson and his parents, because such conduct seemed to all three of them perfectly natural.

Soon after the end of the Ethel Smith affair, Anderson began to write poetry and short stories. One or two of his poems appeared in a local Ealing paper, and one was published in the *Poetry Review*; his short stories, however, were all rejected. At about the same time he gave up the striped trousers and black jacket and began to wear a bright-coloured shirt and a sports jacket when he went to work. He was sacked from the shipping firm for slackness, and for nearly two years was out of work. Most of his time was spent at the public library, or upstairs in his bedroom reading. He made little effort to look for a job, and it took all his parents' skill in mental conjuring to separate the lower-class won't-works who were a menace to the country from the unfortunate can't-get works represented by their son. He did not make life at home very pleasant for his parents, and at times his attitude seemed to them quite incomprehensible. When his father tried to have a heart-to-heart talk Anderson said simply: "You've taken responsibility for me. Very well, keep me." When his father asked what kind of work he would like to do, Anderson said he was not interested in any office job. When his mother asked again why he didn't find some nice girl friends, he said that he feared she would not approve his choice of acquaintance.

It is impossible to know what might have happened to this unhappy household had not the pattern of their family life been suddenly altered. The habit of ignoring unpleasantness can extend from mental to physical matters; when Mrs. Anderson paid a long-delayed visit to her doctor she learned that the fears which had often kept her awake during the night had become reality. It was nine months before the cancer finally killed her, and during that time she was hardly ever out of pain. Her physical suffering was appalling; but the doubts she may have begun to feel about the way in which their son had been brought up were cancelled by the remarkable change in his behaviour. Anderson attended his mother in her illness with extraordinary devotion. He brought her breakfast every day, played endless games of cards with her, and behaved almost in her presence like the charming curly-haired boy she remembered. During the last weeks, when she was too weak to leave her bed, he sat by her side for hours reading light romantic novels to her. In the three days before she died he was with her almost constantly, although at this time her appearance was ghastly, and the stench that surrounded her was so unpleasant that her husband could hardly bear to enter the room. It was Anderson's hand that his mother grasped when, pitifully yellow and gaunt, unrecognizable as the plump middle-aged woman who had visited the doctor nine months before, she completed the long journey to death.

Soon afterward Anderson, now twenty-one years old, obtained a job as a clerk in the accounts department of the Nationwide Advertising Company. At the same time he left home, and went to live in lodgings. His father sold Tudor Vista and became a paying guest with some distant relations in Birmingham named Pottle. Communication between father and son was spasmodic, and soon became limited to two or three letters a year. When Anderson last met his father he greeted a little grey bent man who seemed bewildered by the lack of purpose in his life; his father saw a young man with thin, hard, keen face, unusually serious for his age, who wore a neat blue suit, carefully brushed and pressed. Transferred to the Production Department of his firm, Anderson had attracted the attention of his superiors by making rough layouts embodying new advertising ideas for their clients, which he left lying about on his desk. He had been tried in the firm's Studio, where he showed insufficient artistic ability for a layout man, and then in the copy department, where at last he settled. " Your mother would have been proud of you," Anderson's father said to him shakily. " She always said you'd make good." The young man made no reply. Some three months later his father died suddenly of a heart attack.

Anderson was not a great copywriter, but he possessed a combination of practical common sense and verbal ingenuity which is unusual in advertising. After three years he left the Nationwide, and from that time onward moved from firm to firm, each time improving his position a little, making a reputation as a figure of solid talent. In 1939 he came to Vincent Advertising, a firm which people either left in a month because they could not stand Vincent, or stayed for years because they liked him. Anderson stayed. During the war Vincent Advertising, like other firms, handled their share of government advertising. Anderson was first deferred and finally exempted from the war service, because he was employed on the work Vincents were handling for the Ministry of Knowledge and Communication.

In 1942 Anderson married a girl named Valerie Evans. They had no children.

6

There is a part of London near the Buckingham Palace Road, behind Eccleston Bridge, where the large stucco seediness of once-fashionable squares, Eccleston and Warwick and St. George's, fades into a smaller shabbiness. There are streets here of small, identical red-brick houses, fronted by ugly iron railings; these streets branch off the main stem of Warwick Way, that backbone of Pimlico where large houses converted into a dozen one-room flats offer typists and secretaries the chance of developing an individuality untrammelled by the presence of parents or the inhibiting eyes of childhood neighbours. Such self-contained lives typify the decay that is spreading slowly over the fabric of our great cities; to be part of this decay, to visit the ballet frequently and to fornicate freely, to attain a complete irresponsibility of action—that is, in a sense, the ideal life of our civilisation. And if such a life

42

can be worked comfortably enough in the four-storied houses of Warwick Way, it can be lived more easily still in the little red-brick houses of Joseph Street. You might find similar houses in any London suburb, where they would be the homes of clerks, schoolmasters and small businessmen; but the people who lived in Joseph Street were male and female prostitutes, unknown actors and film extras, artists and journalists who had given up worship of the bitch-goddess Success and were content to earn a few pounds here and there which they drank away at the Demon round the corner in Radigoyle Street while their teeth fell out and their tongues grew furry and their eyesight failed. Among these characteristic occupants of the small red-brick houses, however, were a few eccentrically successful figures, people whose presence in this raffish area could not have been easily explained, even by themselves. Joseph Street numbered among its inhabitants two company directors, a dress designer, an important gynecologist and a retired trade union official. Anderson, who might also be regarded as eccentrically respectable, lived at Number 10 Joseph Street, in a house distinguished from its fellows only by the window boxes carefully cultivated by the Fletchleys, who lived in a self-contained flat on the first floor. Anderson had bought a nine-year lease of the house at the time of his marriage.

He turned out of Radigoyle Street into Joseph Street this evening, passing the bright lights of the Demon without so much as a sideways glance. Flossie Williams, one of the Joseph Street tarts, smiled at him as he passed, and Anderson, breathing deeply, caught a whiff of her cheap scent. He felt a mingled exhilaration and depression as he approached his home, an obscure sense of wrongdoing mingled with an equally obscure feeling of pleasure. His key was in the lock when something touched his shoulder. Pivoting quickly on his heel he faced the great bulk of Fletchley, shaking with laughter in the Pimlico dark. " I crept up on you," Fletchley said. " I saw you pass the old Demon. You never heard me. Me in my rubber-soled shoes."

" Are you drunk?"

" Old boy," Fletchley was reproachful, " I've had a pint to

drown my sorrows, not a snoutful. A snoutful is out of the question, much as I should like it. Tonight I have to write immortal verse. A dozen orders to fill, old boy." He declaimed:

> "*I don't know much of rhyme and meter,*
> *So I'll say God Bless Mummy.' Peter.*

That's from a little kiddy, six months old, to his mother. A nice sentiment, eh?"

"Where's Elaine?"

Fletchley wavered on his feet and then said: "Out. Won't be back till late. I'm turning an honest penny on my lonesome."

Fletchley was a man of many curious occupations, all of them approprite of an inhabitant of Joseph Street. He had made money by starting chain letters and pyramids, he had held at one time a valuable insurance book, he was an agent for the pushboards by which small cricket and football clubs raise funds. His latest way of earning money was by supplying rhymed Christmas and birthday greeting wishes. The customer would give details of the recipient's age and character and Fletchley would make notes reading: "Uncle Bill, birthday, from niece Mary. Big nose, retriever dog Laddie, grand-daughter Phyllis learning to talk. Humorous." Uncle Bill would then receive on his birthday a card which contained two or three printed verses embodying the points Fletchley had jotted down. Fletchley set up these cards, which were of a sentimental humorous or reverent nature, on a small hand press, and his charge for them varied between half a crown and five shillings according to the length of the message. The business was largely seasonal, but there was a steady birthday demand throughout the year.

The house had been clumsily converted into two flats, with a hall common to both. Anderson was just about to open the door of his flat when Fletchley said: "By the way, old boy, that police chap called round to see you this evening. He doesn't seem to be a bad fellow. We had quite a chin-wag."

"You'd better come in," Anderson said. He turned on the light. "What will you drink? Gin or whisky?"

"Won't say no to a little drop of something to keep the cold out. Whisky—and don't kill it. Can't think where you get the stuff."

"Valerie got it—black market." Anderson poured himself a drink. "What did he want?"

"Who? Oh, the copper," Fletchley shook again, a pinpoint head wobbling uncertainly on an enormous sagging body. There were food stains on his jacket, and above a mountainous belly the tapes of pants were visible, held by his braces. "He's mustard," he chuckled.

"What do you mean?"

"Mustard, old boy, mustard. His name's Cresse and he's hot as mustard, see? But what did he want? He wanted to see you. Something to do with Valerie. He's a nice sort of a chap."

"What did he ask you?"

"I didn't give away any secrets, don't worry," Fletchley said and winked portentously It seemed to Anderson that there was something strange about Fletchley tonight. His whole body was trembling slightly, as though convulsed by some elaborate inner joke. Sharply, Anderson said:

"Secrets, what do you mean, secrets? And why should I worry?"

"Only my joke, old boy." Fletchley was momentarily solemn, but Anderson had an uncomfortable feeling that this solemnity was maintained only with an effort, and that if the fat man let himself go he would burst out laughing. "Do you know he's got two kids?"

"Who?"

"He's got two kids and he wants me to write birthday messages for 'em. Fancy sending birthday wishes from a C.I.D. Inspector. He is C.I.D., isn't he?"

"But what did he want to ask you?"

"Pretty near everything from the time I get up in the morning to the width of my pajama stripes. All sorts of questions," Fletchley rambled. "You wouldn't believe the sort of questions he asked." And again it seemed to Anderson that there was something very odd, something almost menacing, about the tone of the fat man's voice. But this impression was no sooner in Anderson's mind than it was gone again, as Fletchley drained his glass and put on his mask of good-fellowship, if indeed it was a mask and not a true reflection

45

of the sentimental birthday-greeting soul within his great bulk. " I must be going. 'Night, old boy."

" Good night."

The door closed and he sat still for a moment in the armchair, staring straigh. ahead of him. Then, as his eyes slowly focused to take in the furnishings of the room, the modernist grey carpet with its jagged pattern of blue and orange picking up the same colours in the curtains, the chromium standard lamp, the Lalique glass on the mantelpiece, the chromium electric fire, the white ghastly light from the fluorescent strips on the ceiling, as he took in the whole brassy brightness of the place he thought: *I must get away from here; this is nothing to do with me.* For if the choice of neighbourhood was Anderson's, reluctantly agreed to by Valerie because it was almost impossible to find a place to live in, the flat itself was Valerie's, just as Elaine Fletchley was Valerie's friend. There was one incongruous element, however, which stood out as an oddity in that room of chromium furniture and tubular lighting; a Georgian writing desk which stood between the electric fire and an angular wall lamp. This writing desk had belonged to Anderson's parents, and his father had given it to him when he moved from home. He walked over to the desk now and opened a drawer below the main body of the desk with a small key. He felt at the back of this drawer, pressed a small protrusion, and another small hidden drawer was revealed, just large enough to contain a book with a cover of black leather and stiff marbled corners. Anderson took this book in both hands, holding it carefully as if it were a fragile object. Then he sat down at the desk, staring at the black cover. Anderson had first written in this book a week ago, and had sat up four nights in succession, writing each night for several hours. Every night since then he had felt compelled to read the story put down between the black leather covers with marbled corners. He had written the story himself, and yet he felt so remote from it that a sensation of utter strangeness overcame him while he read, so that he seemed to be reading of somebody else's life and not his own. And now the craving to read what was written in the book had become so strong that it was the first thing he turned to when he came back from work.

Tonight he had gone to the cinema, but in front of the Hollywood faces he saw quite distinctly the shapes and appearance of the book. Now he sat looking at the cover, holding the book in both hands. I can do whatever I wish, he thought. A movement of the hand and this book returns to the drawer, another movement and the drawer is closed. A movement of the hand: and the hand is controlled by the brain. But if a person dissociated from the figure Anderson recognised as himself—the slick executive, in line for a directorship—if somebody else had put down what was in this book, could not a similarly dissociated figure put back the book in the drawer, with a movement of which Anderson himself had no awareness? Was it possible to experiment, he wondered, to make one's mind a conscious blank? And while he thought this, his grip upon the book must have relaxed, for it dropped to the floor, landing with a soft *plop* upon the carpet. Anderson picked up the book, opened it, and began to read:

Now it is all over. The funeral is over, the inquest is over, the verdict has been given. Two people who had very little in common have ceased to live together. One has fallen down a flight of stairs and broken her neck; the other continues an existence in which he regards his own ridiculous occupation with extraordinary gravity. Is there anything more to be said?

Yes, there is a great deal more to be said. A casual death like this one makes one question the whole of existence. Why should Valerie and I have lived together for years? What possible meaning can one attach to our life together, how can one understand it? And if such a ridiculous end to a shared life is possible, doesn't this illuminate the absolute absurdity of existence itself? Now that Valerie is dead, I see quite certainly that I didn't love her. I am absolutely unable to understand why I married her. I can't see why I didn't push her down the stairs long ago. Wyvern, at the office, has a phrase which he uses every now and again when things are going wrong: "Why don't we all get in one great bed and ——one another?"

Well, why don't we?

But of course that kind of thing won't do—that pure abandonment to the idea that life is nonsense. There must be somewhere an explanation of human activity which isn't purely biological, which interprets life in terms of some kind of meaning. It's to try to get some idea of what it all means that I'm putting down this individual case history of my life with Val.

I met Val first at a party given by Elaine Fletchley. At least it was given by *Woman Beautiful,* the high-class fashion magazine she works for, and Elaine was a hostess. They asked somebody from all the bright advertising agencies, and I went from Vincent's. It was a very dull party. I had a bit of chat with other advertising figures and was just working my way over to say good-bye to Elaine when I bumped into a girl and upset her drink. "Oh dear," she said. "Oh dear, my poor frock." She stared at me with wide-apart eyes of a curious hazel colour. Then she said: "But I want another drinky." There was just the faintest suggestion of a lisp in the way she rolled her r's. So I got her a drink and we talked, and it turned out that she worked for *Woman Beautiful,* too, as an assistant fashion editor. I told her that I was a copywriter and she said: "Oh, but you must be awfully clever." She was so short that she had to look up at me, and she did so with a kind of starry gaze. I can remember wondering what I was doing talking to her. She was just the kind of girl, I can remember thinking, for whom I had no use at all. How is it possible, then, to account for my next action? I leaned over (I can see myself doing it quite clearly) and said: "Let's get out of this din and go somewhere else?" And what did she say? She giggled and answered with quite a definite lisp. "I say, you awe a quick worthker." We left the party, had some drinks—she soaked up the drink like a sponge—and she stayed at the flat I lived in then, in Kensington. When she left in the morning we arranged to meet that evening. We did. And the next and the next. In six months we were married.

So there it is, or there's the beginning of it. During the whole of that six months if I'd ever asked myself whether I liked Val, the answer would have been an unhesitating No.

I dislike girls who lisp, girls who are kittenish, girls who drink too much. Valerie did all of those things. Why did I marry her, then? Partly I'd got into the habit of seeing her—but what made me start the habit? Partly no doubt I was the victim of that feeling war and bombing gave you, that no relationship you formed mattered much, or was likely to be permanent— and how damned mistaken that feeling was. Partly she was good in bed, and although I was over thirty when I met her I hadn't much experience of that sort of thing. Although Val was nearly ten years younger than I was, I gathered she'd had plenty. But although I enjoyed our times in bed, I wasn't all that interested. That certainly won't do for a main motive.

And why did Valerie marry me? If I can't explain my own motives, I certainly can't understand hers. I think she found me attractive—although few women have done so. I believe she liked men older than herself. And—although I may be quite wrong—I believe she regarded me as a very different person from the man I am. Subconsciously I assumed that we should stop drinking and going to parties after we got married. But Val assumed that we should go on drinking, and go to more parties than ever.

So we started off wrong. And then there was trouble about this house. Val was essentially what I think of as an Earl's Court girl—nice gay parties with people in the rag trade as she called it, a few commercial artists, some fifth-rate actors. Well, you can get all that in our bit of Pimlico if you want it, but in rather too sordid a way for Val. She liked a bit of glamour spread over it—not too much, just a thin layer. She was horrified when she first saw the house and even more so when I told her I liked it. " But how *can* you like it? It's so vulgar. That woman Flossie Williams—she's just a tawt." And what are your friends, do you think? I asked her. And what are you? Didn't you sleep with me the first time you met me? The only difference was that she got marriage instead of a spot cash settlement. At that she burst into tears, and it's true I was unfair, because Val was a one-man woman. I say I think she found me attractive, but I'm doing myself an injustice. The fact is that she never looked at anybody else at all. She told Elaine Fletchley so, and Elaine told me. And how can one explain that? That's as nonsensical as the rest of it.

So Val burst into tears. She was always bursting into tears; it was one of the most irritating things about her. Then she asked me again why I liked living here, but I couldn't answer that, because I didn't know. There was just something about the streets and the people and the atmosphere, that's all.

But if Valerie couldn't get her own way about the house, at least she made it look the way she wanted. It's all round me now, as it's been round me for years—the glaring colours, the fumed oak paradise in the bedroom. " It's so bright and gay and new," she'd say—but with the lisp, of course. " I hate old stuff. I'd like life to start again every morning. New people, new job, new places, new everything. Wouldn't you like that?" And when I said truthfully that I'd like nothing less, she'd be upset. And she not only had her way about the look of the place; she got Elaine to live in it as well. First she said the house was too big for just the two of us. Maybe there'll be three one day, I said, but she didn't want children. Then she wanted Elaine to come and live here with us. I didn't want it ; I wanted to be alone. But she had it her way. We turned the place into two self-contained flats and we had the ground floor and the Fletchleys had the first. We shared the cellar, where we both kept a small stock of drink. Elaine is a neat, tarty little piece, slick and smart and hard. What did she see in Fletchley to marry him? That's another problem, but I can't go into it now.

Val had kept her job on *Woman Beautiful*, so when Elaine came the girls would talk office gossip all evening long. Fletchley never seemed to mind, just as he never seemed to mind Elaine going out with other men. " She always comes back," he used to say to me. " She always comes back to old Fletch." But at this time, when they first came here, Elaine didn't go out much. She would talk office gossip with Val in the evening until I was nearly crazy. Occasionally I thought she was intending to make a pass at me, but Fletchley never seemed to notice, so perhaps I was wrong. I got so crazy with their talk that I suggested in desperation to Val that we should go out and drink. Six months ago she'd have leaped at the suggestion, but now she didn't much want to do anything but drink a pint or two of black-market whisky by her own comfortable electric fireside while she chattered to Elaine. And when we did go out it wasn't any good, because I didn't really care for drinking and I could hardly even be polite to Val. "You're never nice to me, Andy, the way you used to be," she'd say tearfully, and look at me with her head slightly on one side. Was it true? Had I ever been nice to her? I can't believe that I ever was. She'd invented my niceness in the past to contrast with my howwidness in the present. We can't re-create the past, but we can always soothe sorrow and vanity by inventing it.

So drinking was no good, and after a couple of years there was another thing that was no good, too. I couldn't work up the least flicker of interest in Val while I was with her. When I was away from her—in the office writing copy, interviewing a client, sitting round a conference table—then very often I would positively shiver with desire for her. The most powerful and violent sexual images came to my mind, and they were not merely vague images—they had a positive association with Val. As soon as I saw her, though—as soon, even, as I knew I would see her within half an hour—they vanished altogether. It would all have been comic if it had not been deeply humiliating.

All this sounds like a good case for divorce, or at any rate separation. But strangely enough, Val never wanted a separation—throughout the whole of our life together she was absolutely devoted to me. And why did I stay with Val? I find the question absolutely unanswerable. It would have been difficult, I suppose, to arrange a separation. She would have wanted to go on living with Elaine. I should have had to get out of Joseph Street, and I didn't want to get out. Then again I should have been lonely. She had become a habit, and we live by our habits. But there was something outside all that, something that held me to her. It was, it seems to me, precisely *because* I disliked her, because she filled our home with hideous furniture and empty chatter, that I wanted to live with her. The things that I most detested were the things I most desired! Shall I put down the image that came to me most

51

often when I saw Val, tearstained and reproachful, or limply acquiescent in my unkindness? It was of my mother, and the ghastly house we lived in so many years ago—and of holding my mother's hand as she lay, a pitiful and repulsive skeleton, upon her deathbed.

But now I come to the real reason for writing in this book —the effect Val's death has had on me. We lived together for several detestable years. For the whole of that time I had seen with irritation the grease on her face at night, and her intolerable cheerfulness in the morning. I'd listened all that time to her inanities about clothes and film stars. Unconsciously, I must dozens of times have wished her dead. But now that she *is* dead, and the bathroom is free when I want to use it and I no longer find hairpins in the bed, I am oppressed by an extraordinary sense of loss. Not loss of Val exactly—that seems not to enter into it. Rather, part of myself seems to have disappeared. I feel like one of those insects that goes on living even after being cut in half.

On Monday, February 4th, we went to work as usual. Val sang "Berkeley Square," out of her repertory of out-of-date songs, in her bath. I had a worrying day at the office.

There the writing ended. Anderson's perfect absorption in the black book had been such that he had forgotten to turn on the electric fire, and he now became conscious that he was cold. He was sitting also in an uncomfortable position, so that something in his pocket pressed sharply into his side. He put his hand in his pocket, drew out the pot of Preparation Number 1, and placed it upon a red-topped table with chromium legs. He flicked a switch, and the firebar glowed. But there was some other cause for disturbance—what was it? Sickly-sweet chimes sounded in the room. Of course! Val's musical doorbell. Anderson put the book back in the small secret drawer, and closed and locked the desk. Then he went to the front door, and opened it to reveal a burly figure. The street lamp cast the shadow of this patiently waiting figure into Anderson's hall. The face was left dark, but Anderson recognized Inspector Cresse by his bowler hat.

"Come in," Anderson said with self-mocking gaiety. "Come in, Inspector." With a catlike, almost mincing step, he led the way into the room he had just left. The Inspector followed more deliberately. Under the tubular lighting his face showed large, blue-white, slightly dented, with two strongly marked lines running from nose to mouth. The whole face was flattish, the nose a large, blunt wedge, the mouth broad and shapeless, but turned down slightly at the corners in an expression both clownish and severe. But the balance of these heavy features was changed altogether when the Inspector took off his bowler hat, revealing a great white head that was completely bald. What had been menacing now appeared ludicrous; and such sudden changes of appearance and gesture appeared to be part of the Inspector's stock-in-trade. He had presented, Anderson thought, a quite farcical figure at the inquest; and yet at odd moments there was something in the firm fit of his clothes and his blank forward-looking stare that gave an impression of intellectual strength, though not of subtlety. Behind the figure of farce lay the man of power, behind the man of power lurked the irrepressibly clownish comedian. The comedian was uppermost when the Inspector took off his hat, and placed it, with a wonderfully whimsical gesture, upon the red table by the pot of cream.

"A drink?" Anderson almost danced round the thickset figure. "A cigarette? Sit down. It's rather cold in here, I'm afraid." He shivered in an exaggerated manner.

The Inspector sat in one of the chromium-armed chairs, his hard bulk filling it without overflowing. His voice was rich and thick, and at times he did not articulate with absolute distinctness. "I'll take just a little whisky. Thank you, Mr. Anderson. Nothing in it." He held the amber liquid in one large blunt paw. "I called earlier this evening."

"Fletchley told me. You wanted to know the width of his pajama stripes. You Gallup Poll policeman!" Soda water sizzled in Anderson's glass. He almost giggled.

"We had a little chat," the Inspector said vaguely. "He's a man with a sense of humour, which is something I always enjoy." On another chromium chair, bent deferentially a little forward, Anderson smiled agreement, rocked by an obscure secret merriment. " A nice idea of his, to write those cards for birthdays and Christmas. Ingenious, too."

" A nice sentiment." Anderson rocked again.

" That's right. Or don't you think so?" A vacant orb, emptied of expression, the Inspector's eye rolled.

" I'm not called upon to express an opinion." Anderson spoke a little huffily.

" But I'm interested "—the Inspector's great head nodded in puzzlement—" to know what you think. An intellectual man like yourself; you'd call yourself an intellectual now, wouldn't you?"

" An advertising man merely."

" Those verses he writes—you couldn't call them great art now?" Anderson shook his head. " But they help to increase friendliness between human beings, don't they? Isn't that a good thing?"

With complete self-possession Anderson smiled at the heavy face opposite him. " The verses Fletchley writes are in every way contemptible. They pander deliberately to the vulgarian who lives in all of us. They exploit the lowest depth of public taste. That's what is wrong with Fletchley's rhymes."

With clownish pleasure the inspector said: " I do admire the way you talk, now. But tell me—as a plain man now—if there's a demand for something, can it be wrong to supply it?" The vacant eye rolled round the room. " You don't have a woman in," he added. Anderson was taken aback.

" What?"

" Dust." The great bald head was slowly shaken. " You're letting things go, Mr. Anderson. This room looks altogether different from the way it did when I first saw it. That was three weeks ago. Your wife kept it very nice, if I may say so. Not my own taste, of course, but—" The great flat hand moved embracingly to include carpet, curtains, chairs, lamps, everything. " Very nice. And now look." One great finger moved on the red table, sketched a face in dust, skirted the bowler hat and picked up the pot. " Preparation Number one," he read as slowly as a peasant. " Preparation for what, if it's not a rude question?"

Anderson leaned forward again, pleased that the conversation had moved away from his wife. "That little pot, Inspector, contains a cream designed to eliminate shaving from our lives forever. It is a small part of the twentieth-century revolution."

"And what might that be, when it's at home?"

"Hygiene, asepsis, artificial insemination."

The lines on the great blue-white face deepened as the Inspector laughed. "You're in favour of modernity, though, Mr. Anderson. How about the refrigerator in the kitchen? And "—his hand moved embracingly again—" all this."

Anderson said stiffly: "My wife furnished this flat."

"Ah, she was a modern," the Inspector said sepulchrally. "I'm old-fashioned. But hygiene and asepsis—I'm modern enough to believe in them."

"But don't you see that they're unimportant?" Anderson cried. He was moved suddenly by the need for explanation.

"Unimportant?"

"When a doctor saves human lives he is committed to the belief that they are valuable. But he may be quite wrong. It's only during the past few hundred years that we've come to assume that there is something intrinsically important about the fact of life itself, and now soil conservers are telling us that the world's population is too large for the amount of food available, that we are slowly starving to death. Improved maternity statistics and better dental treatment have no importance in themselves. The important thing to find out about any man or woman is whether he's preserved his soul alive."

The Inspector looked at Anderson. Anderson looked at the Inspector. "Have you got a match?" the inspector asked vacantly. Anderson gave him a box of Swan Vestas, and the Inspector lighted a cigarette. "Matches," he said absently. "That's what I was going to say."

"What?"

"Nothing." The vacant eyes rested on Anderson. "Have you got any enemies?"

"Enemies?"

"We have received a letter—in fact, we have received two

letters." Suddenly two pieces of paper were in the great hand. "We don't pay much attention to such things in general, but just in this case we'd like to know who sent them." Anderson read the letters. The first suggested that he hated his wife and made her life miserable for years. It asked why Anderson's statement at the inquest that his married life had been "normally happy" had been left uncorroborated. The second said that Anderson had been persistently unfaithful to his wife. "And then he insured her life for £5,000. And then she fell downstairs. Cui Bono?" Anderson read the letters and returned them without comment.

"Typed on a Remington 12 machine, posted in Central London, no fingerprints," the Inspector said. The clownishness had dropped from him, the heavy face was alert, the eyes' vacancy might be interpreted as alertness. "The first of them came a week ago, the second three days after it. Nothing since. You've no idea who wrote them, I suppose?"

"No."

"Stuff like this now—in one way it's beneath contempt. And yet in another it's interesting. It's the sort of thing that sets us thinking." With a return to clownishness, the Inspector ran a hand over his great bald head; the humorous action was somehow more menacing than a threat could have been. "A clever chap like you now, you're thinking all the time. But a policeman only thinks when he needs to, and that's not very often. A bit of low cunning's enough for our purposes usually, when we're dealing with the uneducated classes. But with a gentleman like yourself——"

"I went to a grammar school," Anderson said sharply, to check this ponderous humour.

The Inspector was unperturbed. "That's just what I mean. You're a well-read man, an intellectual. A policeman's got to be clever to keep up with you. When we got these letters we thought back over the case, and you know what we discovered? We hadn't been clever enough. But that won't be any surprise to somebody like yourself." The Inspector slapped his knee with a meaty hand, and laughed.

"Not clever enough?"

"We had failed to read our Sherlock Holmes. The curious

incident of the matches. Although, of course, in a way the reverse of *Silver Blaze*. You have read that, of course."

"I'm afraid not, no."

"Detective fiction," the Inspector said with a sigh. "But the box of matches worries me, I must confess. You don't understand me?" Anderson shook his head. In his thick voice the Inspector said: "Your wife left the sitting room——"

"The kitchen. She was cooking the supper."

"Left the kitchen, passed through the sitting room, went out into the passage, to the head of the cellar stairs, turned on the switch and found that the light had fused. Unhappy that the light should have fused, is it not, just at that particular moment? Tragic, even Then she struck a match, began to descend the stairs, slipped——" The Inspector paused delicately, and then looked up. "But did she strike a match? Where did the box of matches come from that was found by her body?" The question was asked in a gentle voice. Anderson goggled at him. "She would hardly have taken matches from the kitchen when she supposed that the cellar light would be on? Of course she wouldn't. She would not find matches in the passage. She didn't come back or call to you when she found that the cellar light was out of order. And yet—a box of matches was found by the side of her body."

"Her frock," Anderson said. His voice was hoarse.

"Woollen. No pockets."

"They must have been there for days."

"No, you'd had the cellar cleaned out the day before, don't you remember? Your charwoman gave evidence. *She's* quite certain there was no box of matches down there then. It's a problem. I don't see where the box of matches could have come from, do you?" The Inspector's voice rumbled softly; it was ridiculous to think that his eyes could ever have been vacant. "What the anonymous letter said about the five thousand pounds insurance—that was right, wasn't it?"

Like a man emerging from water, Anderson shook himself. "Inspector Cresse, are you insinuating that I killed my wife?"

The Inspector looked astonished. "Why, what a question to ask! I came here about those anonymous letters."

"Then why did you ask about the insurance? You know

perfectly well that we each had an insurance on the other's life. I am not short of money, Inspector."

"Now now, Mr. Anderson." The meaty hand was raised, soothingly. "Nobody said you were. You don't get the point. Nothing was mentioned about that insurance at the inquest. The person who sent that letter must know you pretty well. You might think it over and see if you can identify him—or her. But the whole affair, that unfortunate business about the light that fused, and so on, raises what you might call a moral problem."

"Oh yes, a moral problem." Shall I say it? Anderson wondered, and then gripped the arm of his chair and spoke earnestly. "Tell me, Inspector, if I told you that I killed my wife, would you arrest me?"

"Ah ah." Like gigantic scissors the Inspector's legs shifted and were crossed from right to left instead of from left to right. "Precisely the moral problem." Anderson poured out fresh drinks for both of them. When he passed the Inspector's glass, however, some of the whisky splashed on to the hard, fleshy thigh. Anderson exclaimed in dismay, drew out his handkerchief and rubbed the offending spot. The Inspector, apparently unconscious of these ministrations, stared ahead of him at the pentagonal looking glass fixed over the fireplace. "Precisely the moral problem. You killed your wife, Mr. Anderson." Anderson sat perfectly still, holding his own glass, staring. "You killed her, I mean, in the sense that had you pursued some other course of action she would not now be dead. You might have taken her out to dinner. You might have gone down into the cellar in her place, might you not? And then perhaps when you found it in darkness, you might have mended the fuse—you are a handy enough electrician for that? Or perhaps you might have accompanied her to the head of the cellar stairs instead of reading the paper in the sitting room. Then you would have cautioned her, doubtless—you would have said: 'Be careful of that slippery step halfway down.' And then, who knows—perhaps she wouldn't have slipped."

"You attach blame to me? You think me guilty?"

"Ah ah," the Inspector said again. He drank three quarters of the whisky in his glass. "That question is not for an ignorant policeman, but for an intellectual. A man like yourself. It is a problem of morals." He spoke with gravity to which Anderson, his partner in this curious verbal knockabout, responded with restrained jocosity.

" So you will not arrest me?"

" Arrest you?"

" Even though I said '*Mea culpa,* I confess my guilt.'"

Anderson beat his breast in mock despair. "What do you propose to do about it? Supposing I said that—just supposing!" With a revival of his earlier gadfly spirit, Anderson walked mincingly across the room to straighten a picture.

" What do *you* propose to do?" The Inspector's features had lost altogether their joviality. The strong lines threw into prominence the great blunt nose; the loose lips were joined in an appearance of resolution. "We can do nothing without you." He stood up and clapped the bowler hat on to his bald head. It was like the curtain coming down on a play.

" Nothing!" Anderson echoed triumphantly.

" Nothing."

THE 26th OF FEBRUARY

The sickly light of morning, filtering through pink curtains, illuminated Anderson asleep in a double bed. He slept in a position curiously contorted, one arm thrust over his head like a signal, the other holding a pillow tightly to his chest. His knees were drawn up like those of a man making a jack-knife dive. His yellow face looked younger in repose. The top of his pajamas, opened, revealed a body surprisingly white.

An alarm clock rang by the side of the bed. Anderson opened his eyes. They stared at his wife's photograph, which stood beside the alarm. While a hand silenced the alarm clock, Anderson continued to stare. His wife, head slightly to one side, eyes melting, lips bent upward to a smile, seemed joyfully to meet his gaze. Anderson's stare shifted from the photograph to the pink curtains, to the pink quilt on the bed, to the china knick-knacks on the mantelpiece, to the pink ribbons tied round the top of the dressing table, back to the photograph. A slight film seemed to be spread over the glass. He touched it gingerly, and exclaimed: "Dust," remembering the Inspector. The flat had not been dusted or cleaned since his wife's death. Groaning slightly, Anderson got out of bed, ran a bath and put two slices of bread in the electric toaster. Plates and dishes with small pieces of food in them stood in the sink. He bathed quickly and looked at his face in the shaving glass. Magnification made the pits of removed blackheads look like craters of the moon, but he stared particularly at the blue growth on and underneath the chin. Each hard bristly hair was plainly distinguishable; the total effect was exceedingly unattractive.

Anderson put his watch in front of him and then, like a nervous bather, dipped a finger in the pot of Preparation Number 1. Gingerly he smeared the stuff onto his face. He felt at first nothing at all, then a prickling and burning that was not unpleasant, then again nothing. Obviously, the stuff had failed to work. He checked by his watch, waited another half minute to give the preparation a chance, then damped a washcloth and wiped his face. He looked to see the blue stubble. It had gone. His face was absolutely clean to the eye, and to the touch of fingertips felt babyishly soft. The preparation, in fact, did exactly what had been claimed for it; Anderson, an advertising man accustomed to publicizing goods that did perhaps a quarter of what was claimed for them, gasped with astonishment at such a consummation.

2

The swing doors hissed behind Anderson. Miss Detranter was reading from notes, ticking off each item as she read. "Flowers," she said to Jean Lightley. "Flowers for the directors' rooms. Flowers for Mr. Anderson's room. Flowers for each department. Secretaries' typewriters neat and tidy. Tell the Studio they must get straightened up. All of them working, but everything bright and clean. Tell the production boys to get blocks stacked one side of them and proofs the other. Tell Miss O'Rourke——"

Anderson stared and listened. The black book with marbled corners, the Inspector's visit, belonged to another time and world; within these doors he was an advertising executive, a man with a purpose in life. "Hey," he said, "that's my secretary."

"VV's orders," said Miss Detranter sweetly. "He rang up in a flap and said get all the girls to work on it. I can't leave Reception. Jean won't be half an hour, will you, Jean?" Jean looked startled.

"Flowers in February. What's it in aid of?"

"Mr. Divenga's coming round."

"And who's Mr. Divenga?"

"I simply haven't a clue," said Miss Detranter. Anderson made his way down the corridor. As he turned the corner, he heard: "——Tell Miss O'Rourke she must have some vital statistics on hand. Charts and graph on the wall——"

Anderson went into his room! Figures scurried past in the corridor. Reverton's secretary, Miss Flack, came in with a duster. "Just dusting," she said with a smile and flicked rapidly at cupboard, chair back, hatstand and desk. "Mr Divenga's flown over," she added with a bright smile, and went out. The telephone rang. "Oh, Mr. Anderson," the operator said, "Mr. Vincent said to tell you that Mr. Divenga's coming in this morning."

"I've grasped that."

"If you have an outside appointment, will you please postpone it if possible. If it can't be postponed, please let me know. Otherwise will you please be available."

"I'll please be available." The operator giggled. "Who's Mr. Divenga?"

"I don't know him from Adam, I'm afraid, Mr. Anderson." The operator giggled again.

Anderson sat down in his chair. As he did so he noticed that Miss Flack, when she dusted the desk, had shifted a letter at the bottom of his pile of mail, so that it was out of place. His hand moved to replace it, and then he noticed the handwriting. It was a letter from Val.

Anderson sat quite still. His head seemed to be the centre of a whirlpool, going round and round and round and round. He closed his eyes, and in the whirlpool there were faces—the round bland face of Lessing, the square dependable face of Reverton, the triangle of VV's great forehead and small pointed chin, the long chalky nose of Molly O'Rourke. Anderson opened his eyes again, and gripped the sides of the chair to stop himself from falling. When he felt better he picked up the letter and read the hastily scribbled lines: "My darling. I love you so much, and it seems so long since I held you in my arms." Somebody has stolen the letters she wrote to me, Anderson thought with a bitter anger that surprised himself. And then, as he turned the page and read the unfamiliar words, he realized suddenly why this letter had been put on his desk. This was not a letter Val had written to him; it was a letter she had written to somebody else. "I love you *dearly*" were the last words, and then came the scrawled signature "Val." Val had loved Anderson—or so he had always thought; but she had never ended a letter "I love you dearly." And yet this letter, written in the light blue ink she used, on dark blue paper, was unmistakably in her writing.

Anderson sat looking at the letter for a period that might have been seconds or minutes. Then he pushed it clumsily into his pocket, and almost ran out of the room. As he slammed the door the telephone rang. With blundering emphasis Anderson moved along the corridor, head down. His swinging arm struck something soft, and a voice said " Good morning." Anderson looked up to find Mr. Pile regarding him severely through his rimless pince-nez. " Is anything the matter?" Anderson muttered. " You don't look well, Anderson. Perhaps you had better go home." Mr. Pile's tone made it clear that he did not care for executives who were unwell and went home.

" Mr. Divenga," Anderson said.

A withered smile passed over Mr. Pile's face. " Ah yes, he is coming round this morning. But he won't expect to see our senior men rushing about head down. Are you quite sure you feel all right?" Anderson nodded. Mr. Pile stood still, fumbling for the true and appropriate phrase. At last he found it. " Well, more haste less speed." He passed on.

Anderson went into the Copy Room. The neat brown-suited figure of Greatorex rose to receive him. " I put that list of names on your desk——"

" Where's Lessing?"

" I haven't seen him this morning, Mr. Anderson." Greatorex was apologetic. " Shall I ask him——"

" Doesn't matter." Greatorex looked at him in surprise. Outside the door of the Copy Room, Anderson stood and wiped his hand over his forehead. Anger and urgency drained away, and his body felt simply weak. He walked along slowly and aimlessly, turning right and left, until he came to a door marked RESEARCH DEPARTMENT. Molly O'Rourke's head popped out. " Oh, it's you," she said. " Come in." He went in. " You can lend a hand with this chart. Just pass it up to me, will you." She stood on a chair, and he passed up to her an enormous chart made up of different blocks of colour. Above each colour block, on the left-hand side of the chart, was a percentage figure. The centre part of the chart was divided into geographical areas. The blocks on the right-hand side were split into months of the year and had cash figures over them. " Take this," she said. He held one end of the chart while she pinned it to the wall. They both stood looking at it. " In case you wonder what it all means, it tells you the percentage of cakes of Happiday Soap sold in England in comparison with all competitors. It gives you an area breakdown. It relates advertising cost to sales returns in all districts. It tells you——"

" Wonderful," Anderson said. " And when you've got it what have you got?"

" You haven't got much and that's a fact. This is all two years out of date. Fortunately the date was at the bottom and we've cut it out. It looks good on the wall. Part of the red carpet for Mr. Divenga." She stared at Anderson. " You look terrible. What's the matter? Here, never mind, take a nip." She drew out a bottle from the drawer of her desk. Anderson looked round for a glass. " Ah come on, drink it like a man." He took out the stopper, tilted back his head, and drank until tears came into his eyes. " My my," said Miss O'Rourke, " that must have put several hairs on your chest. What's the matter? Tell mamma." Her black curls shook, her chalky nose was near to his face.

" Look, Molly," Anderson said. " Did you see anybody go in my office early this morning?"

" Since I can't see round several corners the answer, old cock, is No. Don't tell me somebody's been stealing your ideas."

" Somebody's playing a funny kind of joke on me, and I'd like to find out his name."

" Sure it's a him?"

Anderson fingered the letter in his pocket. " Quite sure."

" Girls can play some pretty funny jokes sometimes."

" This one was played by a man." The house telephone rang. Molly said: " Yes, you've run him to earth. Yes, I'll tell him." She put the telephone down. " Birdseed is on your tail. Something about some drawings——"

" Christ!"

" But more important, Mr. Divenga is on his way round. Will everybody please be in their rooms. You'd better run along. Feeling better?"

" Yes."

64

Molly was casual. " Care to repeat the dose this evening if you've got nothing better to do?"

Anderson hesitated and then said : " All right."

She put her hand on her heart and grimaced. " My, you just sweep a girl off her feet. Come here, your tie's crooked." She straightened Anderson's tie and gave him a little push out of the door. On the way back to his room Anderson met Reverton, walking down the corridor pipe foremost, with a look of intense concentration. He raised his hand and would have gone on, but Anderson stopped him. " I say, Rev, who's Mr. Divenga?"

Reverton stared at him in surprise. " I thought you knew, old boy. He's the managing director of Multi-African Products. Just flown over unexpectedly. Going to meet him now. Will you be available?"

" I'll be available."

" All a lot of bull, of course, showing him round, but you know how it is."

" I know how it is," said Anderson.

3

Falsely hearty voices roared along the corridor in waves. The door opened and they all came in, laughing. But where was Mr. Divenga? " And this is Mr. Anderson," VV said. " Our copy chief. He will be in control of the creative side of your account—under me, of course—and if I may blow somebody else's trumpet without immodesty, you couldn't have a finer man on the job. Anderson, this is Mr. Maximilian Divenga of Multi-African Products." Anderson stood up and from behind the smiling Reverton there darted a little figure something less than five feet high. He was dressed in a tight-waisted lilac suit with a fawn waistcoat, he wore spats above crocodile leather shoes. But it was not these things that made Anderson gape at Mr. Maximilian Divenga, nor his beaky nose, but the fact that the lower part of the little man's large head was almost completely covered by a great black spade beard.

" You are happy, yes?" Mr. Divenga asked, gripping Anderson's hand with fingers like pincers. "Are happy in creation?"

"Mr. Divenga thinks it most important that the creative minds in charge of an account should feel thoroughly integrated with the work they are handling," said Mr. Pile plummily. He turned to the gaily dressed dwarf. "That is a consideration we always bear in mind, my dear Mr. Divenga. We pondered very seriously the problem of which of our creative minds should handle your account. Mr. Anderson already has the whole question of shaving at his—ah—fingertips. He handled another shaving cream account with great success when he was —ah—working with a rival agency some years ago. Isn't that so, Anderson?"

"Iss goot," said Mr. Divenga before Anderson could assent to this complete untruth. Then he turned menacingly on Mr. Pile, and gave his chest several steely prods. "But iss not *another* shaving cream account. Preparation Number One iss not shaving cream. *Shaving iss finished.*"

"Finished," said VV triumphantly, and the others took up the cry. There was a short silence. Were they all thinking as he was, Anderson wondered, of Mr. Divenga's great black beard?

"I've been giving your preparation a test, Mr. Divenga," he said. "My chin's pretty blue normally, but Number One leaves it smooth as silk."

The little man stepped up close to Anderson, passed a hand over his chin and breathed "Ahh." He turned to the three directors. "You have felt?" Obligingly VV and Pile touched Anderson's chin and exclaimed in wonder, although as Pile retreated Anderson seemed to remark a slight frown behind the pince-nez. Mr. Divenga turned to Reverton. "You have felt?"

"Don't need to, Mr. Divenga. Tried it myself yesterday morning. Absolutely miraculous."

"Miraclus, miraclus," said Mr. Divenga. "Always in South Africa are performing miraclus. Have marketed many miraclus—clasp knife changes to tooth drawer, paper flower breathe on and opens, card of pretty girl with clothes on—hold to the light and is pretty girl without clothes on." The three directors

66

and Anderson laughed heartily, but with a trace of puzzlement, VV became oratorical.

"Engaging toys, Dr. Divenga, but this is something different. I assure you, my dear sir, that I believe—that we believe—your preparation to be the greatest boon ever brought to twentieth-century man. It is——"

"Iss miraclus," said Mr. Divenga, whose attention seemed to have wandered. "Pleased to meet, Mr. Anderson. Shall we go on now?" The directors about-turned.

"Is Number One the final form of your preparation?" Anderson asked. "I ask partly because I think we should impart a slightly different odour from the one it has at present before putting it on the market, and partly because I felt a rather curious sensation when I used it this morning." Then Anderson made the most awful error of his advertising career. "I don't know whether you've tried it yourself, Mr. Divenga——" Three directorial faces looked back at him from the doorway, frozen in expressions of horror. Anderson stopped, speechless. But Mr. Divenga seemed merely puzzled. "Senashun, what is senashun?" he asked.

"A kind of burning feeling just for a moment or two."

An expression almost of alarm appeared on the little man's face; but it vanished in a moment. "Iss sample," he said, pointing to the pot on Anderson's desk. "Iss all the time more miraclus. Experiment lavatories," he said with a smile at Anderson which showed a mouthful of splendid teeth, "Soon get rid of senashun."

He had gone, and the directors followed him. Mr. Pile cast one backward glance over the top of his pince-nez at Anderson, and the glance was not friendly.

4

Jean Lightley stood awkwardly in front of his desk, with her weight resting on one foot.

"So you brought in my mail at about twenty-five past nine."

"Yes, Mr. Anderson."

"You're absolutely certain that this letter wasn't with it?"

He held up Valerie's letter upside down, and some distance away from Jean.

" I'm sure, Mr. Anderson."

" And it wasn't lying on the desk when you brought in the mail?" She shook her head. " How do you know? It might have been put under another paper. That's possible, isn't it?"

A tide of colour went up from Jean Lightley's neck into her face. " Yes," she whispered, " but I don't think so."

" Now look, Jean, this is important. Are you sure you didn't see anybody come into my room between half past nine and the time I came in this morning?"

" I didn't, Mr. Anderson," she said. " But of course I wasn't watching the door. I passed up and down the corridor though." She sounded doubtful.

" All right, Jean." He remembered the calendar. " Has that magic calendar of mine been behaving itself?"

" Yes," she whispered. She almost bumped into Charlie Lessing at the door in her eagerness to get out. The copywriter looked after her.

" What's on your mind?" Anderson asked. " And by the way, where were you at nine forty-five this morning?"

Lessing looked injured. " I was at the B.M. historically researching into the history of shaving. The old English was ' sceafan,' perhaps derived from the Latin ' scabere,' which means scratch, or the Greek ' skapto ' which means dig. ' We're not going to sceafan any more '—yes?"

" No."

" A shaving tool was first known in the twelfth Egyptian dynasty," Lessing said imperturbably, " and became common in the eighteenth. ' The Egyptians had a word for shaving— modern man uses Depilo.' "

" Don't keep calling it Depilo, that's no good. Have you seen Mr. Divenga?"

Lessing grimaced and spread out his hands. " Depilo? De pillow? Ain't that what you sleep on, no? So there's nothing to history, eh? Out, damned history."

" Keep it up your sleeve. But I don't think we'll ever get past VV. Let's look at that list of names Greatorex has made."

" Some of them aren't bad."

They bent over the list. " All these portmanteau names are no good," Anderson said. " Can't be patented. And things like Secshave are no good either. But we might put forward—" The house telephone rang and he picked it up. VV's voice said: " Hey presto."

" What's that?"

Gleefully the voice repeated: " Say hey presto."

" Hey presto."

" No no. Say ' Hey presto '—can you see that at the top of an eight-inch triple? ' Say Hey Presto—and forget about shaving.' ' Say Hey Presto for a silk-smooth jawline.' ' Say Hey Presto and no more cottonwool.' "

" Cottonwool?"

" After you've cut yourself shaving." VV's voice was faintly dubious. " Perhaps that one's a bit obscure. But you see the possibilities. I think we've really got something with Hey Presto, don't you?"

" I thought we were out for humanity, not humour."

VV chuckled happily. " This is human and magical at the same time. Think it over, boy. Then come in and see me."

Anderson put down the telephone, and began methodically to tear up the sheet of paper containing Greatorex's names. Reverton's square head was poked round the door, for once pipeless. He said with mild interest: " Copy Department having fun tearing up copy?"

" VV's had a brainwave. He's found a name for our anti-shave preparation. Hey Presto." Decisively Anderson tore the sheet of paper across again, and dropped it in the wastepaper basket. " There go about a hundred ideas for names."

Reverton's square face and Lessing's round one both looked serious. " It's got something," Lessing said.

" ' Say Hey Presto—and forget about shaving.' " Anderson was ironic.

" Yes, I can see that," Reverton said. They were his highest words of praise. " You don't like, Andy?"

" It's not whether I like it—though I think it stinks. But it's just exactly the line he told us not to work on." Reverton raised his eyebrows. "Humanity, not humour, he said, and I think he was right. Is 'Hey Presto' human? It sounds pretty comic to me."

"Now look, Andy," Reverton said earnestly, "You're losing your sense of proportion. It's good this name, don't you agree, Charlie?"

"I think so, yes."

"All right then. You know me, Andy. I'm one of the boys myself; I think like you, I know what's on your mind. You like ideas to come from the copy boys and the Studio and then go up to the directors, not come down the other way. So do I. We all know directors are pretty dumb—I ought to know, I'm one myself." He laughed heartily. "But it can happen that a director gets hold of a bright idea. This is it."

Perversely, against the sense which told him he had better keep silent, Anderson said: "I still think it stinks."

The telephone rang. Anderson picked it up and made a face. It was Bagseed. Reverton and Lessing went out. With an effort, Anderson adjusted a tone of false joviality over his voice and said, with the forestalling technique familiar to advertising executives and others engaged in selling material which they have had no hand in producing, "I know what you're after, Mr. Bagseed, you're after those drawings." The forestalling technique was justified upon this occasion by the fact that, at the moment these words were spoken, Jean Lightley came in with drawings in her hand. Mr. Bagseed whined, cajoled and threatened until Anderson said brightly: "Those drawings are on the way up to you *now*, Mr. Bagseed." He looked at the drawings, which showed odiously fat little girls and unnaturally demure little boys wearing a variety of clothing, and told Jean Lightley to send them up immediately to Kiddy Modes. When she had left the room he tilted his revolving chair back against the wall, and sat staring at the green carpet. Looking up, he was surprised to see the neat brown suit of Greatorex in front of the desk.

"I knocked, but you didn't answer." Greatorex coughed. "I wondered if you'd had a chance to look at those names for the new preparation."

Anderson pointed to the wastepaper basket. "There they

are." He held up a warning finger. "Don't get the idea they were no good. I thought two or three of them were pretty bright. But that doesn't matter." He let the revolving chair drop to the ground with a bump. "What matters is that VV has had an idea himself."

"That's Mr. Vincent?"

"That's Mr. Vincent. He's decided to call the stuff Hey Presto. That's the decision and there's no argument about it, unless VV changes his mind. So——" He indicated the torn-up pieces of paper.

"Hey Presto," Greatorex said. "Well, that's a pretty good name."

"I think it's a terrible name. I'm the creative man on the account. But that doesn't matter either." Anderson tapped the desk with his finger. "Lesson number one in advertising. Be original, but don't be too original, because people won't like it. And remember that until you get near the top nine-tenths of what you do won't even be considered. You'll sweat your guts out for no purpose whatever. It's disheartening, but that's the way it is. Now, here's advertising lesson number two." He laid another finger on the desk. "Have you got another copy of that list? All right then, don't throw it away. VV may change his mind—or the client may not like VV's idea —then that list may be very useful. Understand?" Greatorex nodded, but looked at him oddly as he left the room. Anderson reflected again that he was a fool to be saying such things. A month ago he would not have said them. Why was he saying them now?

He pulled out of his pocket the letter from Val, spread it before him on the desk, and read every word of the letter carefully as though in the hope that the wording of those hurried phrases or the shape of the handwriting or the texture of the blue paper would tell him something of the circumstances in which this letter had been written, and to the utterly unknown and unsuspected lover who now lay like a shadow across his past life. Who had been her lover? Somebody in his own office, somebody to whom Val had talked of him, laughing about him as a cuckold almost too easily deceived. Who could it have been? Reverton, Lessing, Wyvern, Vincent? She had

71

known them all slightly, and thought little of them. It was impossible that she could have written to any of those men the words on the sheet of paper, that she should have said to any of them, " I love you dearly." And yet she had done so; in death she triumphed over him through hasty words of love. What assignations did this letter represent, what clandestine meeting, what furtively delightful brushing of hands even in his presence, what pleasant deceits! Reverton, Lessing, Wyvern, Vincent: which of them had been her lover? The letter gave him no answer.

5

The small window of Anderson's office looked on to the backs of three similar blocks of office buildings, separated from Vincent Advertising by a deep, narrow well. On three sides, looking out of Anderson's window both upward and downward, one could see through other windows girls typing, men surrounded by sheets of paper, girls looking in filing cabinets and sharpening pencils, men making notes in books or speaking to strange machines, tea being made and drunk. Wyvern was fond of standing at the window and saying that the contemporary world could be seen in microcosm; with, he added too aptly as he stared down the dark well, the bottomless pit which was the destination of all worshippers of Mammon, all those who sold their souls for a mess of pottage, all who had installed a piece of clockwork in their heads in place of a mind.

Anderson's room was never fully illuminated by sunlight, but on sunny afternoons a bright searchlight shaft would cut across his desk, liven the colour of a small, sharply defined area of carpet, and play upon the hatstand. This February afternoon was sunny; and, giving himself an occasional quarter turn in the revolving chair, Anderson sat watching the parallelogram of sunlight become narrower and narrower until it was a finger strip touching one edge of his penstand and gleaming on a worn segment of carpet. The telephone rang, people came in and out asking questions and bringing tea; he made no attempt to do any work, but sat staring in front of him. He thought—although the word is not truly applicable,

72

for the images that passed through his mind seemed almost wholly casual and involuntary—of Val in relation to those four men, of her gestures and actions in their company. One day at the annual outing Lessing had helped her out of a charabanc. Anderson saw now with strange clarity the grip of Lessing's hand upon her arm just below the elbow, fingers pressing deeply the soft flesh of the upper arm. Lessing, Lessing, a randy married man? Once at a party, Val had been missing for half and hour and then had returned, dragging somebody by the hand, saying: "Look what the cat's brought in." There, smiling behind his pipe, letting himself be pulled into the room, with a great show of good-humoured reluctance, was Reverton. But Reverton, like Lessing, was a man happily married, with two children. Surely not Reverton. Wyvern? A disappointed artist, tediously cynical, always droning on about his obligation to his mother. But then Val had always liked them to go out drinking with Wyvern because she said he was such good company. There was a particular ridiculous phrase they used instead of saying "Cheerio." Anderson saw Wyvern raising his glass and saying "Shorter days," and a clink as Val's glass struck it and she responded: "Longer nights." And VV? But he could recall nothing about VV in connection with Val, except a vague impression of the elaborate courtesy with which he always treated women.

The afternoon passed away; the sunlight faded, and the daylight; Jean Lightley came in, touched the electric switch and exclaimed: "Why, Mr. Anderson, you're sitting in the dark. I thought you had gone home."

Anderson, slouched in the revolving chair, moved a little. "No, Jean, I have not gone home." And I should like, he thought as he caught among those other glimpses of the past a picture of the pink bedroom, the modernist sitting room, the dishes in the sink, the thin layer of dust over all, I should like never to go home.

6

"Down hatches and mud in your eye," said Molly O'Rourke. "This is my fourth and I can't feel a thing. They've doctored the whisky. I say, I say," she called. The barman came up. He was a large man with a sad, ugly prizefighter's face. Several strands of almost colourless hair were plastered down on his head. Molly thrust her nose and her glass forward at the same time. "Is this stuff doctored?"

"I beg your pardon?" The barman's voice was surprisingly almost a tenor.

"Castrated, if you'll pardon my French. Do you a-dul-ter-ate," Molly O'Rourke said with a twitch of her chalky nose, "The poten-cy of this allegedly Highland dis-till-a-tion with an ad-mix-ture of——"

"What's that?"

"Skip it. Care to tickle your tonsils?"

"What's that?"

"Lift the elbow. I mean to say," said Miss O'Rourke patiently, "have a drink."

"Oh ah. Just a little drop of It then. I like a little of It." The barman poured a drop of It. "Good luck. You've certainly got a funny way of talking."

"We're in advertising. That explains everything, doesn't it, Andy?" She swung her body in its uncreased blue tailored suit round on the bar stool.

"If you say so. Look, Molly, there's something I want——"

The barman leaned forward a little. "All sorts we get in here, you wouldn't believe." He made a gesture that embraced the empty bar. "Had a raid last week and it's done for business. But they'll be back?"

"Who'll be back?"

"The boys'll be back. You don't scare 'em away for long."

"What boys?" Molly asked, and the barman's sad look lightened. He put a hand on his thick waist.

"You know—the boys. The boys that wish they were something else."

"Oh, *those* boys."

"Antics they get up to sometimes. I could tell you——"

"Two more whiskies," Anderson said. "Look, I want to talk to you, Molly." He pointed to the little empty tables in one corner of the bar. The barman was offended.

"All right, then, all right; you want to be alone, that's all right. I can take a hint. I know when I'm not wanted." He poured two nips of whisky. "But I've got my feelings like anybody else. Your young lady got into conversation with me, don't forget that. I was passing the time of day in conversating when asked, that's all."

"No offence," said Anderson. "Have another drink, Jack."

"No offence at all. I shouldn't like you to think I was pushing, that's all. I'll just have another drop of It. But my name's not Jack."

"What's your name?"

"My name's Percy."

They left him at the bar, and sat down at one of the empty tables. Molly O'Rourke's knee was warm against Anderson's leg. "What's on your mind, Andy?"

"Molly, how well did you know Val?"

She leaned back and let out breath in a sigh. "Still chasing lost causes. Why don't you give up and make a fresh start?"

"What did women think of Val? Did they like her?"

Molly placed one lean bony hand upon the breast that pushed out her jacket. "If you're asking one woman the answer is No. I thought she was a snake in the grass. I never went for that dewy innocence. Whatever she got was what was coming to her."

Anderson put down his glass quickly upon the table top. Some drops of whisky bounced out. "What do you mean by that?"

"Mean? I'm not using up any spare handkerchiefs on her, that's all."

"You said she got what was coming to her. What did you mean?"

"Oh I don't know, Andy, I don't know." She looked away from him and said: "I suppose the thing is I never thought she was good enough for you. That's all I meant."

"What about men friends? Did she know anybody well—anyone in the firm?"

"Here, here." She moved her knee away from Anderson's leg. "What's all this about? What does it matter now, anyway?"

"Oh, it doesn't matter." Anderson was elaborately sarcastic. "It's just that I'd like to know who she was running round with, that's all. Just that I'd like to know how long I'd been wearing horns."

"Look here, Andy, I don't know anything about this. But I think you've got it wrong somehow."

"I've got nothing wrong," he said violently.

"I mean I don't think there was anyone in the office."

"There was someone in the office."

"If there was I don't know about it. You believe me, don't you, Andy? But I tell you who would know all about it—if there was anything to know. That girl she worked with—Elaine Fletchley."

They were both silent. Then Anderson said: "Let's get out of here."

"All right, let's go and eat."

"I don't want to eat."

"Right you are, then, let's go and drink. Where shall we drink?"

"I know where to go," Anderson said.

As they went out Molly called: "Good night, Percy. Don't mix any gin with that It." The barman ducked his head and looked pleased. Outside, a thin rain blew into their faces. Anderson called a taxi. When they went inside Molly placed her bony hand on his. Charing Cross Road went by, the bookshops all in darkness. Irving's statue stared under the lights of flourescent blue.

"Look, Andy, I know it's none of my business, but you're taking this too hard. People are talking. Little Jean had some tale about your giving her a calendar and saying it was magic. It's all over the office."

"Somebody was altering my calendar." Anderson leaned back on the cushions. "Every time I was out of the room it was changed to February the fourth. That's the day Val died."

"Why—you poor darling." Molly's hand gripped his convulsively. "Who would have done that?"

"That's what I want to find out."

"Sure you didn't imagine it?"

Anderson pulled his hand away. "What do you take me

for?" The taxi lurched as they turned into the park and he was thrown against her. As they kissed her hard fingers dug into him, moving furiously over his back, holding him tightly as if he were a plank that might save her from drowning. In the flickering darkness her head moved down to his neck, and her corkscrew curls bobbed over her face. He jerked his head back and pushed her away. " I like you, Andy," she said. " I've always liked you. There goes Buckingham Palace. Good-bye, Buckingham, and good-bye Palace. I'll tell you something, Andy—shall I tell you something?" Her body rested in the crook of his arm. " Percy didn't doctor that drink."

He grunted. How many times, he thought with a nostalgia that surprised himself, how many times have Val and I ridden in petrol-scented darkness past Buckingham Palace and down these streets. The bombs dropped a mile away, pieces of shrapnel clattered on the pavement like toys, reminders of the delightful impermanence of life. On such nights Anderson had come as near as it was possible for him to come to a confused love for everything around him, love for the people who might today or tomorrow be killed quite casually, love for the civilization being reduced to rubble under his eyes, love even, momentarily, for Buckingham Palace and his companion in the cab. Such possibility of sudden death imposed upon life a design. But tonight there were no bombs and life had no design and a different companion rested in the crook of his arm.

They stopped. " Here we are," Anderson said. " My home ground." He glanced upward at the sign, faintly visible in the light streaming from the saloon bar, of a grinning figure with cloven hoofs, harlequin clothes and flames coming out of its hair. Underneath the sign, in mock-Gothic lettering, could be read THE DEMON.

Molly seemed disappointed when they got inside the pub, although she did not refuse a drink. " I thought we were going home."

" Home, home? I have no home." Ironically Anderson declaimed: " Let Rome in Tiber melt and the wide arch of the ranged Empire fall. Here is my—home. Drink up."

" Oh, be your age," she said a little impatiently. " Where

77

can I go to spend a penny?" When she had gone he stood pressing his fingers upon the glass and looking at the imprint. He slipped one hand into his pocket, and fingered Val's letter, assuring himself that it was still there, a perfectly tangible proof of disaster. Why disaster? he thought. Why disaster when I never loved her? Because, he answered himself, because the letter had opened up one of those terrible gaps in personal relations which we all know to exist, but are generally able to ignore, the sudden revelation that, in the lives of the people we know best, there exist great unexplored areas of jungle, places where primitive loves and hatreds battle silently together like tigers. Anderson asked for another drink. " Sorry, Mr. Anderson, no more whisky." He ordered gin and paid for it. A boy came round selling the Greyhound Special, printed slips which showed the results of the evening's dog racing. A big dark man with a broken nose standing near Anderson bought the sheet. A man with a checked cap and the pointed nose of a weasel looked over his shoulder. The third member of their party, a small faded blonde woman wearing a pink dress and white high-heeled shoes, sipped a small port apathetically.

The big man exclaimed angrily. " Your bleeding Melksham. The bleeder never even showed."

" You musta got the wrong race, Jerry. Couldn't come unstuck, Melksham." The weasel nose appeared over the big man's shoulder, little eyes looked hastily over the sheet, thin lips exclaimed : " Would you Christmas Eve it! Never showed."

" I thought it couldn't lose," The big man said bitterly. " I thought it could win on three legs. I thought the others weren't in the race."

" It was a racing certainty, Jerry."

" And what kind of a bleeding certainty do you call that? Never even showed."

" It couldn't lose on the book, Jerry."

" Couldn't lose. Couldn't lose. What about your info that cost me half a nicker?" The little woman moved convulsively, but did not speak. " What about the others being ready to lie down?"

" Do you know what I reckon, Jerry?" the checked cap

78

asked solemnly. Molly came back. Anderson, absorbed, pointed to her drink upon the counter. " I reckon it's next time out."

" Next time out! "

" Look at it this way. It's a good thing tonight, see. It can't lose. So it's three to one, maybe five to one on. So nobody can really make a killing. Next time it's odds against, see, and you get right in with both feet."

" Next time! It's cost me ten bleeding nicker *this* time."

Like a clockwork toy suddenly moved to action, the small blonde woman gave a small scream, and spoke in a voice of the utmost refinement. " Not ten pounds, Jerry. Oh really, not ten pounds."

The big man did not look at her. " He's smart. He knows it's a good thing. He has the inside dope it can't lose. He tells me to step in with both feet and help myself."

" You got no call to say that, Jerry."

" But ten pounds, Jerry. What about the rent?" The little woman stared with horror at her port.

" Now don't you stick your nose into this."

" But the rent, Jerry. Are you sure the rent's all right?"

"——the rent."

" Oh, Jerry, you've spent the rent money. I never thought you'd do it."

The big man shook his head like a dog. " That's enough now. Let's get out of here." But the clockwork toy, wound up, was not now to be denied action. Without a word the little woman launched herself at the checked-capped weasel. The table at which they sat went over. Beer flecked Anderson's trousers and Molly's stockings. Red marks appeared on the face of the checked-capped man. He pushed at the woman, not hard, and she fell over. The big man roared angrily and advanced, not upon the checked cap, but upon the woman. With one hand he pulled her to her feet and with the other struck her in the eye. She would have fallen again, but for the hand that held her up. Molly cried out. The barman ducked under the counter, caught hold of the big man by the neck and waistcoat and ran him out of the door. The big man made an attempt to resist, but maintained firm hold of the

79

woman, who was crying and holding a hand to her eye. The man with the checked cap picked himself up, dusted himself and went out after them. The barman came back, looking rather pleased. Molly said to Anderson: "Aren't you going to do something?"

"Never interfere. That's my good-neighbour policy."

"But he might kill her."

"Not he. She'll have a black eye tomorrow, that's all."

Her nose was twitching. "It's horrible."

"Haven't you seen a fight in a pub before?"

"That's not what I mean. It's the way you just get them out of your sight and then don't worry about them. Suppose he *did* do some injury to her—we should be responsible." Anderson shrugged. She put down her glass and ran out of the pub door. Anderson followed her. Under the sign of THE DEMON the faded woman in pink sat propped on one elbow crying feebly, and trying to staunch a flow of blood from her nose. There was no sign of the two men. Molly knelt by her side, Anderson stood above them. A confused flow of words came to him: "Nose . . . rotten little devil . . . the rent . . . Rampole Street . . ."

"We've got to get her home," Molly said. "Forty Rampole Street. She says it's just round the corner. That swine!" she said encouragingly to the woman. "I'll tell him something if I see him. Give her your handkerchief, Andy." Reluctantly Anderson applied his handkerchief to the woman's bleeding nose, and helped to lift her to her feet. She was as shapeless as a feather pillow. "I suppose there isn't a spare room at your place for her," Molly said.

"There certainly isn't."

"She shouldn't be left with that man." Together they supported her, each with an arm around her. The woman took not the least notice of them. She lurched forward with Anderson's handkerchief against her nose, muttering. A policeman looked at them suspiciously. They turned the corner into Rampole Street and suddenly the woman came to life again, darting out of their arms to a figure half visible in a doorway. "Jerry!" The big man with the broken nose emerged.

"Oh Jerry, take me home."

"Come on, then," the big man said. With one malevolent glance at Molly and Anderson he strode away along the street. The woman followed a step or two behind him, still clutching Anderson's handkerchief to her nose.

Anderson burst out laughing at the expression on Molly's face. "You've worked in advertising too long; it's softened you up. Come to my place and have another drink." They walked back. Anderson felt suddenly and unreasonably gay, but as they passed the Demon he was oppressed for a moment by a sense of forboding. Something had happened when he came out of the pub; he had seen something strange, something out of place. What was it? The thought escaped him, and he put it away.

The tubular lights flickered, and then illuminated their two figures. "Drink," Anderson said, and poured it. Molly looked round the room curiously.

"Not your taste." With his back almost turned to her, Anderson shook his head. "Val's, eh? Just what she'd like. My my, you need a spring clean, don't you. What's here." She opened the door to the bedroom and stood, hands on hips surveying it. "Blime, a symphony in pink." When Anderson came in she had Val's photograph in her hand. Something about her tall, bony figure drinking in the room and the photograph, sniffing it all up with her big nose, shamed and excited him. "Put that down," he said, and then as she turned in surprise he gripped her by the shoulders and pulled her over to the bed. The glass of the photograph frame broke as it dropped to the floor. Like a man burning with fever dropping into a cool stream, he coupled with her.

7

He was conscious at first only of a sound rhythmically repeated, the pattern of a train's wheels, perhaps, the sound of a sewing machine, but more nearly—more nearly—the scream of a train's whistle as it passed through a tunnel. One tunnel and another and another, and then the noise was transformed into a long thin whistle pulled, one might almost say, through the hole of a needle that was stubbornly resistant to it. And then, as he opened his eyes and stared upward, he realized that the sound was a snore. Awake, on an instant awake and aware of what was happening, he turned to see the white shoulder turned away from him mounting high among the bedclothes. For a moment he hesitated and then touched that shoulder with his forefinger, half expecting to find a marble statue by his side. But the shoulder was warm, it shuddered to the finger's touch, the arm moved slightly and was then flung out along the pink quilt. The whistling ceased, the body turned to him, he saw the face. It was the face of Val. In the half-darkness of the early morning he could see the features distinctly, the wide space between brows, the short nose and upper lip, the tiny mole by the side of the chin. As he traced those familiar features he saw, with a shock of terror, the eyes open slowly and heavily like a doll's eyes and stare at him. His hands moved to push away that face, to close those eyes . . .

A shrill cry awakened him, and a thrashing and beating like that of a trapped bird. Talons tore at his arms. Molly O'Rourke sat upright and naked in the bed, clutching her neck. "Christ," she said, "Christ, you nearly strangled me."

He stared at her without understanding. "But you're not Val."

"And thank God I'm not if that's what she was let in for every night." The marks of his fingers were on her neck.

"I had a dream—a nightmare," he said humbly.

"Well, don't have another. Go to sleep." She turned away from him, and in a few minutes the whistling sounds began again. Anderson lay on his back, staring up into the half-darkness which became slowly half-light. He thought about the letter, and then he remembered what had disturbed him when he came out of the pub.

THE 27th OF FEBRUARY

Upon Anderson's desk there lay an envelope, white, with no name written upon it, placed centrally on his blotting pad. He stood above it, staring down, passing a hand over a chin treated with Hey Presto, which felt remarkably like polished glass. A jumble of thoughts moved in his mind, thoughts of fingerprints and of Val's face as he had seen it in the night and of the red marks round Molly O'Rourke's throat. The telephone rang and he picked it up, staring at the still untouched envelope which contained, perhaps, nothing at all, nothing related to Val. Listening with less than half his mind, he heard Bagseed's voice, nasally imperative: " Action."

" What's that?"

" I say they won't do, Mr. Anderson. Mr. Arthur has never seen anything like them in his life."

For ten minutes Anderson argued about the merits of the drawings at which he had merely glanced. The neck of a frock had been too much rounded, a sleeve was too short and a lapel too wide. The effect was to depreciate the class of goods sold by Kiddy Modes. Mr. Arthur had been much upset. Anderson made notes on a pad and said that he would send up for drawings and get alterations made.

Bagseed's voice took on a note at once conspiratorial and gleeful. " One more point, Mr. Anderson. Have you looked at drawing number eleven?"

" Number eleven?"

" I don't think you can have looked at it closely. Mr. Arthur said, and I was bound to agree, that it really is disgusting."

" Really."

" Disgusting. It's the one with the gym tunic."

" The gym tunic, yes."

" A gym tunic must always be treated carefully, Mr. Anderson. It's a risky garment."

" And you feel the artist hasn't treated it carefully enough."

"My dear Mr. Anderson, your artist has shown her almost doing the splits."

"Oh."

"And she looks—can I be quite frank with you, Mr. Anderson?"

"Quite frank, yes."

"Not many vamps do the splits."

"I beg your pardon."

"Nothing, nothing," said Anderson. "We'll scrap that pinup schoolgirl. Send her back with the others." He hung up and carefully, as though he might be touching a bobby trap, picked up the envelope. There was something inside it, and he slit the top with a paper knife. A piece of paper fell out. It was blank.

He turned the paper over and over in his hand. What had he expected to find? Relief flooded over him; strength seemed to come to his body and resilience to his mind. He laughed aloud, crumpled paper and envelope and threw them into the wastepaper basket. And then, when the first exhilaration was over, he became thoughtful. What was the purpose of this curious pursuit of him? The letter of today was a sheet of blank paper, but the letter of yesterday had been, quite unmistakably, written by Val.

Something in his head moved round and round, round and round. Lessing, VV, Reverton, Wyvern. One of four. Or—he remembered what he had seen in the pub last night. He spoke to Jean Lightley and told her to have the drawings collected from Kiddy Modes. "And ask Mr. Greatorex to come and see me." Then he was there, in front of Anderson's desk, blond, neat ever so slightly deferential.

"Sit down, Greatorex." He looked down at the desk pad. "Didn't I see you last night? In Pimlico?" Would he deny it? But the neat blonde head moved in agreement.

"You were there with Miss O'Rourke." Mildly and pleasantly, Greatorex smiled. "You were in the saloon and I was in the public."

"A long way from home, weren't you, Greatorex?"

"Yes. I live in Islington. I go to see friends in Pimlico sometimes." Now Anderson lifted his head and stared. Greatorex shifted nervously in his chair. "The beer's good in the old Demon."

"You know it? Perhaps you've seen me in there before."

"I don't think so."

"With my wife? A small woman, fair?" Anderson hesitated and went on: "She died three weeks ago."

"Yes, I heard that. I'm sorry."

Greatorex raised his own head and Anderson's stare was met, it seemed, with candour and sympathy. "There's no need to mention that you saw me with Miss O'Rourke. We were just having a drink together, you understand."

"I understand." And now the long gaze, held upon both sides, seemed to be one of deep complicity and comprehension.

2

"Hey Presto," VV said. "Hey Presto, Hey Presto, Hey Presto." Sheets of paper fluttered round him. One dropped into Anderson's lap and he stared at it. A rough pencil layout showed the reflection of a face looking out of a shaving glass, fingers reflectively touching jaw. The drawing had been made with a B pencil. Above it VV had written in a crude, powerful script, "Say Hey Presto," and below, "And forget about shaving." When he looked at the other pieces of paper Anderson saw that they embodied the same idea with different slogans. Wyvern looked at the layouts with positive distaste; he regarded any work of this kind done outside the studio as a reflection upon his own capacities. Reverton's expression was enigmatic as he collected the layouts when they had all looked at them, and replaced them on VV's desk. The little man turned his dog-brown eyes upon each of them in turn. His hands fluttered like butterflies.

"Listen to me now. I am about to make a confession." He bowed his head in penitence. "I asked you to forget that you were advertising men, and remember only that you were human beings in dealing with this thing. *Mea Culpa,* I was wrong. Don't hold it against me." Anderson watched with reluctant admiration as VV joined both hands together in prayer. There it is, he thought; that's the way to do it. He knows he's been contradicting himself right and left and he's persuading us that black's white, like a conjurer. " Let me tell you the result of much cogitation and burning of the midnight oil. I see a need here for drama. There must always be drama in advertising—advertising is the drama of the masses; but here we have a product which is in its essentials dramatic. But there is also, as Rev here has seen with his particularly practical mind, a need for education. How can we combine the two?" Behind the pipe Reverton's face was serene, but he did not look at Anderson. So he's been doing a little idea-stealing again, Anderson thought. Was it possible to imaginé that square jaw, that placid face, belonging to Val's lover? Was it Reverton's hand that had placed the envelope, neat and square and empty of writing, upon his neat, square, empty blotter? He would never have the imagination, Anderson thought, and felt momentarily amused.

" Run the two schemes side by side " VV's hands moved outward. " For big spaces the dramatic scheme. This face reflected in the glass, the face of a supremely contented man. The face of a man who has done with shaving for ever. And to drive it home simply the slogan. The basic slogan will be ' Say Hey Presto—and forget about shaving.' I have indicated some others very roughly, and the genius of our copy boys will find some more. For the smaller spaces an educational campaign. What is this wonderful new cream that has revolutionized men's lives? What are its properties and its make-up? What precious oils enter its manufacture?"

" What do?" croaked Wyvern. He spoke so rarely in conferences that they looked at him in surprise. VV regarded the question rhetorically.

" What do? That's the question to which we give an answer, sober yet interesting, lively without being sensational. Jack, my boy, here's your chance as a typographer. Something chaste, something discreet, something elegant. Andy, here's an opportunity for good straightforward and educational copy. Don't be afraid of packing it. Be factual. Be informative. Let yourself go. Set out what you've got to say under headings. One. Two. Three." VV punched one hand into the palm of the other

Reverton scratched his nose with his pipe. " Doesn't sound too lively."

" It *can* be lively," VV insisted. His eyes were gleaming with love and inspiration. " Make it question and answer. *What is Hey Presto?* It is a cream that etcetera. *What are its constituents?* The rare oils of the tgojumba tree are blended with etcetera. *How is it prepared?* Analytical chemists working in conditions of aseptic etcetera. Christ, do I have to write them all for you?"

While VV talked Anderson had been staring at his mobile face, alight with enthusiasm. He was moved suddenly by a desire to turn that constant enthusiasm and good humour to anger. He coughed. " Did you say this was factual advertising or a patent medicine campaign?"

There was a moment's silence. Then VV spread out his hands again, imperturbably good-humoured. " Ah now, Andy, you expect too much. Advertising is persuasion, not medical science. But do you see what I'm after? We've got to persuade, yes, but we can do it decently not vulgarly; we can set out persuasion in Times Roman instead of . . . " He let the sentence die away and sank back in his chair. His doglike eyes, half closed, moved from face to face.

Reverton scratched his nose again. " Silence reigned," he said humorously. " And we all know what happened after that. Shall I tell you what I think, VV, speaking as one who's seen a bit of life on both sides of the fence—Board Room, Copy Room and Studio?" Body flung back, too tired completely to open his eyes, VV slightly nodded. " I think I'm speaking for the boys when I say that they'd like to feel they're not bound by this scheme of yours, that they——"

Anderson ceased to listen. How many solemn conferences of this kind had he attended over the years? Conferences on the best way of selling boots and toothpaste and machine tools, vacuum cleaners and antiseptics and motorcars? They peeled off in layers from his mind, the ridiculous failures and even more ridiculous successes, the occasion when by a mixture of wheedling and bluster he had jockeyed a superior or a client into accepting his own presentation of an idea. To win it was necessary above all to know when to fight, when to laugh, when to argue earnestly. To an equal the rueful smile: "I'm sorry, but I just can't see it that way, old man." To a superior propounding ideas the youthfully enthusiastic tone: "I say, sir, this really is grand stuff; this'll knock 'em sideways." He had been accomplished in playing those parts and many others, but now something had gone from him, and he could think only that one of these three men might have been his wife's lover.

"Isn't that so, Andy?" Reverton looked at him with a slightly quizzical gaze. "The guinea pig's come to no harm, has he? Hey Presto really works?"

With a conscious effort Anderson brought himself back. "Girls, just feel my chin."

"No five-o'clock shadow?"

"No five o'clock shadow." He ran a hand over the slightly chilly smoothness of his face. "If I were a boxer I'd say I had a glass jaw."

They laughed. That's it, Anderson thought; you can still do it when you try, you can't teach an old dog new tricks but he doesn't lose the ones he's learned. Providing, he noted mentally, he can summon up the energy and interest to go through them. Consciously summoning up the necessary energy, Anderson spoke for ten minutes in a manner both passionate and serious. He said that it was absolutely essential that they should obtain more information from Mr. Divenga. He said that informative copy, even if dedicated to the art of persuasion, must have a firm basis of fact. He was judiciously doubtful about the proposal to split the campaign into halves. He suggested that they work on this idea of VV's, but keep their minds open to other possibilities. He suggested also that a memorandum should be prepared covering the whole subject. Reverton listened with every appearance of interest. VV still lay back in his chair, but his eyes stared at Anderson keenly. Wyvern looked out of the window.

Ten minutes later the meeting broke up. Anderson was the last to leave the room. He was at the door when VV said softly: "Andy." Anderson pivoted on his heel. VV hesitated and then said: "What are you doing for lunch?"

"Nutmeat steak, jacket potatoes and salad with grated new carrot," VV said. "Is that all right?"

The waitress, a brick-red girl with a fanatical eye, bent over him. "Perhaps you'd sooner have the mock-chicken with seakale? or spaghetti and tapioca savory?"

"Nutmeat steak," Anderson said hurriedly, and when she had gone away, "I didn't know you were a vegetarian."

"My boy, I haven't touched meat for six weeks," VV said with the enthusiasm of the reformed drinker. "My stomach was a terrible state. Insomnia, indigestion, sharp pain after food. I knew there was only one thing for it—a clean break. I've made a clean break with meat."

"Do you feel better for it?"

"Of course I feel better. If it weren't so difficult I'd eat nothing cooked, nothing but raw food. Do you know the protein of grated raw cabbage? Do you know what percentage of protein value is destroyed by cooking?" He stared at Anderson indignantly, and then suddenly burst out laughing. "Andy boy, I'm getting to be a bore in my old age."

Anderson joined in the laughter politely. "Last year it was steam baths."

"And before that it was brown paper next to the skin." VV's hearty laugh rolled round the restaurant, startling pale longnosed men crouched over their date and nut salads and their large-footed bare-legged wives munching raw vegetables. "Do you know the trouble with me, Andy? I'm an advertising man. It's an incurable disease. There's nobody more easily sold on a simple nostrum for all human ills than a good advertising man. And do you know why that is?" He flung himself back and stared at Anderson.

"Why?"

"Because we make such a mess of our own lives. We know how to sell other people on happiness, but we've never been able to sell it to ourselves." VV's brown eyes melted with self-pity. The waitress brought the nutmeat steaks. She carefully wiped the edge of each plate and stared at its contents lovingly before she moved away. "I'm a failure," VV said as he stuffed nutmeat steak into his mouth. "I've made a mess of my life."

VV had several moods well-known to his immediate subordinates. They fell into the chief divisions of self-congratulation, self-condemnation and self-pity. These were all capable of refinement into subdivisions by characteristic modifications. There was, for instance, self-congratulation with mock self-mockery: "You struggle to get to the top of the tree, and when you've clambered up it what do you see? A desert." Thus also VV's moods of self-condemnation were based upon recognition of his own wasted genius, and his self-pity was compensated by recognition of his courage in surviving the hard knocks of fate. Anderson ate some food which tasted like sawdust covered with breadcrumbs, and waited for self-condemnation to be replaced by self-esteem.

"And why have I failed?" VV pointed a finger and turned it into a fist. "Because I possessed too many talents. You think that's a good thing? Andy, my boy, it's as fatal as having no talent at all. Composer, singer, painter—did I ever tell you that I had a picture in the R. A. when I was sixteen?" Anderson, who had been told this story many times, made a surprised noise. "I composed an opera when I was twelve. But one's restless, one turns from this to that and at last one becomes—what? An advertising man." VV attacked his jacket potato furiously. "It's a sad end for an artist. I always say thank God for the wife and kiddy, Andy, thank the Lord for the personal life. Though even that——" He sighed heavily and left the sentence unfinished.

"How is Mrs. Vincent?" Anderson scraped pieces of underdone potato out of a burnt jacket. It was Vincent, he thought; he is an attractive man—Vincent was Val's lover. This kind of histrionic nonsense is the kind of thing all women enjoy. Vincent and Val rolled together on the pink bed in the pink room. Anderson had once gone swimming with VV and noted the remarkable furry hairiness of his body. It was this furry animal that he now saw holding Val in a firm grasp, her gaze adoring while out of the animal's mouth poured a sickening stream of self-pity and self-praise. Suddenly Anderson thought of Molly O'Rourke, and of the mask that had turned to him in the night. Nausea overcame him as he stared down at his plate. "I can't——" he said, half rose from his chair and sat down again. One or two long-nosed men looked round.

VV said in alarm: "Andy boy, are you all right?"

"Quite, thank you."

"This stuff takes a bit of getting used to. You have to stick at it." VV pushed his own plate away and played with a toothpick. His stare at Anderson, for all its self-absorption, was remarkably shrewd. "I'd like you to know, Andy, that I feel for you about Val."

"My wife? Yes." Was this, Anderson wondered, the prelude to a confession?

"She had gaiety. That's a great quality in a woman. My wife, now—she lacks it. Never well, you know. A nervous condition. The doctor can't find a cure for it." VV spoke with a touch of pride. He leaned forward and said gently, almost lovingly: "Why don't you take a holiday, Andy?"

"You haven't eaten your nutmeat? Didn't you like it?" the waitress asked accusingly. Anderson shook his head. "It's very good for you. What sweet, please? Prune mould is recommended." They ordered prune mould.

"A holiday," Anderson said vaguely, and then: "You called her Val."

"That was only a manner of speaking. I hardly knew her, of course. You need a holiday, Andy; you're not looking the thing. Let the office do without you for a couple of weeks."

"Did she ever write to you? You'd know her handwriting if you saw it, wouldn't you?"

VV's spoon dipped into a confection of a purplish colour and blancmangish texture with a strip of arsenical green running along its spine, and then was carefully put down. "I don't understand you. What are you trying to say? I'm telling you that you need a holiday, Andy. Don't make it too hard for me."

As though he were outside his own body, Anderson could hear his voice, shrill: "What do you mean?"

"It's being talked about. You're losing your grip—only temporarily, of course, but people get to notice. There was something Rev told me about a desk calendar——"

"Rev? That snake?" Anderson cried. He heard himself and was appalled. "You want to get me out of the way, is that it? And what about the letters?"

"The letters?"

"You'd send them on, I suppose, Post Restante. But I'm not going. You can put them on my desk as usual. There's nothing wrong with my work. This is Rev's plot to get rid of me."

VV was trying to be jocular, not very successfully. "Hold on now, Andy. I'm a democrat, but remember Rev's on the board. If there's anything you want to talk over, let's talk about it sensibly."

"A plot," Anderson shrieked. His outswept arm jerked the glass dish containing his own prune mould to the floor. The purplish mould mingled with the red carpet. There could be no doubt that they had attracted attention. One or two of the women were talking urgently to their companions. There was a flurry at the end of the room. The brick-red waitress was hurrying up to them. At the next table a young man writhed round in his chair and asked politely: "Were you asking for a clergyman?" Anderson stood up. Below him and, it seemed, small, as if seen through the wrong end of a telescope, VV's face stared in astonishment and distress. The waitress confronted him, a solid wall of flesh, her face redder than before with annoyance. "You haven't eaten——" she began. Anderson stepped aside to avoid her and his heel crunched on the glass dish. Pushing aside her statuesque body so that she staggered across a table, he ran out of the restaurant.

4

Few interesting or reliable statistics are as yet available regarding the course of mental breakdown. We can chart with certainty the thought patterns only of those unfortunate people who are incarcerated, more or less permanently, in mental homes; but these are extreme cases, and they must surely be

*unsafe guides to the psychopathological conduct in which
every human being now and then indulges. Anderson's conduct in the restaurant was, beyond doubt, irrational; but it
was the result of extreme emotional pressure, and it would
not be safe to make assumptions from it about his future
behaviour, or about his competence to fulfil his functions in
everyday life.*

These reflections passed through Anderson's mind as he
walked aimlessly about the streets of central London, wandering from Tottenham Court Road through Soho, thence
down to Piccadilly and into Mayfair. He thought of himself
in the third person, so that responsibility for the actions of
this hypothetical Anderson did not concern him. Nevertheless
he *was* concerned, concerned in the sense that he felt a need
to trace the illogicality of Anderson's actions. Such concern
led him to ignore the corporeal universe in which he moved
and with his mind set on problems which he knew to be
insoluble. Anderson's body cannoned into other bodies,
crossed the street against traffic lights, bought a paper and
looked at it without noting its contents, and behaved generally
like a rudderless boat. Some people when drunk lose all surface
knowledge of their intentions, and yet are able to fulfil them.
In much the same way Anderson, after an amnesiac interval,
found himself standing outside a small hairdresser's shop in
Melian Street, near Shepherd Market.

There was nothing remarkable in the shop's appearance.
A sign over the door said in letters of faded gold,
ANTOINE'S, and in smaller letters LADIES' AND
GENTLEMEN'S HAIRDRESSING. Two flyblown
windows offered toothpaste, powder and lipstick. The door
was closed, and the pane of glass in it opaque; but
Anderson had been here before, and knew what he would find
inside. Like an echo, as he stood on the pavement, words
came into his mind that he had read long ago: *In dreams
begin responsibility.* He pushed open the door and was in a
narrow passage between plywood walls. A door to the left said
GENTLEMEN, a door to the right said LADIES, and
from behind these doors came the clip of scissors and the mur-
mur of voices. At the end of the passage a young man sat

behind a counter on which was displayed shaving cream, tooth-paste, face powder and razor blades. The counter, like the front window, was dirty. The young man, on the other hand, was very clean. His dark glossy hair was waved, his nails were manicured, and there were two rings on his fingers. He was playing a game resembling Diabolo, in which he threw up a marble-sized ball and caught it in a small ornamental cup. A spring in the cup released the ball to varying heights, but he invariably caught it. Anderson waited. When the young man had thrown up the ball three times and caught it with unfailing dexterity he gestured toward the counter and said: "Was there something?"

"Lily." This was the first word Anderson had spoken since leaving the restaurant, and it came out harshly.

"If you're wanting flowers you'll do better round the corner."

Anderson cleared his throat. "My number is MM51. Is Lily free?"

The boy paused with his fingers on the spring. "Just now she's busy. Was there anybody else?" Anderson shook his head. "All right, MM51, you said." He picked up a telephone by his side, spoke into it inaudibly and said: "You know where to wait?" He gestured at a red curtain behind him.

With his hand on the curtain Anderson paused. "That's a clever trick. You must have put in a lot of practice."

"And where does it get me?" The boy flipped up the ball again. Anderson passed to the other side of the curtain, let it drop behind him and walked upstairs. Miss Stepley met him at the top. She was a neat woman of forty-five with graying hair. She wore a white coat, and looked like a doctor. She said pleasantly: "Lily's engaged. Will you come into my room? I'm afraid we're rather busy today." She opened a door and stood holding the handle. Anderson was about to move past her into the room when he stood still, immobilized by something extraordinary that he saw. It was, at least, Anderson's impression that he saw this thing: at that moment he believed fully the evidence of his eyes, but perhaps, he thought afterward, he had been mistaken. He was standing on the landing, and Miss Stepley was in front of him, holding open the door to her room. A long passage lined with red plush stretched ahead, and the passage was dim, because there were no windows and the only light came from small fittings set into the ceiling. The door of a room just down the passage opened and a girl came out. Anderson had seen her before; her name was Marjorie. She nodded to him as she handed a small card to Miss Stepley and then pushed open a door neatly labelled REST ROOM. That was not the extraordinary sight: but when Marjorie left the room she did not close the door completely, and through the gap a man's figure was visible. The man sat on the edge of a bed with his hair disarranged. He was engaged in pulling on some full-length underwear, and he looked up, with an expression of annoyance on his slightly flushed face, at the open door. As the man looked up Anderson saw, for a moment, his face; only for a moment, because Miss Stepley quickly moved across and closed the door. There was nothing extraordinary, either, about seeing a man in that room; the extraordinary thing was the man's identity. For the man Anderson thought he saw in the room, pulling on winter underwear, was Mr. Pile.

" This way," Miss Stepley said brightly. Her room contained a large desk, filing cabinets, a table, four spindly chairs. On the wall were a number of machines that looked like time clocks. Miss Stepley looked at the card given her by Marjorie, and pressed a lever on one of the clocks.

" That looks like a time clock."

" It is a time clock. We have one for each of our girls."

" Really? That's a new idea, isn't it?"

" Absolutely. After every engagement a girl fills in a card like the one which Marjorie handed to me. It tells us the length of time for which she was engaged. By clocking in on this machine we can tell her working hours each week. By comparing that with fees paid we can also asses her hourly rate of pay. Of course, the recorders reveal a number of other things, too, like peak periods and slack times. We can tell which girls aren't pulling their weight in the organisation."

" What happens then?"

" We warn them. This is a free enterprise organization, and there is no room in it for inefficiency. The customer is always

95

right, and if a girl's earnings drop it is because she has ignored that elementary fact of economics. If she shows no sign of improvement——"

"You turn her out to look after herself."

"Good gracious, no." Miss Stepley looked shocked. "What do you take us for? This is a business like any other, and we recognize our responsibilities toward our staff. Besides, it is not in our interest that girls should be on the streets in competition with us. No, the organization finds them jobs elsewhere. Girls who have no particular talent in our profession may make excellent assistants behind a shop counter."

"Don't you find that girls ever try to cheat you out of money?"

"Unhappily, yes," said Miss Stepley with real distress. "It's very difficult to obtain a thoroughly satisfactory staff-management relationship. But we obviate that difficulty as far as possible by arranging payment in advance. If, after that, clients still offer gifts to our staff, we can't stop them doing so. But it is an antisocial practice like tipping, and we hope before long to have educated our clients so that they realize our fee covers a full service from the staff. And by the way"—she ruffled through a card index—" you're MM51, aren't you? I see you've paid us three guineas on previous occasions. Would you care to——"

Anderson placed three pound notes and three shillings upon her desk. "Does MM mean anything?"

Miss Stepley looked up from her cash box and smiled briskly. "Speciality masochism, quality mild."

"And everyone's known by a number?" she nodded. "Then it's no use asking you who it was I saw through that open door—he's just a number, too? I thought I knew him for a moment, but I don't think it can have been the same person."

"He is simply a number to us. But in any case it would be a breach of professional ethics to discuss one client with another."

"Yes, I suppose so. You seem to have everything excellently organized."

"Love is a business like any other," Miss Stepley said solemnly. "It was high time somebody understood that."

"It's rather unromantic."

"But hygienic. Frequent staff inspections are carried out. We deal with reality here. Romance can be left to the women's magazines." There was a buzz from the switchboard by Miss Stepley's side. She put on a pair of headphones. "Yes, Lily. I have another appointment for you. Category MM. Can you receive him?" She smiled brightly at Anderson. "Lily is ready for you now. Room 5."

Anderson went along the corridor to his appointment.

Afterward Lily said: "Ten minutes to spare. Got a fag?" She lay on the bed naked, smoking, a big blonde Cockney girl.

Anderson passed his hand over his face, which felt slightly numb. He felt empty in mind and body, curiously light-headed. "Do you like it here?"

"It's all right. Only, of course, you're not free like the way you used to be. It's like living at home."

"Really? I should hardly have thought so."

"You don't see what I mean. They're always going on at you, wanting to do things for your own good. Makes you sick, sometimes. We get three evenings off a week, see, and we have to be back by eleven or our pay packet's docked. Then there's the pension scheme—they dock so much for that. Very good it is, but I'd sooner have the money. Then if you ever pick up a man outside there's trouble if Step gets to know about it. So I generally just go to the pictures with one of the other girls. I love the pictures, don't you?"

"Sometimes."

"I saw ever such a nice film last week, an old one; it was on at our local fleapit. *Mrs, Miniver,* it was called. Walter Pidgeon and Greer Garson. Have you seen it?"

"I haven't, as a matter of fact."

"Oh, you ought to. They're ever such nice people, Mr. and Mrs. Miniver, and it's the war you see, and——" Lily's voice went on. Anderson closed his eyes and wondered why he had come here. What the relation between his urgent bodily need and that awful scene in the restaurant? His mind shied away from thought of the exhibition he had made of himself.

"—and the planes are flying in formation and they stand watching them from the ruins of the church. That's the end."

Anderson opened his eyes and saw that Lily was crying. "It's so sad," she said. "Have you a handkerchief?" She lay on the bed naked with Anderson's handkerchief to her eyes. As Anderson put on his shirt and trousers and stared down at her, he felt desire for her again. "Lily."

She looked at him and then sat up on the bed. "If you want another appointment you'll have to speak to Step. Time's up for this one."

"No." Anderson was not sure that he wanted another appointment, and anyway he was not prepared to spend another three guineas. He finished dressing, walked along the corridor and down the stairs. Outside the red curtain the boy was still playing cup and ball. He did not look up as Anderson passed him. In the street Anderson saw a broad-backed bowler-hatted man in front of him. Something about his figure was reminiscent of Inspector Cresse, but the man turned down a side street and when Anderson reached the corner there was no sign of him.

5

The time was four o'clock. It was difficult to return to the office, but more difficult not to do so. Anderson looked up at the sign which read V I N C E N T A D V E R T I S I N G V I N-C E N T A D V E R T I S I N G V I N C E N T and settled his black Homburg hat firmly on his head. Then he walked in and the swing doors hissed behind him.

Upon his table lay the drawings returned from Kiddy Modes and an envelope addressed to him by VV. He tore open the envelope and read in VV's sprawling hand:

Andy,
    What was all that about? Come and tell me when you feel like it. Not today—I'm at a conference all afternoon, New World Coolers.   VV.

There was a postscript in small writing: "Dare I repeat that you need a holiday?" Anderson laughed. VV was a good chap. He put the note in his pocket, and looked at the drawings.

Bagseed had made notes upon every one of them in a gentlemanly copperplate hand. "Collar on this jacket won't do. Refer to model. J.B." "This dress hangs wrongly. Refer to model. J.B." "Neck of frock incorrect as per our discussion. J.B." The drawing with the gym tunic was marked with a large cross and the word "No" simply. This "No" was also initialled "J.B."

As he looked at Bagseed's comments Anderson found himself becoming angry, and by the time he had read the curt letter that accompanied them he felt the kind of fury known only to advertising men who think they are being treated unfairly. He called in Jean Lightley and pointed to the drawings. "Do you see anything wrong with these?"

She saw Bagseed's comments and gasped: "Oh, isn't he fussy?"

"He is."

"Mr. Crashaw won't like making alterations, will he?"

"He will not. Write to Bagseed and tell him that we have looked at the drawings and cannot agree that they are of a nature to depreciate the class of goods sold by Kiddy Modes. We are, however, having alterations made upon the lines laid down in his instructions. Yours, etcetera. Then write to Crashaw: 'Dear Crashaw, Kiddy Modes have shot these drawings back at us with comments made and bureaucratically initialled. Out of our many pestilential clients Kiddy Modes are perhaps the most pestilential of all. As far as I can see their criticisms on this occasion, as on others, are incompetent, irrelevant and immaterial, and can hardly blame you if you decide to throw in the sponge on this job. I hope, however, that you'll feel able to play along with us and make the necessary alterations. We have to take the rough with the smooth as you know, and Kiddy Modes are just about the roughest there is. They demand just about six times as much attention as any other client of their size. If you can help us out on this occasion it will be much appreciated by me. Sincerely.'"

Miss Lightley murmured, "That's very strong."

"So are my feelings. Get those typed as quickly as you can and send them up by hand." When she had gone Anderson took Val's letter out of his pocket, read it again and put it back. The telephone rang and the switchboard operator said: "Oh Mr. Anderson, Mrs. Fletchley, Mrs. Elaine Fletchley, rang twice while you were out. She said it was important."

"Try and get her for me, will you? at *Woman Beautiful*." The house telephone rang as he picked up the other receiver. He put it to his ear and said: "Anderson."

"O'Rourke."

There was a pause. "What do you want?"

"Haven't we got a date for tonight?"

"We haven't. I'm busy."

"What about a drink?"

"I'm sorry. I told you I'm busy."

There was another pause. "I want to see you, Andy."

Somebody opened the door. "All right," Anderson said. "I'll come in in five minutes."

"Am I interrupting something?" Wyvern asked. "I can come back."

Anderson waved him to a chair. "Not a bit. What's on your mind?"

"I dunno. Bloody old Hey Presto, I suppose. What do you think of that scheme? Tell me honestly, if there's any honesty among account executives. I've got the boys working on half a dozen different ways of presenting that face in the shaving mirror idea, but they all look pretty corny to me."

"Ours not to reason why," Anderson said absently. Was he mistaken in finding something strange about Wyvern, a suppressed excitement in his manner, a hint of uncomfortable revelations about to be made? Wyvern's long legs in corduroy trousers were stretched out against the carpet, his lopsided smile seemed to have a special meaningfulness. Anderson slipped his right hand into his jacket pocket. The telephone rang. He pulled out the letter and placed it on the desk, looking all the time at Wyvern.

"Switchboard, Mr. Anderson. Mrs. Fletchley's in conference. They'll tell her you're in the office as soon as she comes out."

"There's another thing," Wyvern said as Anderson put down the receiver. "Do you know where VV got his bright idea from that he's thought up all of a sudden? I've found the identical layout presentation—face in mirror, product name up above and slogan below—in an old *Saturday Evening Post*, used by Topmost Shaving Creams. What do you know, eh? Doesn't it stink?"

"We all know there's nothing new." Anderson began to play with the sheet of blue writing paper on which Val's letter was written, curling it up in his fingers and uncurling it, looking steadily at Wyvern.

"Nothing new—it's bloody well dishonest, and you know it."

"Dishonest—come now." Anderson opened out the letter carefully and began curling it the other way.

"Perhaps it's not in a way—I know what you mean, old cock. You mean VV probably doesn't realize his own dishonesty; it's just something that's stayed in his mind. And you're quite right, of course; if there's one thing advertising men do better than taking in the public it's taking in themselves. This whole bloody hullaballoo shows that."

"How do you mean?"

"Why, nobody but an advertising agent would believe this story about a magic cream extracted from the juice of whatever it is. That stinks, too. Don't tell me there isn't something phony about Mr. Divenga. With that beard!"

"But——" Anderson raised the letter coiled round one finger and tapped his smooth chin with it. The house telephone rang. Molly's voice said: "Five minutes, remember?"

"When I'm free." He put it down.

"I know, I know," Wyvern said amiably. "Don't tell me. It works. It's the most revolutionary etcetera that homo sapiens has ever invented to ease his spirit in the era of the atom bomb. I see it. But I still don't believe it." During all this time Wyvern had not appeared to notice the letter in Anderson's hand. Now he suddenly said, almost with embarrassment: "What the devil are you doing with that bit of paper, Andy?"

Anderson hesitated for only a second. "That bit of paper, as you call it, is a letter from Val."

"A letter from Val!" Wyvern stared and then said: "Poor old Val. It was a damned shame; the sort of thing that makes you wonder what life's all about. You know what—I was remembering only the other day that silly toast we used to drink."

"Shorter days—longer nights."

"That's right." The suppressed excitement had gone from Wyvern's manner, if it had ever been there. He now looked simply uneasy. "Forgive me for saying so, Andy, but it's no use harking back. We all do it, I know. I often wonder what would have happened to me if I'd left home when I was twenty-one. My mother wasn't bedridden then, and I could have done it. If I had done—but you see it's no use harking back. Get rid of memories, destroy letters, otherwise they haunt you."

"Haunt you?"

"When I was out in the desert I used to look up at the stars and think about my mother, make decisions about what I'd do when I got back. I was going to leave home and make her an allowance. I was going to get out of advertising for good. And there you are—look at me now."

Anderson was not listening. "This letter arrived yesterday morning," he said.

"Yesterday morning! But, Andy, Val died more than three weeks ago."

"That's exactly what I'm getting at. I found this letter on my desk yesterday morning."

At last he had spoken out, and for the first time he had told another human being the incredible truth. The moment remained in Anderson's memory through a pattern of colours. The green carpet, the brown panelling on the walls, Wyvern's stone-coloured corduroy trousers, the white hands resting on them that tightly pressed his knees. He felt, with a kind of triumph, the tension in the room. Something significant had happened, something more significant still would happen in a moment, a gesture would be made or a word spoken that had the quality of a revelation.

The house telephone rang. Molly. He snatched at it and shouted: "I said when I'm free."

"This is Rev here, Andy. You sound het up."

"I'm sorry, Rev. I thought——"

"That's all right. I know you're up to the eyes. Can you come in just for a minute? It's just a little job to be done."

" Right away."

He replaced the receiver, and the moment had gone. Wyvern was standing up, a long thin figure looking down with the oddest expression on his face. " I wanted to know if you had any other Hey Presto ideas we could work on, but we can talk about it some other time." He stopped at the door and said: " If I were you I'd forget all about that letter. I wouldn't tell anyone else about it."

When Anderson left his room to go in to see Rev he heard the sharp rings of the house telephone, but he did not go back. The little job that Reverton wanted done was, as he had said, only a little job: what he had omitted to say was that it was a job he was supposed to do himself. The job was connected with the Crunchy-Munch account. Vincent's had obtained the Crunchy-Munch advertising on the strength of a slogan invented by VV: " First you Crrrunch it Then you Munch it—that's C R U N C H Y - M U N C H." This slogan, with a few variations, had been the basis of Crunchy-Munch advertising for several years. Now they had suddenly become dissatisfied with it ; and although every bar of Crunchy-Munch was sold on the chocolate ration, they had begun to worry about the effect of the advertising on their sales when sweets were un-rationed. " Shall we be ready to go full steam ahead," the Crunchy-Munch advertising manager had asked, in one of those metaphors favoured by all advertising men, " when we get the green light?" He was paid a handsome salary for worrying about such things, and it was customary to send him a yearly memorandum, which had become a sophistical exercise in evolving theories about the effect of various advertising approaches on the techniques of sweet-selling, if it ever became necessary to sell sweets. The purpose of this memorandum was to give the Crunchy-Munch advertising manager something to occupy his time, and also to present a picture of the situation which implied both that a continual jockeying was taking place for future leadership in the confectionery field, and that in this race Crunchy-Munch, thanks to the mental agility of their advertising agents, were always leading by a quarter of a length. This year, however, the memorandum would be a little different; it would have to justify the new scheme which was to be discussed the following morning. Reverton suggested that, since Anderson was in charge of the new scheme, he should write the memorandum, too. " It's not the kind of job I like to delegate," Reverton said with a shake of his square sensible head, " but I've got so much on my plate I think I'll just have to. Anyway, you're right on top of the new scheme, Andy; you're the man to write the memo." Reverton paused and added casually: " By the way, what is the new scheme?"

" We're putting up two ideas." Reverton raised his eyebrows. " One's Lessing's and one's mine. The studio is working on them now. They'll be on the table tomorrow, for you and VV."

" Two schemes, eh? Differences of viewpoint?" Reverton said mildly.

" Just two ways of presenting it. When will you want the memorandum finished?"

" If we pass the scheme through tomorrow, Andy, early next week for the memo. Can do?"

" I suppose so. I don't know when I'm supposed to work on Hey Presto."

" Better hand it back, then, if you haven't got time for it. Mustn't let anything stand in the way of Hey Presto. I was going to give you the dope, but it can stay here." Something in the way in which Reverton tapped the papers on his desk, the readiness with which his own mild grumble had been accepted, seemed curious to Anderson. He felt, with no obvious reason, that he had fallen into a trap.

" That's all right," he said; " I'll manage."

" Grand. Weight off my mind." Reverton handed over the papers with a smile and tamped the tobacco in his pipe thoughtfully. Anderson felt, as he had done a few minutes ago with Wyvern that there had been a sudden drop in the emotional temperature. There had been a moment of crisis, and now it was over; but the nature of the crisis baffled him. He expected, nevertheless, that Reverton would pursue the subject of the memorandum, so that the next remark took him completely by surprise.

" What do you think of Charlie Lessing?"

Anderson quite frankly stared. "Charlie Lessing? As a copywriter, you mean?"

"All round. There's more to being a copywriter than writing copy; you know that." He waited expectantly.

Anderson said: "I don't know just what you want me to say. He's good at classy copy, stuff with plenty of snob appeal, not so hot when something down to earth is wanted." He ended almost with a question. Reverton puffed away at his pipe.

"A nice chap, is he? Easy to get on with?"

"I get on with him. Some don't—think he's a bit superior. Why?"

"One just likes to keep a finger on the pulse," Reverton said with quite uncustomary vagueness. "Harmonious running and all that. So you'll tackle that memorandum after our meeting tomorrow."

Anderson said he would tackle the memorandum. Back in his own room he found Jean Lightley and Molly O'Rourke. Jean was standing guard over the two letters he had asked her to type; Molly was at the window, staring out at the figures on the other side of the well, moving about in their little lighted boxes. She looked round as Anderson came into the room, and then turned her back to him and stared again out of the window.

"Your letters," Jean said.

Anderson looked at his watch. "You could have signed them yourself. It's late."

"I thought perhaps—that one to Mr. Crashaw—you'd like to look at it."

"You're quite right." He signed the letter to Bagseed, and then read the one to Crashaw. It was strong, but not too strong. He signed it. "By hand."

"Oh yes, Mr. Anderson." She brought out hesitantly: "Mrs. Fletchley rang through and spoke to me. She's had to go out and you can't reach her. She'll be at a party later on this evening—at the Pollexfens', she said. She said it was something important."

Anderson looked at Molly's hostile back. "The Pollexfens' yes; thank you, Jean." She went out. Without turning round Molly said: "Five minutes."

Anderson put down the Crunchy-Munch papers and said with elaborate patience: "I told you I was busy."

"Too busy to come in and see me."

"That's right."

"Too busy to see me tonight."

"That's right."

"But not . . ." Since Molly was standing with her back to him, addressing the window, Anderson could not hear her.

"If you'd turn round," he said, and at that she turned round and showed tears running down either side of her great nose. Her voice was choked.

"Not too busy to see Elaine Fletchley."

"I haven't seen Elaine."

"You've been trying to see her. Ringing her up."

The tears blotched Molly's powder. Anderson contemplated her with distaste. "You know why I want to see her. I asked you last night if Val had an especial boy friend. Now I'm going to ask Elaine."

"Why?"

Suddenly Anderson's control left him. He smacked the desk lightly with the palm of his hand. "Because Valerie was somebody's mistress."

"So what?"

"And it was somebody in this firm." Now, Anderson thought, I've done it; the cat's really out of the bag. But to his surprise Molly seemed not to find the news exciting.

"What does it matter? She's dead. It won't bring her back. And anyway, you never loved her." Molly dabbed at her eyes. "I must look awful. I'm making a fool of myself. I've never met a man who didn't give me a runaround. And do you know another thing—I've never failed to come back for more. I'm a fool that's all, I'm a fool." She began to cry again, weakly and without conviction. Anderson picked up the Crunchy-Munch papers again, and pretended to study them. "You don't want to make love to me."

"Not at this moment, thank you."

"You don't even want to kiss me?"

"No."

She tottered toward him on her high heels. "Give me a kiss to show you don't hate me."

"For God's sake, Molly, we're in the office."

"It's time to go home. Everybody's going home. Nobody will come in. Just one kiss."

"Very well." Anderson got up and advanced toward her round the desk. Her nose at this distance, and under harsh electric light, was revealed as one of gastly shape and size, almost like a false nose put on for a charade. Was it possible, if one kissed her, to avoid a jarring contact with that forward and hunting proboscis? It appeared not; and yet it had been possible, no later than last night. Very gingerly Anderson's lips approached the tear-ravaged face. Reluctantly he felt the warmth of her body against his own. He closed his eyes, like a child about to drink medicine, and thus he did not see Molly's withdrawal from him, but simply felt it in terms of decreased warmth. He opened his eyes again. Molly was staring past him. He turned round and saw VV standing in the doorway, hatted, overcoated, staring at them.

6

At one moment VV was standing there before Anderson's astonished eyes. In the next moment, without speaking he was gone. Had he really been there at all? With vigorous gesture Anderson pushed Molly away from him and opened the door. He ran down the corridor in time to see the door of VV's room close and present to him so blank an oak face that he was moved by the kind of fear he had known in childhood when he had been found out in wrongdoing and had been locked in his room, not, as his mother impressed on him, as a punishment, but so that he could "think it out." He felt at those times a weight of guilt that could be dispersed only by contact with the judge, his mother, even though when he saw her he had nothing to say. So now, with the sense of betrayal strong upon him, he felt it essential to see VV. He crossed the landing, tapped on VV's door gently and entered.

The bright, inquisitive, intelligent face that was turned to-

ward him seemed wholly friendly; it showed no consciousness
of having witnessed that scene in Anderson's office a moment
ago, no recollection of that appalling luncheon. Anderson felt
again, as he had felt several times in the past forty-eight years,
that the events in his life somehow failed to be interconnected
as events should be in a life properly organized and rational;
the happenings of yesterday, the errors of luncheon, the visit
to Miss Stepley's establishment, seemed to bear no relation to
what was happening here and now. Had these things really
happened? If they had, Anderson thought, they must be on the
tip of VV's tongue; they will surely be mentioned. But VV,
instead, presented him with two thumbs triumphantly raised.
"New World Cooler," he said. "Everything went like a
dream. Approved this, approved that, approved the other—
only two small copy revisions. Lessing's scheme, wasn't it?
Well, it's very good work. Congratulations all round are in
order. Copy, Studio—even the man who took it up and sold
it to them takes a bow." Gracefully VV bowed, and added
solemnly: "It's times like these—intelligent scheme, intelligent
client, no squibbling—that make one feel advertising is worth
while." He looked at his watch and showed a rare trace of
nervousness. "What are you doing for dinner tonight? Can
you come back with me? Belsize Park, you know. Only
en famille—but it's rather an occasion in a way. And we
should have time for a talk." With an upward look, humorous
and shy, he said: "We ought to have a talk, you know."

Anderson had dined once before with VV and his wife, but
that had been in a restaurant. Was it a mark of favour to be
asked to dine with him at home? While he was pondering
this point, VV said with a small intimate smile: "Better get
your hat and coat. And get rid of your—visitor."

"I'd like you to understand, it's——"

"Not another word. I do understand, my boy. I understand
perhaps better than you think."

Molly was still in Anderson's room. She looked at him as
if he were a stranger. "Where are you going?"

Anderson put on his overcoat. "I'm invited out to dinner
with the boss."

She continued to stare at him. "There's been a telephone

call. It was a policeman named Cresse. He wanted to know
if you'd be at home tonight. I told him I didn't think you
would. He said he'd call anyway."

"That was absolutely right." Anderson adjusted his black
hat at a jaunty angle. "Did he say anything else?"

"He said that the air was unhealthy in Melian Street. He
said you'd understand."

VV's high spirits were gradually dissipated on the way out
to Belsize Park. In the underground train they were packed as
close as tinfoil, and he talked about travelling conditions. "I
admire," he said loudly to Anderson as they swayed on the
same strap, "the enormous capacity of modern man for endur-
ance. But it's unhealthy. The real, healthy thing is the capacity
for rebellion. I don't see any sign of that around us." His
waving hand, with a large parcel in it, described a small
part of a semicircle and then was stopped by contact with
a bulky figure in dungarees. The figure glared. VV glared back,
but he stopped talking. After they got out at Belsize Park he
was monosyllabic, and they trudged up Haverstock Hill in
silence. Then VV said: "Marriage is a terrible thing."

"What's that?"

"I say marriage is a terrible thing. Have you met my wife?
She's a terrible woman." Anderson found nothing to say.
"Sometimes I wonder why one does it all. Advertising, I
mean. Working, working, working—abandoning an artistic
career—and for what? To support a woman who just doesn't
care." VV's rich voice was low and emotional, as though he
were about to cry. "I sometimes think you've got the best of
it. A girl like Molly——"

"Look here," Anderson said, "I shouldn't like to think that
was anything serious. It's not."

This time VV was able to make the semicircular arc without
obstruction. "I'm a man of the world, Andy. I understand
these things. I don't want to inquire into your private life.
Probably none of our private lives will bear inspection."

"But——"

"Though there are compensations. Did you know I had a
stepdaughter? Her name's Angela. She's a nice girl. It's her
birthday today. Fourteen."

109

"Shan't I be in the way?"

"Oh, not at all," VV said gloomily. "Quite the contrary. And we must have our talk, don't forget that." His voice was now almost threatening.

VV lived in a large block of flats. They went up three floors in a lift and down to the end of a corridor. As he turned the key in a highly varnished maplewood door VV gave a low-pitched whistle. There was a sound of running feet. The door opened and a large girl flung her arms round VV's neck. "Daddy!" she cried. With a look almost of idiocy VV put his arms behind his back. "Daddy, what have you got? Oh, who's this?" Anderson found himself shaking hands with the girl. She was large-boned, red-haired, slightly freckled, and attractive in a peasant-girl manner. She looked at least sixteen years old. "It's my birthday," she said. "Have you brought me a present?"

"I'm afraid I haven't," Anderson said. "But many happy returns, all the same."

"Thank you. Oh, Daddy, what are you hiding?"

With ghastly agility VV skipped behind Anderson, holding the brown paper parcel still concealed. Angela shrieked and pursued him. Using Anderson as a fixed central pole, they danced round the little hall, giving cries and shouts of pleasure. At last Angela caught her stepfather and they struggled together as she tried to get the parcel. "Catch," VV said. The package came flying through the air to strike Anderson chest high. He hugged it in both arms as the door opened and a voice said: "What is this brawl?"

Anderson remembered Mrs. Vincent as large and bony. She now appeared smaller, but bonier, than he remembered. Her face was long and thin with a knifelike nose between high cheekbones from which the flesh fell away. Her breastless body was clothed in a long dark sack tied at the waist. Her hands, dropped at her sides, were long and colourless. She stood framed in a dark doorway, looking at her husband and daughter. "Victor," she said, "don't be disgusting."

VV removed his arm from Angela's waist and took off his overcoat. "My dear, I'm glad to see you up." His tone was one that Anderson had never heard him use before, the gentle

110

placatory tone that an actor uses to a stage invalid. "This is Mr. Anderson from the office. Perhaps you will remember him."

"Go and wash your face and hands, Angela. You look grubby." With awful gentility Mrs. Vincent said to Anderson : "How do you do? We have met at the firm's dances, have we not? But this is an unexpected pleasure." Anderson tucked the parcel under one arm and took her limp hand.

"VV was good enough to invite me at very short notice. I hope I haven't put you out."

"Nothing puts me out," Mrs. Vincent said, not reassuringly. She was staring at the parcel under Anderson's arm.

VV made a gesture towards the parcel. "And what do you think? He's brought a present for little Angela's birthday."

"That was kind," said Mrs. Vincent. "And particularly clever, at such short notice. But unnecessary. What is the gift, may I ask?"

"A pair of ice skates," VV said hurriedly. Anderson patted the parcel and idiotically repeated the words. Angela ran out to the hall again and cried: "A pair of ice skates."

"Happy birthday," Anderson said, and dumped the parcel in her arms. She looked at him uncertainly. Mrs. Vincent's thin voice said: "Thank Mr. Anderson for his gift."

Angela opened the parcel. A card dropped out, which she glanced at hurriedly and put into her pocket. "They're lovely," she said. "Thank you awfully."

In words as clear as drops of water Mrs. Vincent said: "A card too. How very thoughtful Mr. Anderson is. What does it say?"

"It just says happy birthday."

"I am sure it must say something more interesting than that. Give it to me, Angela."

"Would anybody mind," Anderson said, "if I took off my overcoat?"

"My dear boy." VV rushed forward. There was a little flurry. Anderson was freed of his overcoat. He turned round to see that Angela had torn the card to shreds. She faced her mother defiantly and said: "You shan't see what's on it." Mrs. Vincent's limp hand came up and struck the girl upon the cheek. To Anderson she said with perfect politeness: "You'll excuse me, I am sure, Mr. Anderson. I have a sick headache." She was swallowed up in the darkness behind her.

Angela stood facing her mother's closed door, cried two words at the top of her voice, and ran into another room, holding the ice skates in her hand. The first word Angela cried was "You." The second pulled Anderson's mind away from his surroundings to the establishment in Melian Street. Would there be any place for such words in Miss Stepley's aseptic sexual paradise? Probably not. Or perhaps they might be uttered only by special dispensation as erotic stimulants.

VV sighed. "I expect you'd like a drink." He led the way into a pleasant but untidy sitting room. "You see how it is. Of course, she's not well. Any excitement upsets her and she has to go to bed. Nervous trouble—but I told you that, didn't I? What can you do?" VV fiddled with the glasses. He was so unlike the benevolent dictator of the office that Anderson felt he was talking to a stranger.

He said with a shade of understatement: "She doesn't get on with Angela?"

"That's the trouble. The fact is that I love Angela like my own daughter. You'd think Mary would be pleased. But is she pleased? Instead she does everything she can to make life miserable for all of us. Do you know the cause of all this trouble just now? The theatre."

"The theatre?"

"We were going to the theatre tonight for Angela's birthday. But—Mary has a sick headache." VV laughed without amusement, and yet with a faintly histrionic air. "I know what you're going to say—why don't we go without her? Impossible, my boy, impossible. She goes to our neighbours' flats and becomes hysterical. She sleepwalks if she knows she's alone. Once she fell out of a window. That was not here," VV said in a regretful voice. "It was a first-floor window. Little damage was done. But she can't be left alone."

"I don't see where I come in."

"We've got to have our talk." But VV said it with little energy or interest. "And the fact is, she's been more than

112

usually intolerable lately. I thought a visitor might—ease the strain. Perhaps I was wrong. Ah, here comes Angela. Now we can have—ah—have supper."

Supper had a certain surrealist quality. VV ate only lettuce, seedless raisins, grated carrot and nuts, but he was anxious for Anderson's welfare. "Eat up," he said. "Take plenty of everything." Anderson found it difficult to follow this advice. The food had come from the delicatessen counter of a very high-class store, and it was all covered with jelly. Anderson ate gingerly of cold consommé followed by prawns in aspic and by chicken in a huge square jelly casing. The jelly stuck like glue to his teeth; the Russian salad that accompanied the chicken, on the other hand, tasted like small cubes of ice. Angela told him that Mrs. Vincent had put it into the cold storage department of the refrigerator by mistake. The white wine afforded a contrast to the Russian salad, for it had inadvertently been placed by the electric fire, and was luke-warm.

"Mother ordered everything from the food department of Jockney and Hanson," Angela said demurely. "Did you think she had done it all herself?" She had changed both her dress and her appearance. She was now wearing a green evening frock and had swept up her red hair to reveal neat ears remarkably like her father's. Only, of course, Anderson reflected, he was not her father, but her stepfather. The effect of the new hair style was to make her look eighteen instead of sixteen.

Anderson sloshed some warm wine about in his mouth. It removed pieces of jelly from his teeth and unfroze some small cubes of Russian salad. "Are you really only fourteen today, Angela? You look much older."

"Do I?" She glowed. "You hear that, Victor?" VV nodded gloomily. She turned again to Anderson. "You didn't buy me the ice skates, did you? The card said: 'For Angela, with love.' You wouldn't have said that, would you?"

"I might have said it," Anderson replied gallantly, "but I didn't buy the ice skates."

"But still it was sweet of you to try to get us out of trouble."

113

She looked archly at VV, who was scooping the last mouthful of carrots and raisins from his plate. "We're always in trouble with Mummy, Victor and I. Do you like ice skating?"

"I've never tried."

"It's so graceful—you just fly along. Victor sometimes comes with me, don't you? I say, this wine is nice, isn't it?"

"Delicious."

"Mummy doesn't let me drink wine. Isn't it lucky she's ill?" She gazed from one to the other of them.

Anderson coughed. "Perhaps she would like a little—a little consommé."

"Oh no, Mummy enjoys being ill. I say, shall we have some more wine? I know where there's another bottle."

VV said weakly: "You've had enough to drink."

"It's my birthday," she pouted. She was certainly remarkably pretty. "And I want it. I'm going to get it." She jumped up and ran out into the kitchen. While she was out of the room VV rolled his brown eyes ceilingward in mock appeal. Angela came back with another bottle. VV pushed away his plate with an air of hunger. "I think I might have a little sweet. What is it?"

"Fruit and ice cream." Anderson brightened, but the fruit arrived embedded in jelly. His spoon slid off the stiff surface of the ice cream. He thrust furiously at the jelly and succeeded in extracting small, tasteless pieces of cherry, pear and banana. VV pushed his sweet aside and sat picking his teeth with a silver toothpick. Angela ate the whole of her sweet with much apparent enjoyment. Anderson tried a mouthful of wine and found that the second bottle was, if anything, warmer than the first.

"It's good wine, isn't it?" Angela said. "I mean, I don't know anything about wine, but I like this, don't you? Oh, but I asked you that before. You are a couple of deaf mutes, you two, aren't you? I mean to say, can't we do something? Oh well, if you're not going to talk, I shall go out and make coffee." She disappeared again.

Conspiratorially, VV leaned over the table. "I suppose you wouldn't like to take Angela to the Palladium? I've still got the tickets, you know, and——"

" I'm afraid not," Anderson said firmly. " I mean, I should like to, but I have to go along to a party."

" You could take her with you."

" And what about our talk?"

" Oh that—that can wait. Will you take her to the party?"

" Well really, I'm afraid——"

" No? No, I suppose not. You don't mind my asking, do you?"

Angela came in a little unsteadily with coffee and biscuits on a tray " I say, let's dance. You do dance, don't you?" Anderson admitted that he did. " And so does Victor, only he never will. But tonight you *must* because it's my birthday." She darted over to VV, took his hands and pulled him from the chair.

" But what about the noise? Your mother——"

" Oh, she won't hear it if we have it low. After all, it's my *birth*day. Next to ice skating, I love dancing more than anything in the world. Don't you, Mr. Anderson? I say, what's your Christian name?"

" That's something I never reveal."

" Then I shall call you Andy. I'll turn on the radio. Oh, but I suppose you want some coffee." Anderson half expected the coffee to be warm jelly and was pleased to discover that it was quite drinkable. Encouraged, he bit into a biscuit, but his teeth refused to close on it. The biscuit bounded from his mouth on to the table. Angela was convulsed with laughter, as she explained that these rubber bouncing biscuits were kept specially for guests. Even VV came out of his abstraction to venture a sad smile. Anderson did not find himself much amused. The incident made him aware that he was painfully hungry.

In the sitting room the radio was playing dance music very softly. Only one light was switched on faintly illuminating walls and chairs and bookcases. " Come *on*," Angela said. " Let's dance." She seized her stepfather by the waist and they began to shuffle over the carpet together. Anderson dropped into an armchair and twiddled with the half-full wineglass which he still held in his hand. Like somnambulists the two figures swayed in their erotic clinch as the radio played

115

It was all over my jealousy;
My crime was my blind jealousy. . . .

The *Radio Times* was by his chair. Anderson picked it up and
saw that the programme was "Hit Tunes of 1942." Nineteen
forty-two, he thought, nineteen forty-two. What did the date
mean? That was the year when he was thirty-two years old.
That was the year when he married Val. That was the year
when he might have been called up—when, in fact, he would
have been called up, but for Reverton. In that year Vincent
Advertising had been told that they must cut down their staff.
They cut, and cut again; and at last there came a day when
either Anderson or a man named Goble had to be relinquished.
Goble was a studio artist who made layouts for the Ministry
of Knowledge and Communications schemes, on which Anderson was then writing the copy: he was thirty-five, two years
older than Anderson; he had two children. Anderson would
have had to go, there was no doubt about it, but for good old
Rev. Good old Rev had been a tower of strength; good old
Rev had not much liked Goble, who was inclined to be inde-
pendent and sometimes came in late and had a habit of taking
things to VV direct, over Rev's head; good old Rev saw a
chance of placing Anderson permanently in his debt. All
this had been understood when good old Rev said: "It's a
toss-up, I don't mind telling you that, Andy, but I'm going into
that Board Meeting to fight like hell to have you retained.
We've always got on together, haven't we? But it's not a
question of that; it's just a matter of which man is the most
valuable to the organization." And then good old Rev had
paused, had taken the pipe out of his mouth shrewdly and then
had looked shrewdly at Anderson. "Unless, of course, you
feel that you must go, Andy." That was the decisive question,
the decisive answer, that put you in Rev's power. For after
you had equivocated, after you had said that if you had to go
you'd do your bit as well as the next man, that if you really
thought you'd be more useful in the army than here doing
essential propaganda work you'd go like a shot, but it was
obvious that you weren't. . . . After you'd said all that
you'd delivered yourself over to good shrewd old Rev, and you

116

could never really argue with him on even terms again. And that was all recognized when good old Rev put his pipe back again and said: " I want you to know, Andy, that I'm going to do my damnedest to swing it for you." And good old Rev had swung it (or perhaps there had been no question of swinging it, perhaps that was just Rev's fun, perhaps the votes of all the directors had gone to him without question), and Goble had been released from deferment and conscripted, and had died on the Normandy beaches, earning himself a posthumous M.C. And the curious thing, Anderson thought as he sipped his lukewarm wine, is that I shouldn't have minded the army at all, that I shouldn't have minded dying, that I should have been very capable of the act of enforced heroism, the action to which there existed no alternative. And why did I accept good old Rev's offer? Because it was the smart thing to do, because it was always foolish to stick out one's neck. There, but for the grace of good old Rev . . .

" Andy, Andy," Angela was calling him. " Come on, Andy. I've kept this dance for you on my card."

VV's face was very red. He dropped into a chair which was completely in shadow.

" VV," Anderson said, " will you tell me something. Do you remember Goble?"

" Poor old Goble." VV nodded.

Good old Rev and poor old Goble. " You remember we had to release him. Either he or I had to go; that's right, isn't it?" VV coughed. Anderson waved his hand impatiently. " I know that's how it was. What I wanted to ask was this. How did the discussion go at the Board Meeting?"

" It's a long time ago, Andy."

" Don't tell me you can't remember," Anderson said rudely.

With a trace of his vanished Olympian office manner VV said: " I was going to say it's a long time ago, and I don't see it can do any harm to tell you. There wasn't any discussion. We knew you were the man we had to keep." He sighed. " And so poor old Goble went."

" Oh, come on," Angela said. " Don't start jabbering." She pushed herself into Anderson's arms and he smelled her hair.

117

Good old Rev, Anderson thought; he fought for me right to the last ditch, only there wasn't any fighting to do. He became aware that Angela was speaking. "I beg your pardon."

"I said don't you think this is a miserable way to spend a birthday?"

"I'm sorry, I'm afraid I'm not exactly gay company."

"Oh, I don't mind. I don't suppose you like me at all, though, do you?"

"Certainly I do." As much, he said to himself, as I like any girl or woman.

"I've always liked older men. I mean, you're fairly old, aren't you?"

"In my thirties."

"That's what I mean." They shuffled round and round. A crooner sang

> *I never said thanks*
> *For that lovely week end,*
> *Those few days of heaven*
> *You helped me to spend . . .*

".I never did hear such a soppy old song," sang Angela. "Did you?"

"Perhaps not. It was popular when I married my wife."

"Oh, you're married. Where's your wife?"

"She died this month."

"Oh yes, I've heard about you."

"What have you heard?"

"Only that you were upset, behaving oddly, couldn't forget her. I bet I could make you forget her." She moved closer to him.

"Behaving oddly?"

"Excuse me cutting in on you." Anderson felt himself pushed away. Angela giggled and slipped into her stepfather's arms. They swayed together, making the beast with two backs, the single and intolerable beast, in the deeply shadowed room. In the very darkest recesses of the room, in the deepest double beds of shadow, Anderson thought, what secrets might be drawn forth by this sickly music and this sweet warm wine? He stood with one arm on the mantelpiece and, with a slight alcoholic drowsiness, watched the beast swaying.

The lights went on. The recesses were exposed to light. The whole room was rich with it, yet strangely the effect was that of a torch shone directly at a face in sleep. The sleeper turns and twists, but he has been speared firmly by the hook of light; and behind the torch he knows there is a judge's hanging face. So, wrenched from their private dreams and lusts, Anderson and VV and Angela blinked and rubbed their eyes and stretched like figures dropped from a congenial extra-terrestrial existence into the real unpleasant world. The cause of the translation, Mrs. Vincent, stood in the doorway. She still wore the dark sack, but her hair was disordered, and Anderson saw with dismay that she had been crying. She strutted slowly, like a breastless pigeon, into the room, infecting them all with her overpowering sense of guilt and shame. Anderson, certainly, waited expectantly for some final pronouncement to drop from her tongue, some word that would make plain the nature of the lotus-land into which they had inadvertently strayed. He found it incongruous that the word she finally ejected like a stone from her lips had a positively banal appropriateness. " Disgusting," Mrs. Vincent said, and without warning dropped with firmly closed eyes on to a convenient sofa.

Her faint, however transparently simulated, had the effect of jerking into action the three figures who seemed set in their surroundings like flies in amber. Angela darted off once again into the kitchen. VV, crying " Her salts, her salts . . . " ran out of the door that led to the hall. Anderson, left alone with the recumbent figure, rather feebly patted its cold, long hands which showed no awareness of his touch. The application of smelling salts to the narrow nostrils, and the pouring of brandy between the colourless lips, however, proved more effectual. As suddenly as she had dropped down Mrs. Vincent, with rather the effect of a jack-in-the-box, sat up and stared at the three faces bending over her. She spoke, but only to Anderson, as though the scene she had interrupted proved a theorem long argued between them. " You see."

But as she straightened Anderson straightened also, so that the effect of her confidence was lost, " I must be leaving, I fear.

An appointment." VV also straightened and nodded to Anderson, as though in relief.

"An appointment," Angela said mockingly. "It's not an appointment; it's a lovely party. I heard you say so when I was in the kitchen. And you won't take me. Why won't you take me?"

Mrs. Vincent, whose comments at this time had the merit of brevity, ejected another stone, this time directed straight at Angela.

"My daughter," she said witheringly.

"And why shouldn't he take me?"

"You should be in a reformatory," Mrs. Vincent said faintly.

"You only think so because you're repressed. You look through keyholes. You ought to be in a home."

"Ha ha ha!" Mrs. Vincent's falsetto laughter was positively frightening. She dropped her voice, most effectively, to a conversational level, as she said: "A period in a reformatory school would do you a great deal of good. I shall make inquiries——"

"They'll put you in the loony bin," screamed Angela. She began to dance round her mother, rolling her head idiotically, flapping her hands, and chanting: "The loony bin, the loony bin, they put her away in the loony bin." Anderson and VV left the room unnoticed. Anderson put on his coat in silence, while VV ran his hands through his hair over and over again, saying: "Sorry, sorry, I'm really awfully sorry."

"Say good-bye to your wife and stepdaughter for me."

"I'll see you downstairs." When they stood in the vast gilt hall that was the entrance to the flats, VV sighed. "A problem child."

"There are no problem children," Anderson quoted sententiously. "Only problem parents."

"And stepparents?"

"And stepparents."

"I must go back there. We don't seem to have had a chance to have our chat, do we?" VV took Anderson's hand and gripped it. "I'm sorry about the way everything's turned out."

"That's all right."

" I hope it's a good party." VV stood on the steps, waving good-bye. He looked extremely forlorn.

7

Adrian and Jennifer Pollexfen had a tiny mews house at the back of Portland Place. They were the constituent elements of a firm named Pollexfen and Pollexfen, and in that capacity called themselves " Design Consultants." They were prepared, for a suitable fee, to design in a modern manner anything from a teapot to a motorcar, an electric toaster to a radio-gram, a hockey stick to a new range of cosmetics. The occupation is one recently discovered, but once discovered quickly seen to be indispensable to industry. It will be readily appreciated that the design consultant has an honoured place in the advertising profession, and also that each design consultant will be likely to have his particular variation of style. All design consultants, of course, adhere, in their fashion, to modern conventions: but some are still old-fashioned enough to be stuck in a Le Corbusier doctrine of fitness for purpose, while others have passed beyond that to the belief that some form of ornamentation, or even of free idea association in design, is permissible. The particular distinguishing feature of Adrian Pollexfen's style was that he managed to make the most disparate objects look like pieces of sculpture by Henry Moore. " U.B.D.," Adrian would say, which being interpreted meant " Unity plus Beauty equals Design "; and he would point to the teapot with its hollowed centre and its lid strongly resembling one of the pinheads to be found on Moore's gigantic figures ; to the surprising radio cabinet which had dials for breasts and was divided at the crutch; to the abstract shapes he had designed for Mary Magdalen cosmetics. Jennifer added the weight of an enormous mass of statistical information to Adrian's artistry on the drawing board; she was very ready to show the design development of a particular article since its invention, and to analyse the reasons for the various modifi-cations of existing shapes in historical, economic and artistic terms. Jennifer, it was said by the unkind, first blinded prospec-tive clients with science and Adrian then slew them with

121

charm. The Pollexfens were great party givers. They were anxious to be intimate friends with as many people as possible; and it is well known that there is no better way of being intimate friends with people than by introducing them to other people at parties.

Anderson wondered, as his footsteps rang on the cobblestones, what he was doing here. Why did Elaine want to speak to him? What could she possibly have to say that was important? In the dark mews the Pollexfens' house was a block of light. A kind of subdued hum came from it, a medley of sounds such as one might expect to hear at the recording of a meeting at the Tower of Babel. Anderson went up the narrow staircase, giving a glance at the alcoves on either side where Pollexfen designs were displayed under perspex; the electric iron like a recumbent woman, the double-headed refillable shaving tube which squirted brushless cream from one head and talcum powder from the other, the toys resembling elemental human figures. At the top of the stairs Jennifer Pollexfen met him, her round face grave at usual, her hair hanging down her back in two long pigtails. They had met once or twice before, but he was surprised by the warmth with which she greeted him. Anderson looked at the thick wedge of humanity behind her, and was reminded of the pictures he had seen of American football.

" There's someone you'll like to meet," Jennifer Pollexfen said. " But a drink first. We'll have to fight, I'm afraid."

" I don't mind about a drink. I'd hoped to see Elaine."

" She's about somewhere," Jennifer Pollexfen said vaguely. " But let's——" He could not hear the next words for, beckoning him to follow, she threw herself, pigtails waving behind her, into what seemed the most crowded part of the scrum. surprisingly, it parted for her; arms were withdrawn, legs seemed to bend away as though made of plasticine, and miraculously they came out into a backwater occupied by a square-headed man with cropped hair and a grey beard who stood munching a sandwich from a paper bag. Jennifer Pollexfen beamed with the consciousness of achievement; her round face was rosy. She spoke, but the words were inaudible, until Anderson suddenly heard " Professor Protopopoff." He extended a hand and the Professor, stuffing his sandwich into the bag and the bag into his pocket, squeezed the hand in a powerful grip and grinned as widely as a cat. When Anderson looked round Jennifer Pollexfen had vanished, swallowed up in the scrum. The Professor was talking, but the noise around them was so great that Anderson could not hear a word he said. This failure in audibility by the Professor was like a break in the sound track of a film—except that the break involved the Professor alone, for all around them the sound track was only too plainly audible. A beefy young man at Anderson's side had obviously just made a joke. He roared with laughter. " Ha ha ha," he yelled, and dug at Anderson with his elbow at each roar. " Ha ha ha," cried a girl in poison green and a man in an egg-yellow pullover. The three of them rocked gently before Anderson's eyes. And then suddenly the Professor's sound track was working. In perfect English, but with a slight accent, he said: ". . . of the syntagma."

" I beg your pardon."

The professor was perfectly audible. " I said that, for me, a syntagma is a grammatically free group of signs correlating a determining with a determined term in a binary structure. Now, from the mnemonic point of view——" his eyes rolled alarmingly—" from the mnemonic point of view, a partial syntagma of discourse is a complete mnemonic syntagma if by a mental association it can be reduced to a sentence, of which the determined term is the subject."

" Oh."

" Take advertisement."

" What?"

" I say take advertisement. That is a virtual syntagma, is it not? And yet it is reducible to——"

" You'll have to excuse me," Anderson said; " I'm looking for somebody."

" But, Professor——"

" I'm not a professor. My name is Anderson."

" You are not Professor Protopopoff? The grammarian? No?" The grey-bearded man looked extremely offended. " You have been trying to make a fool of me." He turned his back on Anderson and took out his paper bag again. Anderson lowered his head and charged into the crowd. But the bodies that had parted before him when he had followed Jennifer Pollexfen's pigtails now seemed to have taken an obstinate quality of resistance. At one point his way was blocked by two men with enormous stomachs which swelled out of their bodies like balloons. A long way above these touching balloons their mouths were opening and shutting; below, the balloons were supported on spinetlike trousered stalks. For a moment Anderson was seized with a desire to drop down and crawl beneath that bridge of stomachs. Instead he stared angrily at the men and said: "Excuse me." The two heads, as he spoke, seemed to diminish, the stomachs to expand threateningly; then normality returned, the men were men and their stomachs were merely sizeable, and he pushed a way between them. At another time, and quite unexpectedly, he found himself transformed from the outside to the inside of a conversational group. He had been beating on them unvailingly with apologies, with "Would you let me pass" and "Excuse me please," with unnoticed shoulder taps and unsuccessful sidelong shuffles. They seemed not to notice his existence. And then suddenly he was in the middle of them, a drink was pushed into his hand, he drained it with a confused impression that it was something unusual, and received another, he was clapped on the back and the chatter, instead of moving away from his ears, was all aimed directly at him.

"So this bastard said to old Jock, he said, every well-read man reads *The Economist*."

"And then Jock says, well, I'm as red a man as most, and e con o mist comes over my eyes when I see that paper."

"And this bastard says I tell you frankly, Jock, I don't think you're pulling your weight."

"Weight, Jock says, weight, you could do with losing some weight, and I tell you what, says Jock, you've lost me. You know what you can do with your job, says old Jock."

"Trust old Jock."

"He's a lad is old Jock."

"Stay out the month, the bastard says, and old Jock said I'll not stay a single day."

124

"Swept up the things from his desk, packed them in his briefcase."

"Raised two fingers to Smallbeer, the managing director."

"Turned Smallbeer's secretary over on her desk and whacked at her with a slipper."

"Kissed the telephone operator good-bye."

"Said a soldier's farewell to the Art Department."

"Blew a raspberry at Production."

"Cocked his leg up as he walked through Space."

"Wished Research joy of it."

"Walked down the street to Rafferty, Hay and Pilkington and got a job at another five hundred a year."

"Taking the lung tonic account with him."

Anderson drained the second glass, said "Hurrah for old Jock," and flung himself at a gap in the circle of figures surrounding him. The figures parted and he was through, but not with a clear passage, for now he bumped against another enormous mass of flesh. A voice said: "Hey there, Andy, watcher doin' to y'r ol' pal Amos." The mass of flesh, great hands and thighs, large feet, blubber face with small twinkling eyes, was resolved into Fletchley.

"Fletchley!"

"My ol' pal Andy's lookin' a little the worse for wear." With his hands round Anderson's waist, clasping him with the insistence of an anaconda, Fletchley sniffed the glass which Anderson still firmly held. "Dat ol' debbil Pernod's bad ol' debbil," he said, and shook his head.

"Where's Elaine? She said she'd be here."

The comedy was wiped away from Fletchley's face. The corners of his mouth turned down in an expression of stage misery. "Gone."

"What do you mean? Gone home?"

"Oh no, she's not gone home. She'll never go home again, Andy boy, she'll never go home again."

"She's left you, then?" Anderson asked brutally. He now had Fletchley not only in focus but in colour, the bluish bags under the eyes, the pasty white cheeks, a hint of carbuncle on the nose.

125

" She says she's left me, but she'll never leave me. That's one thing Elaine could never do to her old Fletch. She always comes back. She's been here tonight. Now she's gone again, but she'll come back."

" Then where is she?"

" At this moment, old boy, she's probably careering round Regent's Park in a taxi, making love to a young man. Film star—not a star, that is, but film actor. Good looking. Young. Got everything. She deserves everything; she deserves the best, and what's she got? Me?" Tears were in Fletchley's eyes. " But I want you to know, Andy, that I'm not jealous. Whatever I may have said or done, it wasn't done in jealousy." The great drops of liquid overspilled the lids, surmounted the bags beneath them, and coursed down Fletchley's cheeks. He put out his tongue and licked at them.

The realization of Fletchley's condition made Anderson feel fully sober, although he was not in any case suffering from drunkenness in any easily recognizable form. His speech was clear, his mind normally, perhaps even abnormal, active; the room and the people in it had now settled into what was almost a state of slow motion. He could observe in detail every movement of a hand, every flicker of expression. His perceptions seemed to be sharpened so that, for instance, the colours of Fletchley's suit, a close-woven herringbone, stood out with extraordinary distinctness. He put out a hand and touched the cloth, and a remarkable improvement in his tactile sense was also apparent; his fingers rubbed against material not to be classified simply as rough or smooth but identifiable, rather, in terms of emotion. This, Anderson seemed to realize, was the way in which life itself should ideally be apprehended. What stirs in my stomach at the touch of this cloth? What subliminal urges move me when I feel fur? What words can taste buds find in richness of cream? *Softness,* indeed, and *richness*—how inadequate they were.

" Words," he said to Fletchley, " are not feelings."

" What's that, old boy? I didn't quite catch."

" Richness, softness, what do they express? What do any words? Not feelings. Words were deceivers ever. The true

126

feelings lie here." Anderson placed his hand on the top button of his waistcoat.

"Deceivers ever." Fletchley's great head swung pendulously from side to side and two more tears rolled smoothly over the blubber of his cheeks. "Who could 'a thought that a girl like Elaine would go off—go off night after night. A well-set-up girl like Elaine. Who could 'a thought it."

"Take advertisment, a virdual syntagma."

"But I want you to know, Andy, that nothing said or done was in jealousy. You believe me, old boy, don't you?"

Fletchley was obviously much moved. Anderson said: "I believe you."

"A well-set-up girl. Say what you like, at *Woman Beautiful* they're all well-set-up girls. Like Val. Your little woman was a well-set-up girl and where did it get her?" Fletchley began to sob, loudly and miserably. "She died. Your little woman died a miserable, a sudden death."

The words dropped, dropped, how did they drop—like bombs, like vitriol?—into the pool of Anderson's peace. He felt anger and yet the peace, his sense of the profound unimportance of what Fletchley was saying, underlay the anger which (like, perhaps, a thick coating of oil?) rested on the surface and made his own voice say sharply: "A sudden death—what do you mean a sudden death?"

"Sudden and sad. I wrote today, old boy, one of my little pieces. "She will not see the spring, nor hear the bluetit sing, nor see the lambkins gambol in the meadow.' I thought of Val."

"*Sudden* death. You mean——" as Anderson spoke the words their relation to football matches and music hall jokes— "you mean *foul play*."

"My dear old boy." Fletchley's tears stopped.

"That's what you mean, is it? *Foul play*."

"Don't get me wrong, Andy."

"If not *foul play*, why *sudden death*? Out with it, Fletchley." The peace still existed deep down, very deep down, but the surface anger was fairly boiling away, there could be no doubt of that.

Half turning away, rubbing fat tear-stained cheeks, his whole sagging body shivering with distain, Fletchley muttered words well in the tradition of *foul play*: " If the cap fits——"

From the depth of his inner peace, remote in a fastness impenetrable by anger and insusceptible to words, Anderson saw and felt what happened next: the endlessly deliberate action with which his right arm moved, forward and upward (would it never reach?), until it collided violently with an obstacle. Violently, violently; and yet in that happy seclusion where his spirit rested imperturbable, Anderson was almost unaware of the impact of fist on flesh, experienced only as one feels the disturbance of a hair that has strayed across the face. He saw, however, the colour of a fist, strong, brownish, hairy, against unhealthy white; he saw the badly articulated body move slowly backward and sink to ground; he saw the pin of blood, that gathered to a large ruby, and was then comically a river of red tears. But the whole thing became at last a fag, too much trouble to follow: quite deliberately he withdrew his eyes from the body wriggling on the floor, his ears from the orchestra about to spray over him prompted by the fistic overture; deliberately he withdrew from it all and settled in that landscape of the heart which he had always known to exist, but had never before been lucky enough to find.

8

He was walking down a long narrow road which seemed to have no ending. Tall houses upon either side turned upon him their unfriendly night faces. Nobody but himself seemed to be moving, so that it must be late perhaps very late. Where had he been and what had he been doing? He found himself wishing for a door to open and show behind it a rich panel of light from within, for the scream of a radio set, for some footsteps other than his own to tap the pavement. There was something disturbing in this apparently purposeful but actually aimless movement of leg after leg. He could not be quite sure that he was awake.

A hand placed, quite casually, upon his forehead, came away wet. Was it with blood? But beneath a street lamp's yellow light he saw that a fine straight rain was falling. His forehead, of course, was wet with it. But he was conscious that for some reason or another his forehead should not be wet. Why not? And then the same hand passed over his hair revealed that he was not wearing a hat. He must have left it at the party.

At the end of the endless road he turned left into a road apparently identical with it. The circles of faint light round the street lamps; the high, blind houses; the absence of people or noise. But there was something else wrong, some strange stiffness affected him. His movements, he discovered, were like those of one struggling against an impediment. Could he, in some way, have been injured? He began gingerly to prod ribs, side and shoulders. Then he realized the cause of the trouble and began to laugh. He was wearing the wrong coat.

Anderson could not have said why the discovery that he was wearing an overcoat much too small for him should have amused him so much. Crowing and hooting with laughter, he capered down the road, and in a moment heard the distant hooting of a motor horn. The sound gave him much pleasure. He passed a shuttered and silent public house. It was, then, after eleven o'clock—but, of course, he knew that, for he could not have reached the Pollexfen party before ten. And as he remembered the Pollexfen party his mind moved back to the strange triangle at VV's flat and he laughed again, laughed until he felt he must burst the buttons of his borrowed overcoat, and at further thought of the overcoat stood, quite helpless with laughter, propped against a sign outside the pub. He turned his face upward to the sky to catch the rain and as he did so distinguished in the faint light the outline of a figure with cloven hoofs and harlequin's clothes. Above the figure was the word Demon. It was strange, he thought, that there should be two demons in London with exactly the same sign. Then his laughter was stopped as tape is cut by scissors. There were not two Demons. This was the *Demon* he knew, the pub at the corner of Joseph Street.

It is again impossible to explain rationally why the discovery that his legs had guided him home should have cancelled Anderson's uproarious mirth, but it is a fact that he was

remarkably reluctant to turn the corner into Joseph Street and
enter his flat. He felt that some disastrous news awaited him
there; and it was only by a great effort of will that he pushed
away from the signpost that had supported his uncontrollable
laughter and turned into Joseph Street. Then he stood still.
Joseph Street, like the other streets through which he had
walked, was dark and silent. But not altogether dark. Through
the windows of his own flat, inadequately contained by the
gappy curtains, two fingers of light stuck out into the road.

Anderson's next actions, the thirty steps taken to his own
front door, the key inserted in lock, entrance hall crossed, and
the last decisive action of turning the Yale key to open the door
of his own flat, were as difficult as any he had performed in
his life. When they were done he felt relief, although he had
no idea of what lay behind the closed door of the sitting room.
He smelled cigar smoke, which somehow reassured him; and,
opening the door, he saw Inspector Cresse filling one of the
chromium-armed chairs, hands folded on stomach, staring
placidly ahead of him like a musical comedy Buddha. Cigar
smoke was thick in the room, a cigar was in the Inspector's
mouth, and the stubs of two more lay in an ashtray. Slowly,
and it seemed in several movements, the Inspector rose from
the chair. The two men stood looking at each other and then
the Inspector, a courteous host, waved a hand. " Come in,
come in, and make yourself at home. There's been a little
trouble."

" Trouble?" And now Anderson, looking round the room,
saw that a great wind might have blown through it. The
carpet had been pulled up and then thrown aside, a pouffe had
been slit open, seats of some chairs had been removed. The
pictures, stacked against the wall, had their backs cut away.
The Inspector followed Anderson's roving gaze with heavy
interest. " And the tubular lamps," he said, " and the fire
elements. Unscrewed them to see what they could find.
Thorough." He nodded amiably toward the bedroom door.
" In there, too. Chaos, I'm afraid. Mattress and pillows, all
that kind of thing. Even took the back out of that portrait of
your wife. I don't call that playing the game."

130

And the writing desk? Anderson had carefully refrained from looking at it; but that, he realized, might be in itself suspicious. He looked, and the Inspector's eyes, at the moment singularly mild, followed. The writing desk was open. Bills, letters, papers, lay confused within it. The drawer beneath had been opened also. Had the searcher discovered the hidden panel, and the limp black book?

"Quite a neat job," the Inspector said. "Didn't force the lock there. Used a skeleton key." Anderson stared and stared, in bewilderment. Presumably the person responsible for this raid was Val's lover? But what could have been his purpose? To get some more letters, perhaps, which he knew Val had left here? But that seemed ridiculous.

"You're looking a bit under the weather," the Inspector said. "Let me pour you a drink, and perhaps you won't take it as a liberty if I pour myself one, too. I haven't done so, because I never take drink or bite in another man's home without invitation." He stopped in the act of pouring whisky. "Is that really your coat? It seems to be a very bad fit."

Anderson struggled out of the overcoat, and threw it on a chair. "I picked it up by mistake at a party."

"Gadding about." A large finger wagged at Anderson. Behind it the white face with its two deep furrows was placid. "Do you know it's one o'clock? I've been here two hours. But you guessed that, I daresay, by the stubs. They're Upman cigars—take nearly an hour to smoke—two and a half gone. I ought to charge them up to you."

"Why are you waiting for me? What are you doing here?"

"The ingratitude of mankind." Now, for the moment an absolutely farcical figure, the Inspector ran a hand over his shining bald head. "Usually we policemen are slated for inefficiency. Try to be efficient, try to help people a little, and are they pleased? They certainly aren't. But let me tell you about it." He produced a notebook from an inner pocket and referred to it. "At 8.48 this evening P. C. Johnson observed that the front door of Number 10 Joseph Street stood wide open. He rang the bell and, receiving no reply from upper or lower floor, entered the hall. The door to the upper flat was closed, but he found the door to the lower flat standing open.

131

He entered and found——" the Inspector stopped reading——
" this."

" That tells me nothing." Anderson stared now unashamedly
at the open lower drawer of the writing desk. " It doesn't tell
me why *you're* here."

" I take an interest in you." The Inspector's hands were
clasped against his stomach.

" You pursue me."

" Oh now—really." The furrows deepened, the mouth
curved in deprecation.

" What about this afternoon? A message left for me in the
office given to a girl who might make anything of it. ' The air
is unhealthy in Melian Street.' That sort of thing is disgraceful,
I say, disgraceful. It is persecution." Anderson had not
meant to shout, but the sight of this large man sitting in his
wrecked room, drinking whisky, somehow induced anger with
this policeman and all his kind.

" Now now, Mr. Anderson, I'm really surprised at you.
Persecution, indeed. I was trying to be helpful."

" Helpful! "

" A word to the wise, you know. I happened to notice you
coming out of that—establishment, shall we call it? I was
surprised—not shocked, you understand, but surprised—and
I was worried. Within a few days that establishment may be
raided. It would be a pity if you were there, wouldn't it?
Wouldn't look well. I was trying to be thoughtful, but do you
appreciate it? No, you think I was persecuting you. Really,
Mr. Anderson, sometimes I agree with Gilbert and Sullivan."

" Gilbert and Sullivan? "

" A policeman's lot is not a happy one. That's a very true
saying, though not intellectual enough for you I expect." In
the same comfortable voice, almost apologetically, the Inspector said: " But I shall have to ask a few questions."

" Me? Ask me? "

" Why yes, Mr. Anderson. I must tell you that we are not
satisfied."

" Not satisfied? " Anderson repeated stupidly. He sat
looking round at the disorder of the room.

Without ceasing to look at Anderson, the Inspector pulled

a nail file from his pocket and began to file his large well-kept nails. As he did this, he went on talking in the same conversational half-tone; and beneath his quiet, coarse voice there lay the faint rasp of the file. "I'll tell you something now, Mr. Anderson. This morning we had another of those anonymous letters. Very nasty, too; beastly things they are altogether. Don't ask me what it said, because I can't tell you, but you can take my word for it, it was nasty. Take no notice, you may say, and that's all very fine. But then what about this business tonight? A few days ago you told me you hadn't an enemy, but it looks as if you have. Eh, Mr. Anderson?"

"I didn't speak."

"I thought you mentioned a name."

"A name?"

"Your enemy's name. You told me a little while ago that you had no enemy. That's not true, is it? You have got one, and you know who it is."

"You want to know the name of my enemy?"

"That would be interesting." The Inspector stopped filing his nails.

"The name of my enemy," Anderson leaned forward and spoke with an intensity the remark hardly warranted, "is Anderson."

Obligingly, the Inspector leaned forward, too. Poised on their chair edges, they confronted each other like eager dogs. "Your brother, is that? I didn't know you had one."

"Myself!"

The Inspector's interest notably diminished. He dropped back into the lap of his chair and as he did so dropped the emotional level of the conversation. "A man's worst enemy is himself! Well, I suppose you're right, but it hardly answers what I want to know, does it?"

The Inspector's obtuseness made Anderson anxious to disentangle his own fine shade of meaning. "You don't understand me. These things that you describe—the anonymous letters, the wrecking of this flat—they are things that I might have done myself. They awaken a response in me. The anonymous letters—spying through the keyhole and telling the world the secrets we've seen inside the room—that's a thing I

133

might have done. And then the flat—look at it now. Do you remember what this room looked like the last time you saw it, how every ghastly object was in the right place, every filthy little cushion and lampshade just as my wife had them. Now I see it all utterly disordered, everything completely boss-eyed, and do you know what I wonder, Inspector? I wonder why I didn't do it all myself years ago." Anderson had meant to speak perfectly quietly, but in spite of himself his voice had risen a little. The Inspector, nevertheless, continued almost perfectly obtuse.

"Well, you do say the oddest things, Mr. Anderson. I don't hold much with all this modern psychology stuff myself."

It was injudicious to shout, Anderson knew, but now he fairly shouted. "Psychology, nonsense. Don't be a fool, man. I'm saying that the actions of this man, whoever he is, are actions I can understand. The desire to destroy, that's what I'm talking about, is that plain enough for you? Because he wasn't searching here for anything, there was nothing to search for. Hatred was moving, hatred of me, the wish to wreck my life, to destroy anything that belongs to me. And I feel that impulse, too. Do I make myself clear? To make disorder out of order, to wreck, tear, kill——" Abruptly Anderson stopped. The word hung in the air between them, a word for which, in the Inspector's terms, there was no possible explanation or excuse. But, so far from asking him to explain it, the Inspector merely sat filing his nails. When at last he spoke it was to take up Anderson's remarks at one remove and with a rambling clumsiness, a missing of the essential point that seemed, on this evening at least, characteristic of him.

"It's funny, now, that you should be talking about order and disorder, because my wife's great on them, too. Did I tell you I was married? Well, anyway, I am, and two kids as well. Here we are in the front garden." With the pathetic pride of an amateur conjurer the Inspector whipped from his wallet a photograph. Anderson looked at a pretty woman in a smock, flanked by two young boys. Their slightly bovine faces, staring earnestly into the camera, were recognizably of the kind that would later attain their father's flat weightiness. A rather younger Inspector, less bulky and with a thick fringe of hair round the side of his head, looked at them with the affection of an overgrown bulldog.

"Very nice," Anderson said. He handed back the photograph and thought: *Wreck, tear, kill*—what could have possessed him to use such words. He had been drunk, it was true, at one time in the evening, and now it was very late, and he was so tired that he hardly knew what he was saying. He looked at his wrist watch. Two o'clock. Would the man never go?

"The apple of their mother's eye—and their father's, too," the Inspector said earnestly. "But I was telling you about my wife. *Order,* she says, you must have order or how can life go on? And she tells that to the kids, and makes them understand it. There's a time and a place, she says, for skylarking, and the time's not lunch time and the place isn't the dining room. And she makes the punishment fit the crime—to use another Gilbertian phrase. If the kids throw food about at the dining table they have to do the washing up, if they come into the house with muddy boots the wife puts mud on their clothes and makes them clean it off. She's got a sense of humour, and that's a wonderful thing."

Good God, Anderson thought, no wonder the poor little creatures look bovine. But the Inspector was droning on. "I say to the wife that it's only a little bit of fun they're having, but she will have it I'm wrong. Disorder, she says, is wicked. I must tell you, though," the Inspector said with one of his devastating lapses into bathos, "that she was brought up a Non-conformist. I say to her sometimes that the state of disorder is a state of nature. Do you know what she says to that? The state of order is a state of grace. It's from the impulse to disorder. she says, that these Mussolinis and Hitlers gain power. And if she were here tonight she'd say to you that it was quite right to say that the impulse to make disorder out of order was the same as the impulse to kill. Killing is disorder, that's what she'd say. And what would *you* say to that?"

Anderson felt suddenly a quite overwhelming anxiety simply to get rid of the Inspector at any cost. "I should say she was a

135

damned fool," he answered harshly, "and was going the right way to make Fascists out of her children."

Surprisingly the Inspector laughed. "You'd be perfectly right. I made it all up."

"What?"

"All that stuff I was saying just then. The wife's thoughts don't rise above the kitchen sink. I was curious just to see what you'd say. It's getting late." At last, at last, Anderson thought. The Inspector stretched like a hippopotamus and yawned. "But somehow I don't feel tired. Insomnia, that's my trouble; one of my troubles, I should say. Do you mind if I have another little drop of Scotch?" He poured a drink and wandered about the room, stopping to peer out into the street. "Not what you'd call a very salubrious neighbourhood. But I suppose there's no accounting for tastes. One man's meat is another man's poison, as they say. How are you getting on at the office?"

"The office?" Anderson lay back exhausted. As he did so his eyelids, like a doll's thick lids that shutter the staring eye when it is laid flat, closed.

"Everything all right, not feeling the strain or anything like that? You look as if you're feeling the strain, you know. But Philosophical, too. I feel in a way it's my business, and sometimes it worries me."

Behind the closed lids Anderson could see the Georgian writing desk. Put your hand inside, open the secret drawer and there, in the mind's eye, was the black book with its marbled edges. In the mind's eye, ah yes, in the mind's eye.

"Order got to be preserved; we're all agreed on that, I hope," the Inspector said, rather as if he were addressing a public meeting. "But how far are we justified in using disorder to preserve it? That's the kind of question that worries me when I can't sleep. Supposing a man's arrested on suspicion, now; you know as well as I do that the boys give him a little going over on the way to the station. Very useful it is, too, often enough, in taking the starch out of them. But is it right? That's the thing I've started worrying about in my old age."

The doll's lids flickered. "Ethically no. Practically yes."

" I'm very glad to hear you say so—because practice makes ethics, doesn't it? Though I'm out of my depth even when 'm thinking about this kind of thing, let alone talking about t. Still, methods like those wouldn't be any use in dealing with a superior man such as yourself, say. Would they?"

" They might extract a confession. Isn't that always what ou're after?"

The Inspector's voice was plaintive. " It certainly it *not*, Mr. Anderson. Only incidentally. A policeman is like God. He wants to know the truth. And he's bound to believe that any means are justifiable—any means, do you understand me —if he can find the truth through them. The truth, the clean and perfect truth—that is what we shall reach tomorrow if not today, next year if not tomorrow The truth!"

The voice was suddenly loud, and like a bell. Anderson opened his eyes and saw the Inspector standing, overcoated, n front of his chair. Seen from this angle and at this moment, he was no longer a comic figure. The deep vertical lines that ran down the cheeks were cruel: the pudgy features had assumed a coherent severity; power and the will to use it lay n the great bald skull. For a moment Anderson lay defenceless, sprawled in his chair, ready for raping by this ogre of order. From behind his back the Inspector then brought forth —not a whip, but his bowler hat. Clapping upon his head this symbol of order the Inspector turned upon a respectable black heel. " Good night." The words rang through the disorderly room. The front door closed. For perhaps five minutes Anderson lay in the armchair, deprived of movement, looking at the writing desk. It does not matter, he told himself, whether the notebook is there or not. What does the notebook say, after all? It says our marriage was not ideally happy—but what marriage is happy? No, no, he told himself, the notebook does not matter in itself. But which of them could have wanted something in this flat so badly that they committed burglary to get it? Lessing? Reverton? Vincent? Wyvern? But Vincent was ruled out, was he not, by the fact that he had been in Anderson's company? Lessing, Reverton, Wyvern? Or—remember the open door, the figure pulling up the long pants—Pile? Ridiculous, ridiculous.

Like a sleepwalker, Anderson moved over to the writing desk, fumbled, found the protusion, pushed. The secret drawer opened. It was empty.

9

Awake, it seemed that he was still asleep. His feet touching the floor had the lightness of a dream; but entirely real was the pain that beat in his head, and the tightness of his face, which felt as if it had been coated with varnish. He applied Hey Presto and wiped it off. He felt absolutely nothing, for the varnish was apparently impermeable, but the blue growth on his chin disappeared magically. The toast he cooked and ate, the coffee he boiled and drank, had similarly no taste or smell. An automaton pushed food and drink into its mouth.

This numbing of the senses continued on his way to the office. The omnibus came noiselessly along the street; he saw but did not hear the click of the conductor's punch. He stood between a fat woman who breathed in and out, deeply but apparently noiselessly, and a figure holding a newspaper. This figure was interesting. Two delicate hands were visible at either side of the paper which faced Anderson, and occasionally an edge of the paper flicked his face. It became important to Anderson that he should see this newspaper holder. The hands seemed to be those of a woman, and yet the trousers, as he saw on looking down, were a man's. A woman in slacks? Anderson swayed forward against the newspaper, but it remained obstinately raised. When somebody by his side got out he said, although to him the words remained inaudible, that there was a seat vacant. The figure accepted the seat, without for an instant lowering the paper. Infuriatingly, when the man-woman sat down, somebody else pushed against Anderson and he was still unable to see over the newspaper barrier.

The figure rose, still holding the paper before its face—and then in a flash the paper was folded and the figure, presenting its back to Anderson, was on its way out of the bus. Excuse me, Anderson said, excuse me, but by the time he reached
138

the end of the bus the figure had dropped off and was running across the road concealed in a duffle coat which effectively concealed sex as well as indentity. Anderson jumped off the bus. For a moment a taxi was in front of him, then it swerved aside and he saw the driver's shaken fist.

Running, running across the wide road he saw the figure, ahead of him, enter an office block. He ran in after it and found with astonishment that he was in the reception hall of Vincent Advertising. The figure sat at the reception desk with its back to him, but turned as he approached the desk. The newspaper still held in front of the face was slowly lowered, and behind it he saw the laughing features of Molly O'Rourke. He stood still in astonishment. She bowed her head in mock acknowledgement, showing all her fine teeth in laughter, and then pointed down the corridor toward his room. He ran down the corridor and at the first bend turned to look at Molly. He could see nothing but the newspaper held at the edges by two delicate hands.

When he reached the door of his room Anderson paused with one hand on the door handle, and then dramatically swung the door open with such violence that it struck the inside wall (but noiselessly, noiselessly). He saw then how he had been deceived, for a figure stood by the desk, back to him, and this figure also was wearing a duffle coat. Slowly, very slowly, the figure turned to face him, and Anderson saw, with a shock that was yet no surprise, the round face of Charlie Lessing. Lessing, too, was smiling, and he held in one hand, waving it with gentle mockery back and forth, a letter from Val. Even across the room Anderson could recognize the blue paper and the careless handwriting.

"You!" Anderson cried, and for the first time heard his own voice. "You, you, you!" Lessing stood there by the desk, waving the letter, smiling. His smile did not waver even when Anderson in a great spring across the room had him by the throat, forcing the hated face further and further away from him over the desk, gripping tighter and tighter the flexible round neck above which the gums still showed in a ghastly smile, while from the pink gullet came wild and agonized screams, while the eyeballs started outward and the throat screamed, while the face reddened and the throat screamed and screamed and screamed. . .

The screams echoed in his head long after he woke and lay staring at the ceiling in the half light of early morning. A nightmare, he thought; it was nothing but a nightmare; there was no reason to think badly of Molly or of Lessing because in a dream he had invested them with diabolical smiles. He straightened up in bed and saw that the hands of the alarm clock said half past five. On the floor lay Val's photograph out of its frame. He picked it up, put it by the bedside lamp, switched on the light and stared at it. The eyes looked lovingly back at him, the full mouth was smiling.

When one wakens after a nightmare, actuality may seem unreal. Anderson opened his eyes to see a patch of sunlight on the bed. His head ached violently and the skin of his face felt tight. The time by his alarm clock was twenty-five minutes to ten. This is another dream, he thought, and turned over in bed. But his head was still aching, the skin of his face still felt drawn. He stretched, yawned, closed his eyes, and then rolled over again to look at the clock. Twenty-five minutes to ten. He picked up the clock, and shook it, but it continued to tick. Had he forgotten to wind the alarm, or had it failed to wake him? The question was academic beside the fact that he was extremely late.

He jumped out of bed, washed hurriedly, applied Hey Presto to his face. In the dream, he thought, I felt nothing; it was as though my face were covered with varnish. Then when he removed the Hey Presto he felt none of the pricking or burning sensation that had accompanied previous applications —nothing except, perhaps, a slightly increased facial tension. It was not pleasant to have the dream pattern so nearly approached; fortunately his senses of touch and hearing appeared to be unimpaired. He had no time to discover whether his sense of taste was still functioning, because he left without eating breakfast. He put on a raincoat and his second-best black hat, and threw over his arm the overcoat collected at the party. When he had closed his own front door he remembered the Fletchleys. Elaine would be at *Woman Beautiful* by now, but he ought to apologize to Fletchley for the blow on the jaw. His wrist watch, however, said a quarter to ten. He decided to telephone later.

The sense of unreality stayed with him as he ran to the corner and jostled on to a bus. He stood; and there, sure enough, as in the dream, the person standing next to him held a newspaper in front of his face. The bus stopped abruptly and threw them against each other; Anderson, with a movement apparently involuntary, pushed at the newspaper and it was lowered immediately to reveal a petulent, small, indeterminately male face quite unknown to him. The journey continued without incident. Anderson jumped off the bus and ran across the road to the office. At the desk sat not duffled Molly O'Rourke but pneumatic Miss Detranter. She called to him, but Anderson, one hand raised in greeting, hurried down the corridor. At the door of his own room he paused with one hand on the handle, as he had paused in the dream. He flung open the door, and was surprised when it struck the inside wall with a crash. That was a surprise; but he received a shock that took him back to the dream when he saw Lessing standing by the desk. Lessing had his arm round a girl who was crying on his shoulder. He looked extremely uncomfortable, and on Anderson's appearance said with relief: " Here he is." He saw that the girl was Jean Lightley.

" Oh, Mr. Anderson," she said. " Oh Mr. Anderson." Her speech failed in a series of gasps.

Anderson took off his hat and raincoat and put the overcoat over a chair. The telephone rang. He moved over to pick it up and Jean Lightley called: " Don't answer it." She put her head back on Lessing's shoulder.

" Listen," Lessing said. " This is what's happened. It's pretty rough. Yesterday you wrote a stalling note to Bagseed about the drawings he'd sent back for correction. And you also wrote a fair stinker to old Crashaw. Well, somehow the letters got mixed up." At these words Jean Lightley, who had shown signs of recovery, burst into great hiccoughing sobs. " Raper of Kiddy Modes has been on raising hell. That's probably him on the line now."

Anderson listened carefully to what Lessing was saying; and yet he could not forget that the villain of the dream was this same Lessing, spectacled, uncurious, amiable Lessing, who now looked at him with such friendly concern. The telephone rang again.

" You don't seem very worried," Lessing said. " I wonder if I've made it clear. Shall I take this call?"

With a supreme effort Anderson brought himself back to

reality, this kind of reality, the reality of advertising and of holding down a good job. He put on even (but with what an effort, what an effort) the mask of language and of manner that had served him so well in the past. " I'll handle it," he said. " Get that weeping Jenny out of here. No, wait a minute; I want a copy of the letter I wrote to Crashaw."

Jean Lightley removed the handkerchief from her face long enough to say: " It's on the desk." Then she ran wailing from the room. Lessing sat at one corner of the desk and swung his leg.

Bagseed's voice was quaveringly severe. " Mr. Arthur would like to speak to you. Please hold the line." Anderson stared at Lessing's foot. A voice like ice water dripped into the telephone. " Mr. Anderson, this is Arthur Raper speaking."

" How are you, Mr. Raper," Anderson said heartily. " A long time since I've had the pleasure of seeing you."

The voice said politely: " That can be remedied. Perhaps you will make it convenient to come up and see me now."

" Right, Mr. Raper. I'm just making some inquiries about——"

The voice said: " Now, please, Mr. Anderson."

" I should like ten——" The line went dead. Lessing got up. He was plaintive. " I wanted to talk to you about Hey Presto. How's the personal test doing? You look a bit funny."

" What do you mean, funny?" He could feel the tightness of the skin round his cheekbones.

" Strained or something, I dunno. Are you going up now? Is there anything I can do to help out?"

" No, I don't think so. Yes, there is." Anderson remembered the Crunchy-Munch conference fixed for ten-thirty. " Will you present those two Crunchy-Munch schemes instead of me?" Lessing nodded. " Strictly anonymous, you know. They don't know anything about them yet."

" Strictly anonymous," Lessing said and winked. " But I shall do my best on my own behalf. I say, the Crunchy-Munch meeting won't take long. There's something on this

143

morning at eleven-fifteen, Board Meeting or something. Rev's saying nothing, but looking full of it. Maybe they're going to give us all a raise."

"Maybe." Anderson put on his raincoat.

"I say," Lessing's curiosity seemed inexhaustible this morning. "That your coat on the chair?"

"Why?"

"It looks uncommonly like one Greatorex wears, that's all. Got a paint mark on the sleeve like his. Good luck. Don't let Raper rape you."

"Thanks," Anderson went along to the secretaries' office where Jean Lightley sat red-eyed, staring at her typewriter. Anderson said kindly: "Jean, I'm sorry I blew off. I'm going up to see Kiddy Modes now." She looked up at him. Her underlip was quivering. "While I'm up there I want you to find out exactly what happened about these two letters, just how they got sent to the wrong people. Try and trace them right from the moment I handed them to you yesterday afternoon. It's not a question of responsibility; I just want to find out what happened. Understand?" he nodded. As he closed the door he heard a fresh storm of sobbing.

2

Arthur Raper was a small grey man wearing a neat bow tie, who would have been identifiable as a rather respectable elderly clerk if one had met him in the street. But he was not now in the street, but behind a large desk in a large room. To one side of the desk, springing up from an uncomfortable chair at Raper's command, was Bagseed, a stringy, indigestible, nervous, old-middle-aged kind of man, obviously nervous for the security of his job. At the other end of the room, separated from Mr. Raper and his henchman by some yards of mulberry carpet, sat Anderson, bolt upright on the edge of an overstuffed chair. In a thin, polite, exhausted voice Mr. Raper said:

"I am going to read you a letter, and I want you to tell me what you think of it." With a little cough he picked up a sheet of paper from the desk. It was, Anderson saw, the letter to

Crashaw. "Dear Crashaw," Mr. Raper said. He read the letter very slowly, pronouncing each syllable with care. At the word "pest-i-len-tial" Bagseed shook his head gravely, at in-com-pe-tent, irr-el-ev-ant and im-mat-er-i-al," he plucked with dry fingers at his skinny neck. Mr. Raper did not speak loudly, and at the other end of the room Anderson did not hear him very well, but he tried to give the impression of a keen and interested executive. It was necessary to crawl, he had decided in the taxi, but it would be fatal to crawl too fast or too far. We're all human, that was the line, we all blow our top sometimes and write things we regret five minutes afterward. So when Mr. Raper asked him to give an opinion of this document Anderson said firmly: "I take full responsibility for writing that letter, Mr. Raper."

"Are you proud of your handiwork?"

"Far from it. I don't want to excuse writing such a letter. But I'd like to explain it." Anderson launched the speech he had prepared in the taxi. "That letter, sir, was the product of a week at the office in which we haven't known whether we are on our heads or our heels. It's the kind of letter all of us sit down and write a few times in our lives. Five minutes after we've written it we regret it. If we're sensible enough to delay posting it for half an hour we look at it again—and tear it up. I'll be frank, and say I wish I'd done that. I'll be franker still, and say that when Mr. Bagseed received the letter and saw the kind of thing it was, and that it had come to him by mistake, I should have expected him to read it, laugh at it, tear it up, and perhaps write me a line saying that we were the most pestilential advertising agents he'd ever dealt with." Mr. Bagseed's hands clutched at his high, old-fashioned collar as though he were being strangled.

"Do I understand you to say that Bagseed should have concealed this letter from me? That he should have . . ." The rest of the sentence was inaudible to Anderson.

"I didn't quite hear you, I'm afraid."

The ice tinkled more sharply. "That he should have betrayed his duty to me? You suggest that?" Bagseed shook his worn old head in anguished denial of such a possibility.

"Why, of course not. But he's got to make a distinction

145

between a piece of spontaneous emotion like a man swearing when he kicks his foot against a stone——"

"I regard bad language as bad manners at any time," said Raper. Bagseed sucked in his false teeth sharply.

"Ah, you're too good for the rest of us erring mortals, Mr. Raper." Anderson managed a laugh.

"Leaving aside your curious view of Mr. Bagseed's responsibilities, I must confess surprise that I have heard no expression of regret from you regarding the contents of the letter. But perhaps you think no regret is called for. If that is your view it would be honest to say so. I respect honesty, Mr. Anderson, above all things."

It was the crawl then. "Of course, I regret extremely the expressions I used in a heated moment."

"But some of them, perhaps, you still feel inclined to justify." Mr. Raper's lips moved, but no words were audible. Had his voice, perhaps, been deliberately lowered?

At the other end of the mulberry carpet Anderson said: "I beg your pardon?"

"I said, 'Out of our many pestilential clients, Kiddy Modes are perhaps the most pestilential of all.' Does that phrase have the ring of truth to you, Mr. Anderson?"

Not only a crawl, but a belly crawl. "Certainly not. I should like to apologize for the use of that phrase."

"'Their criticisms on this occasion, as on others, are incompetent, irrelevant and immaterial.' Does that seem to you a fair observation?"

"It was thrown off in the heat of the moment."

"That is not an answer to what I asked. Do you wish to justify that remark?"

"No no, certainly not. I should like to apologize for it—to you and to Mr. Bagseed."

Mr. Bagseed looked startled. Mr. Raper made the very faintest inclination of his head.

"'Kiddy Modes demand just about six times as much attention as any other client of their size.' Was that a proper remark?"

"I apologize for that, and for the whole of the letter unre-

146

servedly." Is it possible for the head to get lower than the belly when you crawl? It is at least possible to try. " I don't wish to make excuses, but a few weeks ago my wife died. I have not been myself since then."

" Please accept my sympathy in your bereavement," Mr. Raper said primly. " But I am sure you would not wish that factor to influence my judgment of this deplorable letter in any way."

" Naturally not. I only——"

" I am very glad to know that you agree with me about the nature of this letter. Had you seriously thought us at fault I should have felt bound to make a thorough investigation of the circumstances. Nevertheless, I had to make up my mind whether a firm which expressed such views would be quite happy with our account." The thin voice was now penetratingly clear. " I consulted with Mr. Bagseed, and he agreed with me that once the perfect confidence that should obtain between client and agent has been broken it can never be mended." Bagseed was picking at the knees of his trousers and staring at the floor. " Do I make myself clear, Mr. Anderson?" Anderson was speechless, " Do I make myself clear?"

" You're taking away the account?"

" Precisely. Here is a letter terminating the contract. Formally, it has still two months to run, but I imagine that in view of this," Mr. Raper tapped Anderson's letter, " Mr. Vincent will not wish to argue that point. Mr. Bagseed will make all the necessary arrangements for our change-over to another agency."

So the belly crawl was useless, had been useless even before he contemplated it. He had been a perfect mouse for this neat sadistic cat, a mouse who gave the greater pleasure because he clung to the illusion of free will. And what could he say now? It would be a mild pleasure, perhaps, to call Raper names, but by doing so he would give the little man one more satisfaction. But even while his thoughts moved thus rationally, Anderson was inarticulate with rage. He stood up, walked stiffly over the mulberry carpet to the big desk, and picked up the letter terminating the contract. The temptation to put his fist into the small face upturned toward him was almost, but not quite, irresistible. Anderson folded the letter carefully, put it in his pocket, and left the room.

3

We all of us retain, for the greater part of our conscious lives, the impression that we are in control of events; not exactly in any world-shaking, Hitlerian or Napoleonic way, but in the sense that the performance of certain actions has predictable results. The exact nature of the links that make up the chain of cause and effect is concealed from us, and to most people, indeed, the links are of no interest; but it is essential for our mental well-being that the chain itself shall not be broken. When a switch is pressed the electric light must shine; the formal conversational gambit admits of only one formal reply ; a letter, stamped and posted, must reach its addressee. No common logic is, in fact, applicable to the postal service, the return of conversation and the supply of electricity; few of us are concerned, however, to trace such things to their origins, but merely to receive a traditional result from a tradi-' tional action. It is upon this illusion of free will (an illusion in the cases mentioned because the effect of our actions is really based upon the inventive genius, the courtesy or the labour of others) that our civilization has its slender basis ; damage to this illusion in the case of an individual may render him incapable of dealing with the simplest problems, so that he is afraid to push the bell of a street door or to pull a lavatory chain because he has come to believe that life is in its essence illogical and irrational.

Something like this loss of belief had been suffered by Anderson. His mind had served him well in his work as a business executive; his judgment of people and situations had been almost invariably correct. The realization that he had been hopelessly astray in dealing with Raper affected him profoundly. It had never occurred to him that Raper's action might be the decisive one of severing relations altogether; the whole of his own conduct had been based upon a set of wrong assumptions. It was true that even a correct analysis of the situation could not have saved the account, but that point was irrelevant to Anderson's shocked consideration of his own condition. Such a gross error was out of the natural order of events; so far out of it that Anderson, when he left the room with the mulberry carpet, was a changed man. The change affected his thought and by extension, naturally, his conduct. There are two great classes in European civilization, those who do things, and those to whom things are done. Anderson entered the room with the mulberry carpet as (in his own view, at least) a member of the first class; he came out of it a member of the second. His energies had hitherto been divided between the attempt to preserve his position as an advertising executive and the desire to discover the identity of his wife's lover. The first of these objectives he had now abandoned. Not quite consciously, he felt that his power to apprehend the external world was failing; he had always believed that whatever happened constituted a norm or rationality, so that inability to understand the happenings around him naturally appeared as a defect in rational apprehension. He gathered together, therefore, as it might be said, his remaining forces, and launched an attack on the mystery of his private life, the vital part of the enemy position. His business flank was necessarily left exposed.

It was symtomatic of this changed attitude in Anderson that on return to the office his first move was to telephone Elaine Fletchley, and not to see VV. She was out at a fashion show. He telephoned Fletchley at Joseph Street and got no reply. He asked for VV, who was still in the Board Meeting. Jean Lightley, who had told him this, also gave him the result of the investigations he had asked her to make about the change-over of the letters. It seemed that a boy from the Dispatch Department, in an access of zeal, had taken the letters from Jean Lightley's desk. In the Dispatch Department, where the drawings were being packed up, he had dropped the letters and when he picked them up he had put them into the wrong envelopes. It was as simple as that; and to Anderson, now, it seemed so unimportant that he did not even ask the boy's name. When Jean said that she hoped Kiddy Modes had not been too angry he smiled, but made no reply.

To some natures there is something consoling in the perfect knowledge of the worst that can happen; it is, for a little while at least, satisfactory to be saved from the belief in the possibility of beneficial action. Such false tranquillity blessed Anderson now. He felt as the prisoner condemned to death may feel after his appeal has failed and the Home Secretary has refused to intervene. To know one's fate inevitable—is that not also to know peace? Anderson, a plastic and suffering figure, waited now for what might happen with the resignation he had shown in air raids during the war; feeling now, as then, certainty of disaster. But, in fact, he had come through the war unchipped, and no doubt there remained in some part of his mind the thought of escape, which added an edge of contradictory pleasure to his perfect despair.

Anderson remained in this mood for about half an hour, staring into space unseeingly; and then his eye, coming, it seemed, into focus and roving round the neat room, was caught by something out of place. It was the blue overcoat he had brought away from the Pollexfens' party. What was it Lessing had said? That it looked like a coat belonging to young Greatorex? Anderson got up slowly (his movements, since his return from Kiddy Modes, were slightly hesitant like those of an old man), picked up the overcoat and went to Lessing's room. The copywriter was not there, but Greatorex sat at a desk in a corner of the room with a guard book open in front of him, and the telephone in his hand. He replaced the receiver as Anderson came in.

Anderson held out the coat. "I picked this coat up by mistake last night. Lessing said he thought it might be yours."

Was he mistaken in thinking that the blond young man hesitated before answering? But he must know if he had lost an overcoat. "Yes, it does look rather like mine."

"And you lost yours? At the Pollexfens' party?"

"That's right." Greatorex nodded, and smiled ingenuously and charmingly. "To tell you the truth I had rather a lot to drink and didn't know whether I was coming or going. I wasn't sure where I'd left it. But that's mine. I recognize that mark on the sleeve."

Anderson held out the coat. "You know the Pollexfens?"

"Not really. My uncle, Sir Malcolm, gave me introductions to a few people, and they were among them."

"I didn't see you there."

Greatorex smiled discreetly. "You'd gone, breathing fire and brimstone, before I could make my way across the room to say hallo. You created quite a stir."

Of course—Fletchley! Anderson had forgotten about him. "Was Fletchley all right?"

"Was that his name? I don't think he sustained any vital injuries. He seemed to spend most of the evening crying about his wife. I believe he stayed the night. At least, he was still there when I left. Yes, that's my coat all right." Greatorex looked at the label, put his hands in the pockets. "I suppose you didn't leave anything—" His hand came out with an envelope in it. He looked at it and said: "This is yours." Upon the envelope, in typewriting that somehow seemed familiar, was printed *Mr. Anderson*.

Anderson put the envelope in his pocket and walked out of the room without saying anything. Back in his own room he extracted a cream laid card of medium thickness. On it was typed:

> *Yet Ile not shed her blood,*
> *Nor scarre that whiter skin of hers, than Snow,*
> *And smooth as Monumentall Alabaster:*
> *Yet she must dye, else shee'l betray more men:*

Corny, Anderson thought, corny. Somebody's done five minutes' work with Stevenson or Bartlett. He remembered now why the typing seemed familiar. It was, he felt sure, the same as that on the anonymous letters shown him by the Inspector. And yet the quotation, corny as it was, stirred something in him, probed gently and painfully into a very tender and deep recess. But how had the card got into the pocket of that overcoat? It could not have been put in while he was at the party, for nobody could have known in advance that he would leave wearing Greatorex's coat. In pure theory it could have been slipped into the coat after he had put it on, and was about to leave, but somehow that seemed very unlikely. Somebody, it was much more likely, had put the card into the coat pocket this morning, while it lay in his office. Somebody, anybody,

X. But Val's letter and the blank sheet had been put on his desk. Why should X have chosen to put this card into a coat pocket, rather than on the desk? To that question Anderson could find no answer, until with a flash (there seemed, quite literally, to *be* a flash and a kind of crack inside his head, so that he put both hands to his temples, covering his eyes) an answer came to him. Postulate Greatorex as X, say that the card had been in Greatorex's overcoat last night ready for delivery at some convenient time. By bad luck Anderson had taken away the coat with the card in it; and when Greatorex discovered the fact he must have been on tenterhooks in case Anderson put his hand in the pocket immediately on leaving and discovered the card. In fact, Anderson had not done so; and when Greatorex found that out this morning he had, with the utmost coolness, delivered the envelope as he had meant to do last night. Neat.

By this process of reasoning which, Anderson conceded to himself judicially, seemed remarkably plausible, Greatorex was X; but Greatorex, as far as Anderson knew, had been altogether unknown to Val. Greatorex was in the office only because he happened to be the nephew of Sir Malcolm Buntz. Greatorex as X was, in fact, at once plausible and ridiculous.

When Anderson progressed this far in his reasoning he became aware that something in front of him was shining. The shining came from his desk and was something more than the reflection of electric light upon it's polished surface. Something actually upon his desk was shining, and, peeping through the fingers that covered his eyes, he could not be sure what it was. He must, then, remove his fingers to see the object; but that proved to be, for some reason, remarkably difficult. It seemed to Anderson minutes, although doubtless not more than one or two seconds, before he drew away fingers from eyes; and when he did so he was conscious of a positive screech of separation, as though they had been attached by sticky tape. His eyes, naked and defenceless, were confronted by the shining object. Anderson was looking at a brand new chromium desk calendar. The date showing on it was the thirty-first of February.

The sight of the calendar filled Anderson with an unreasoning terror which nullified altogether the logical process of reasoning by which he had been seeking to identify Greatorex as his wife's lover. He put out a finger and touched the calendar, very timidly, as though afraid that it might contain some poisonous spike that sprang out at a touch. He ran a fingertip over this shining surface, placing it upon the figures 3 and 1 as if to convince himself of their existence. He was still staring at the calendar when the door opened and Lessing said, "How did it go?" and then, "Why, what's the matter?"

Anderson swallowed and spoke. "The calendar."

"What about it? New, isn't it?"

"Where did it come from?"

"How should I know? Probably a gift from your faithful secretary."

Anderson swallowed again and said: "Look at the date."

Lessing looked and sighed. "What little things do amuse little girls. The thirty-first of February. Doesn't it show that the oldest chestnuts are still the ones that rock 'em in their seats?"

"You think it's a joke."

"If you call it a joke for a young girl to be coy."

"Coy?"

"What's the thirty-first of February but a sort of super leap year, quadruple leap year or something? But how did it go with ropy Raper and birdseye Bagseed?"

Still looking at the calendar, Anderson said: "We lost the account."

Lessing's soft mouth rounded into an O of surprise. "Do the big boys know?"

"Not yet."

"They won't be pleased."

With an effort Anderson stopped looking at the calendar and looked instead at Lessing. "Rev's always said it was a pain in the neck."

"Saying's saying and losing's losing. A twenty-five thousand pound pain in the neck is worth having. But it's your baby, not mine. Only I've got some bad news too. Rev's done you in the eye over Crunchy-Munch. He produced a scheme of his own at the meeting and pushed it through against our two ideas.

153

Ghastly stuff. 'The kind of sweet that mother used to make.'
Two curly-headed children and a good brawny housewife
wiping her hands on her apron. VV fell for it like a ton of
bricks. Did you know Rev was working out a scheme of his
own?" Anderson shook his head. "It's a filthy trick," Lessing
said indignantly. "How's Hey Presto?"

"It's made my face stiff," Anderson said and then broke
off. "There's Jean." He was out of his chair and at the door.
Jean Lightley came in, panting slightly. Anderson pointed to
the chromium desk calendar. "Did you put that on my desk,
Jean?"

"Oh *no*."

"Do you know who put it there?"

She stared at him nervously, and blushed. "I thought *you*
did, Mr. Anderson. Because you didn't like the other one, did
you? So I thought you might have bought a chromium one
because you liked it better. It was on the desk when you came
in this morning."

"And you didn't put it to that date."

"Oh *no*, Mr. Anderson." She crimsoned and fled. Anderson
turned to Lessing. "You see."

"So you've got an unknown admirer. Should you worry?
You've got other things to worry about, believe me."

"What do you mean?"

Lessing's gaze seemed innocent of duplicity. "I'd be worrying about Kiddy Modes and Crunchy-Munch and Rev if I
were you."

The door opened, and Wyvern's narrow head appeared.
"Comintern's still in session. It's a general salary cut, never a
doubt of it. Those who stay put will be getting the rise.
Coming for a drink?"

The telephone rang. Anderson picked it up. The switchboard girl said: "I've been calling and calling, but you were
out. Mrs. Fletchley will be in Riley's Long Bar at a quarter to
one if you can manage that. She said be sure and let you
know."

Anderson put down the receiver and said, "I've got a date,"
He arranged with VV's secretary to see VV at half past two,
and went out. As he passed through the swing doors he heard

feet in the corridor, and the sound of the director, voices, loud with self congratulation. Then the doors sighed behind him. In the street outside he cannoned into a little man who was bouncing along in a shuffling two-step, head down, wagging one finger in the air. As they hit each other Anderson distinctly heard the little man say: "Three four *five* six, three four *five* six." After they had collided the little man staggered away, said "Sorry," and resumed counting. He ran past Anderson into the building.

Within two minutes Anderson had forgotten the little man. He was convinced that he would learn something important, something that would destroy the whole nonsensical web in which he was trapped like a fly in a treacle, when he met Elaine Fletchley.

4

Riley's Long Bar was crowded, but Elaine Fletchley was not in the crowd. Anderson bought a beer and settled in to wait. After a quarter of an hour and two beers he asked the barmaid whether she had any message for him. The barmaid clicked her fingers. It had gone completely out of her head that Mrs. Fletchley had telephoned to say that she had to take a couple of clients to El Vino's. Could Mr. Anderson join her there? Anderson went to El Vino's, where a bland blond barman told him that Mrs. Fletchley had left a few minutes ago, leaving a message that she would be lunching at the Chinese restaurant in Frith Street, and that Mr. Anderson should join her there. There is no Chinese restaurant in Frith Street, so that obviously somebody had made a mistake. Anderson tried the Shanghai restaurant in Greek Street, Ley On's and Maxim's in Wardour Street, the Hong-Kong in Shaftesbury Avenue, Shaffi's in Gerrard Street. He looked in the French pub, the Swiss pub, the Scotch House and the Irish House. He did not find Elaine Fletchley. The skin of his face felt as tight as a lampshade.

Molly O'Rourke, wearing a bottle-green coat and skirt with a grey blouse and a red tie, stood outside the door of her room. She caught hold of Anderson by the sleeve and said "Hey." He looked at his watch. "Ten minutes," he said. "I've got to see VV." They went in the room. She shut the door and stood against it, staring at him. "Men," she said, "aren't they all the bloody same! You give them all you've got; they take it without saying thank you, and leave without saying good-bye."

"What?"

"I'm not a floozie, Andy, you know that. They all think I'm hard-boiled, but I'm not a floozie, though God knows I've been unlucky in my men. You've no right to treat me this way, Andy." A tear dropped off her cheek and splashed to the coloured chart on her desk. A little yellow ran where the tear had dropped. "I gave myself to you."

"Don't be ridiculous, Molly."

"All right." She sniffed and stopped crying. A tear hung like an icicle on the end of her long white nose and then dropped, emasculating a little blot of red on the chart. "This kind of thing's no good, is it? not what men go for at all—I know that. Aren't you going to see me again, Andy?"

"What am I doing now?"

"Oh, you know what I mean. What about tonight? Busy, I suppose? And tomorrow night, and the night after tomorrow? I'm a fool to ask, I know that. Don't bother to lie to me. And a fool to buy you a present. You haven't even noticed it."

"What present?"

"A bloody little desk calendar."

"Desk calendar." He began to laugh, but the laughter came out in choking hiccoughs.

"Stinking little chromium thing. Saw you'd got rid of your other one. I put it on your desk this morning. What's funny about it?"

"You put it on the desk." Anderson went on laughing until

he remembered. "What about the date? What date did you put on it?"

"Why the right bloody date of course, today's date, the twenty-eighth of February."

"You're sure of that? You're sure you didn't have a little joke?" He took hold of her arm. "Didn't you have a little joke with me and put the date of the calendar at the thirty-first of February?"

"The thirty-first of February?" She glared at him in astonishment. "Why, there's no such date."

VV sat tapping his desk with a paper knife. His look was friendly but reserved and a little sad. His magnetism was flowing at only about a quarter strength. "You wanted to see me, Andy."

Anderson explained about Kiddy Modes. As he explained and showed VV the letter terminating the contract he felt the absurdity of his own words. A year ago, a month ago, what he was saying would have made sense; today it was merely ridiculous. And what was ridiculous, he vaguely realized, was not simply agitation about losing Kiddy Modes' account, but the whole social structure propped up by advertising campaigns and board meetings. This, he wanted to say to the sad gnome who sat opposite him tapping rhythmically at the desk, this is not reality as I know it, obscene and raw. Reality, Anderson wanted to say, is what I have experienced in the last few days and am enduring now; reality is the cellar stairs, the hidden diary, the changing expressions on a policeman's face, the life torn in ribbons. Reality is the fourteen-year-old red-haired seducer slipping into her stepfather's arms, the disastrous disgust with the world and herself in Mrs. Vincent's thin face. And if that vivid recollection of VV, his face red with suppressed desire, was true, the figure opposite him now who held the power of rebuke or praise, was a preposterous mask if the disordered flat, the open drawer, the stolen diary, were real. This solemn recitation of the significant must be a dream. Now, indeed, he saw with all the minuteness of a dream the yellow pattern on the green curtains that hung before the window, the hairs sprouting richly from VV's nose and ears.

He stopped talking; and, like an actor taking up his cue, VV began. What was he saying? Anderson knew that the words must be important. He tried hard to listen, and even to make apposite replies; but he was all the time aware that what was said and done here could have no effect upon a fate already decided, though still imperfectly known. Snatches of speech came through to him. *Last night,* he heard, *last night* —what did that mean?—and *unfortunate incident*—could that refer to the burglary of his flat? But of course—the realization was delayed, but emerged finally—VV was saying that he had meant to discuss Anderson's position last night, but hadn't done so because of the trouble at dinner. *Holiday*—well, that was plain enough.

" I don't feel inclined to take a holiday," Anderson said firm-ly. He added, with a feeling of rich absurdity: " I have a job of work to do here." He pointed to his face. " Hey Presto!" A joke! But his face felt as though it might crack if he bent it in a smile, and VV's resigned sadness did not change. His expres-sion became, if possible, more serious and he picked up the telephone and spoke inaudible words. They sat staring at each other. Supposing, Anderson thought, that I said: " Let us talk about something important. Tell me, did you sleep with your stepdaughter last night?" Would that open for both of us the floodgates of confession, should we be able at last to speak honestly with each other, to meet face to naked face? But he knew that the alien words would never be permitted to come through in true simplicity by the censor operating in VV's mind, that they would emerge as something quite different from what was intended, as an insult or an attempt at blackmail. And would they not, after all, be that in a sense?

Two figures had crept into the room. How had they done so without Anderson's knowledge? Creeping up behind my back, he thought indignantly; and it was literally true that anybody who entered the room must have done so behind his back, because the chair in which he sat had its back to the door. But it was a dirty trick that these two grotesques, made in the shapes of Reverton and Pile, should have sneaked in on tiptoe as they must have done. Now they sat, solemn as statesmen pondering the fate of Empire in an old *Punch* cartoon, sadder even than VV, mutes at a funeral. But at least their lips were not sealed. The mouths of these Charlie McCarthy characters opened and shut. *Holiday, holiday*, Anderson heard. Surely he had made his position clear? He leaned forward and said again, very slowly: " I don't want to take a holiday."

The dummies shrugged, inimitably lifelike. VV made a long speech. VV was an intelligent man, a man who could tell a Dover sole from a packet of crisps. Perhaps he would tell the dummies about his stepdaughter? But he talked instead about Kiddy Modes. Anderson shut off, as it were, the power current necessary to make connection with the words, and stared at the complicated whorls of smoke rising from Reverton's pipe. While VV talked the faces of the marionettes grew sadder and sadder. *Makes no difference*, VV said. Anderson could not forbear a smile, for they were echoing, a good while afterward, his own thought. It made no difference, absolutely none, whether they lost this account or all of their accounts. Was that not what was meant? Perhaps not, for a moment later, without intending to eavesdrop, he heard another connected phrase: " Extended leave on half-pay." And then—it brought, almost, tears to his eyes—" Sympathy." Ah, sympathy! What errors, casual injustices, deliberate villainies, are covered by thy name!

Now VV had finished speaking, and one of the marionettes would no doubt begin. But instead they waited for him, they deferred to him almost, they seemed to seek his opinion on the nonsense VV had been talking. He felt inclined to let them have it, to pepper these three stuffed or mechanical figures from the unworld of dream with a few rounds from the pop-gun of his private knowledge. *Pile, old boy, what's your sex classification in Melian Street? VV, whose room did you sleep in last night? Who have you laid the finger on now for a judicious spot of emotional blackmail, Rev, do tell.* Or something simpler, something friendly, a piece of personal exhibitionism which might provoke the desired Buchmanite reaction. *Gentlemen—half-magnetizing, half-baked genius of the half world—here it is, what you've been waiting for, the unadmitted revelations of my whole inner life. Listen, and you shall hear.*

There were the words, shiningly visible. Had they, in fact,

159

been uttered. Looking round foxily at the three faces set in their stiff masks of regret, Anderson decided that they had not. It was better perhaps that they should stay unuttered in the presence of these dummies. Sinking back into the comfortable chair provided for him the prisoner at the bar smiled, waved a hand, refused to plead. His judges pronounced sentence. Anderson, now physically and emotionally limp, lounging in his chair almost with insulting ease, felt the immediate slackening of tension as he abandoned momentarily the world of reality. The sound track came back; and like a corpse miraculously granted the power of hearing, he listened to the elegies read at his graveside.

It was not, said good old Rev, removing his pipe from his mouth as a token of respect for the dead, it was not, Lord knew, that any of them wanted to lose old Andy. The copy lads who worked with him had always liked Andy, the production boys liked Andy, the Studio liked Andy, and—last and no doubt least important—the Board liked Andy. He had been a grand team man, consecutive, keen, tireless, a man who was on the job twenty-four hours a day. And Rev spoke with very special feeling, he said, about the question of team spirit, because he had been one of the boys himself not so long ago. He knew the difference between working with an awkward and with a decent copy chief. He would like to say about Andy that Andy had always played the game with everybody. But for the last few months, Rev was bound to say, Andy's work hadn't been what it was. It had been efficient all right—Andy was never less than efficient—but it had somehow lacked the spark. He wouldn't enumerate all the little points he'd checked up on and worried about, Rev said, but Andy would remember them. He'd tried to take some of the work off Andy's shoulders, but there it was—the dear chap was just a glutton for work, and was just the least bit huffy if you suggested he might be overdoing it. And then less than a month ago old Andy had taken just about the hardest knock a man could take. Since then his work—Rev pursed his lips, looked down at his pipe, shook a sad head—it was better to draw a veil. He'd just like to say, though, how pleased he was that Andy was being given this period of six months off duty. Be-

ond that time, of course, they couldn't say anything, on either
side. If he felt like coming back afterward, Rev would be the
first to welcome a good fellow, and a great team man, back into
the organization.

And now Pile, that hard-eyed, dry little old man, L.E.G.
Pile, cast his handful of earth upon the grave, addressing himself as he did so to the virtues of that conspicuously English
institution, family life. Who would have supposed that the old
man had so much sentiment in him? For his voice quavered,
or at least, Anderson thought with too much flippancy, semi-
quavered, as he told what his own family had meant to him,
bustling Mrs. Pile and the four little Piles, four little kiddies
to have their napkins changed, their mouths filled, their clothes
put on (more and more clothes put on, larger and larger meals
eaten), their school fees paid—the two others fidgeted, but
Anderson listened with the closest attention as old dry Mr.
Pile told how the institution of the family had helped to preserve him from fornication, drunkenness and extravagance.
Anderson, said Mr. Pile, had not been granted, alas, the blessing of a family. Might he be forgiven for discovering in the
absence of the infant's cry the lack of that inspiring, energizing
influence that alone could bring a man unharmed through the
valley of the shadow of death. (Who would have thought the
old man had so much poetry in him?) They had seen and
known this friend of theirs for years, they had valued Anderson's advice and respected—nay, in his own case, been dazzled
by—his intellect. His departure from them, unavoidable as it
was by the keen standards of business ethics and efficiency
to which Anderson would be the first to adhere, was nevertheless a tragedy. Might he be forgiven for saying, as he
wished Anderson God-speed and good luck, that it was a
family tragedy?

A family tragedy? Anderson saw the long pants, the thin
ruffled hair, the goatish expression changing to one of annoyance. Aren't all tragedies family tragedies? he heard himself
asking. But these words, like the others, remained unspoken.

With the corpse now firmly underground, VV judged it safe
to attempt a little act of resuscitation—nothing spectacular,
nothing serious, a mere gesture to placate whatever gods may

be, gods who think that full justice had not been done
Anderson. This was not to be looked on, VV then cried wi
a ghastly joviality not meant to convince, this was not to
looked on as a parting. Pull not those long faces. Say
revoir but not good-bye. Andy did not want a holiday-
very well, then, he need not take a holiday. Let him take
rest cure, go to some little place where he would be we
looked after. Let him return in six months' time a ne
man, a well man, not disturbed any more by these terrib
calendars that changed their dates (oh yes, VV injected pare
thetically, *that* story is all round the firm and we can't igno
such things, my boy.) Let him come back to us then and—V
added with a self-conscious drop from grand to commonpla
—we shall be pleased to have a chat.

There was silence. The judge-executioners had done the
work, and now they stared at him. Anderson returned the
looks with a suitably dead gaze. Quietly, conscious of irreve
ence, Reverton coughed, and VV was startled into action. Th
question then arose, he said, of Andy's—we are bound to u
the word—successor. We thought at one time of promotir
young Lessing——

Good old Rev took his pipe out of his mouth to say: But yo
told me yourself yesterday that people didn't get on with hir

And we felt, pronounced Pile, that while excellent at h
present work, he might be weighed down by the position of to
much responsibility. But we have been fortunate enough
find a really excellent executive type——

A man with a distinct personality, said VV.

A friendly type, Rev remarked, and with good connection

A man with a keen administrative sense, added Pile, whos
name is Blythe-Pountney.

VV rang a bell. A man came in. Andy, my boy, said VV
meet Mr. Percival Blythe-Pountney. Mr. Blythe-Pountney, M
Anderson.

Anderson had seen Percival Blythe-Pountney before. H
had been walking along, wagging a finger in the air an
saying: Three four five six. Now the little man stuck out
hand, both guilty and sly. Anderson took it, and burst ov
laughing. The laughter, uncontrollable as last night's laughte

162

ocked him so that he had to lean against the wall. Mr. Blythe-Pountney looked modestly, but still slyly, at the floor, but three pairs of eyes stared at Anderson with frozen disapproval. There is, after all, no return from the dead.

6

There is no return. But was it not possible, Anderson thought again, that the whole thing was a dream? At times during the afternoon he thought so, said to himself: It is quite impossible that I should be showing this man Blythe-Pountney the progress of my accounts, introducing him to the Production Department, the Space Department, to Studio, Research, Vouchers, Accounts, Dispatch. Blythe-Pountney, at first accompanied by Rev, but later left entirely in Anderson's hands, did no more number counting or finger wagging. He developed during the afternoon, however, a nervous tic which caused him to wink prodigiously at awkward moments, and his limb movements were poorly articulated. An arm, moving in a wild unnecessary semicircle, would now and again thud against Anderson's body, or a flying elbow be dug suddenly into his side. Blythe-Pountney seemed able to control these unexpected thrusts in the presence of women, but he gave Wyvern a great dig in the stomach and flicked the manager of the Space Department lightly across the face with his hand. His two-step overcame him at the oddest times and places. He might run a step or two down the corridor, or break into brisk foot tapping while details of space bookings and insertions were being explained to him. It was difficult, certainly, to believe in Blythe-Pountney as a representative of reality.

The news, nevertheless, had to be broken. Anderson broke it, gently and carefully, like eggs into a basin. "I'm taking a long holiday," he said, and added with what he hoped was an obvious note of irony, "At the directors' request." When he told Lessing the copywriter shook his head, eyes grave behind his hornrims. "Bad luck," he said. "Kiddy Modes?"

"No," Anderson answered. "Life. The missing wail in the nursery." Lessing looked puzzled. "This is Blythe-Pountney, who is taking over from me." Blythe-Pountney twitched,

163

winked and shuffled. Greatorex was brought from his corner desk and introduced. "Are you leaving us for good, Mr Anderson?" he asked.

"For good or ill. Never be surprised by sudden departures in the world of advertising, Greatorex."

Blythe-Pountney said to Lessing: "You'll be working for me on that—um, ah—new account, won't you? Hey Presto. Big stuff. I like it. Scope for ideas. Let me see what you've done on Monday."

"With you."

"What's that? What's that?" Blythe-Pountney winked.

"Andy and I work with each other."

Blythe-Pountney twitched. "That's what I said."

"The word is *with,* not *for.*"

"Oh." Twitch and two-step. "Oh yes. Jolly good. Yes, I see." A gargantuan wink. "With, not for. Yes, I see your point."

In the studio Wyvern carefully wiped off paint and took the hand offered by Blythe-Pountney with an accompanying two-step. Wyvern said nothing at all, but Blythe-Pountney seemed hardly to notice silence. He stuck his nose into the rough lay-outs Wyvern was making for Hey Presto, was enthusiastic about some designs for labels that had already been rejected by a client, pinched the arm of a girl working as apprentice in the studio, and criticized a photographic montage of buildings which was being pieced together for a construction company. "Modernistic stuff, eh, modernistic. Very interesting. Like it, do you? Can't say I do myself. Simple, strong, vital, that's what I find clients generally like. Just like the girls," he said with a wink and a sudden dig of his elbow at Wyvern. "Most interesting place in an advertising agency is the studio, I always say. Like to spend all my time in it. Got some layout ideas myself, you know, full of ideas. Be bringing them down to you; you'll be seeing a lot of me. 'Bye till Monday." Blythe-Pountney two-stepped forward, grasped Wyvern's hand, winked and two-stepped away. Anderson said: "I'll be in tomorrow, Jack, to clear up and say good-bye." Wyvern stood, hands on hips, looking after them.

When Blythe-Pountney had gone Anderson sat in his office,

staring at the diminishing finger of sunlight on the carpet. His mind had gone back, for no obvious reason, to the day in his boyhood when, coming downstairs to breakfast, he had seen by his mother's plate the salmon-pink writing paper and recognized Elsie's hand. His mother had wept, shouted, screamed at him; but when she knew that Elsie was going to have a baby shouts and screams were replaced by gentle wheedling. "You don't really want to marry her, do you, dear? A girl of that class. You've made a mistake, but we must see if you can't patch it up, so that you can wait until Miss Right comes along." Patching-up meant the last letter in the salmon-pink envelope to say that Elsie had gone to Bradford, but what else did it mean? His father and mother had spoken of the affair thereafter only as a narrow escape from danger, a trap which through their cleverness had never, quite, been sprung. But what had happened to Elsie? He could recall nothing of her but a nervous giggle, employed upon the most inappropriate occasions. On the common under the bushes Elsie had giggled and giggled, quite unable to control herself. She remained as a giggle and a salmon-pink envelope, but what had happened to the seed within her? Had it been allowed to live?—Was a child of his loins, a young man or woman, now talking with a Bradford accent, training as engineer or student of ballet? How astonishing that in all these years he had never thought of Elsie Smith and of their child. One brings down the curtain, Anderson thought, and never looks behind it. And why was he looking behind it now? Suppose the seed exterminated, might one say that murder had been done when Elsie was sent to Bradford?

The thin beam of sunlight had vanished when, looking up, he saw Reverton standing, pipe in mouth, smiling a little ruefully. Vincent, Reverton, Wyvern, Lessing, which of them gave my wife his—blessing? "I've come to say good-bye," Reverton said, with such finality in his voice that Anderson was startled.

"Good-bye?"

"I shan't be in tomorrow. Going down to see Crunchy-Munch. I was sorry to have to butt in with my own ideas there, but you know how it is sometimes. Anyway, it's over

now. Andy, it's all for the best, believe me. It may be onl
temporary." A far-away look came into Reverton's eyes
"We've had some good times together. I'll miss you, Andy
We've been a great team, but I've got the firm to think of. W
must all think of the firm. Frankly, I've had a feeling latel
that you haven't really been—believing in your work." Tribut
had been paid in sentiment. Reverton took the pipe from hi
mouth, looked at it, tapped it on his heel. "You won't forge
the Hey Presto when you come in tomorrow, will you'
Divenga rang up about it today. As a matter of fact, there'
some snag."

"Snag?"

Reverton was looking hard at his pipe. "This particula:
sample may not be absolutely suitable for every type of skin
He doesn't want us to go on using it. Seems it contains some
substance which may irritate the delicate white skin, though
it's quite all right for dark skins. They're sending over othe:
samples which have gone through some new refining process
They're experimenting all the time, you know that." Reverto:
paused, apparently expectant of a reply. When he did not ge:
one he said again: "You won't forget to bring it back tomor
row. I shouldn't go on using it."

"I won't forget."

"No hard feelings, Andy."

There should be hard feelings, Anderson thought, but in
fact there are no feelings at all, nothing but numbness and a
memory of Elsie Smith. "No hard feelings."

"Sure you're all right?"

"Perfectly."

"Well." Reverton tucked away the pipe, shot out his mus-
cular reliable hand. "Good-bye, Andy, and good luck."

"Good-bye."

The afternoon grew darker. Anderson sat at the desk while
spots of light appeared in the offices visible through the window. At last he got up, put on his hat and raincoat and
reached the door. There he switched on the light and stood
looking at the desk still littered with papers, the green carpet,
the hatstand; items in a dead life. He said aloud, not knowing
what he meant. "It won't do." As he walked away from the

ffice the telephone was ringing. It seemed somehow to be a comment on his career.

7

The sense of impending event, awful in its significance, disastrous in its effect, that hung over Anderson was accompanied by a strange numbness and emptiness. He was frightened at the thought of return to his flat; the disordered presence, the empty drawer, the dirty sink, the Inspector's presence hanging about the place like his cigar smoke, were things that moved through his numbness to cause irrational apprehension. It was with a sense that he had absolutely nothing to do but wait, combined with a contradictory feeling that some kind of action was demanded of him, that Anderson turned into the Stag after leaving the office. There, sitting in one of the partitioned alcoves, hat on back of head, sat Wyvern. He pointed a finger at Anderson.

"Bang bang bang, so they got you. The gipsy's warning was right. Let me set them up. Cheers. Let me guess what my old pal Rev said to you. He said: Good-bye Andy, it's been lovely knowing you; if I were a crocodile I'd weep; I'm sorry, but you've stopped believing in your work. Right?"

"Not far wrong."

"I know I'm not far wrong. Don't say I didn't warn you. But why did they fall for this St. Vitus? Because of his old school tie? He's no advertising man; he just stocks a nice line of bull. Anybody with half an eye can see that. Well, he'd better not come playing around in my department or he'll be out on his ear."

"Another beer."

"Thanks, mine's a Bass. It's a damned shame the way they've treated you. It is the boot, isn't it? Rev said you were taking a long rest, and might not come back."

"I shan't come back."

Wyvern held his long nose with two fingers. "When you smell stinking fish, there you smell advertising. That's my view of the profession."

"There's nothing like that to it," Anderson said wearily.

"They've got as much right to get rid of me as I've got t
leave them. I don't complain."

"Then you bloody well should complain. When I think c
those complacent bastards sitting there and then think of m
old mother——" Wyvern tilted his glass and took a long drink
"Though from what they tell me you've been a bit off the bea
lately. I mean old boy, magic calendars and letters flyin
about to the wrong people—they just won't do."

"Who told you?"

"My ear is to the ground," Wyvern cupped one ear. "Wha
are you going to do for that little girl?"

"Jean Lightley, do you mean?"

"Jean Lightley," Wyvern made a noise. "I mean Molly.

"I'd forgotten about Molly."

"Ah, there you are. But she hasn't forgotten you. She want
you, Andy."

Anderson thought of the long chalky nose, the ride in th
taxicab and the tears staining the little squares of colour. H
said flatly: "But I don't want her."

"Why did you make her think you did, then? Why did yo
sleep with her?" Anderson stared in astonishment at the fac
stuck forward indignantly into his own. "Hell, man, everybody
knows it. You've only got to look at her and see th
difference."

"You can't see a difference," Anderson said mechanically
He was looking at a hat which lay on a table by one of th
alcoves opposite. The hat was a bowler, rather old but quit
respectable. A coat, beside it, was dark blue. The occupant
of the alcove were invisible, but it seemed to Andrson tha
he knew both hat and coat.

"Shall I tell you the trouble with you? I feel all the sym
pathy in the world with you, the dirty way you've been
treated, but shall I tell you the trouble with you? Self-centred
you're too damned self-centred, Andy. Suppose we were a
like that? Take me and my mother now, what do you think
happened the other night? I was just going out——"

A hand, holding a glass of beer, was visible outside the
partition. The beer was placed upon the table by the hat
Before the hand was withdrawn Anderson saw the thick, hairy

168

wrist. At the same time he heard a laugh, light and boyish.
The laugh, like the overcoat, belonged to Greatorex. Anderson
stood up suddenly and knocked over the table. Beer flowed
over the floor and on to Wyvern's lap. " Sorry," Anderson
said. " Sorry." He got out of the alcove and ran from the
pub without looking into the alcove opposite.

8

Trafalgar Square, Leicester Square, Piccadilly, Shaftesbury
Avenue, Charing Cross Road. Neon signs flashed at him in
coloured lights messages which had a desperate depth of
meaning. BOVRIL—BOVRIL—BOVRIL, said the lights in
Trafalgar Square, where the fountains played excitingly their
song of sexual aspiration. In Leicester Square the houses of
pleasure invited him, Gable and Grable, Garbo and Harpo,
Tracy and Lamarr. In Piccadilly Circus a sign said excitingly
DRAIN IT TO THE LAST DROP. Ah, to belong again
to the world of Bovril and Moussec, to know and love the
realities of Gable and Grable, to be unconfused by the agonies
of choice. *Reality,* said Dr. Johnson, leaning forward and
pinching one elegant thigh with his rude fingers, *Here is reality,
sir. Thus I confute you.* Oh, Anderson cried, wandering among
the civilization of the Corner House and the Milk Bar, jostling
gum-chewing girls, passing the contraceptive doorways of chemists—oh to believe that such a visible world exists in its ideal
simplicity; a world away from the disordered flat, the anonymous letter, the unseen figures in the alcove. He stopped
outside a cinema which said MORE BRUTAL BENNY—
MORE LUSCIOUS LUCY—FIERCER AND FRANKER
THAN EVER. Lucy Lalange presented an expanse of thigh
ten feet high. Brutal Benny Baily stood snarling by her side.
Anderson passed over his pieces of silver and went inside.

Within the air was warm, delicious; he shivered with ecstacy
in his thin raincoat; his shoes sunk in rubbery pile. From
the walls, as an epauletted attendant conducted him towards
Mecca, looked down benevolently the gods whose names were
music, whose words were law, whose look was love—Astaire,
Iturbi, Goodman, Dorsey, Bogart, Cagney, Scott and Ladd,

Turner, Stanwyck, Lockwood, Bergman. Under different names from those given them at birth, serenely fixed in one attitude, displaying forever a smile or a fist, the gods watched the progress of this neophyte in the service of reality.

Upon the screen, when Anderson first saw it, enormous faces met, blond and dark hair mingled, Benny Baily's voice right, warm, American, said to Lucy Lalange *Everything is going to be all right.* But everything was not all right. The music emphatically discordant, recorded the progress of Benny Baily, sitting grimly at the steering wheel of a long, lean car. Rain drove at the windscreen, scenery slipped by, Benny stared ahead, moving the steering wheel rapidly from time to time as the car shaved others by the width of a coat of paint. Round and round, ceaselessly, Benny's jaw moved masticating the juice of the healing gum. Now a barrier had been placed across the road to stop him—poof, he was through it without so much as a batted eyelid, his jaws moving a little faster to indicate strain. And now a rapid patter of shots came from behind bushes, the windscreen glass splintered. Benny drew a revolver from under his armpit. Crack, crack, crack through the car window and a villain, his face distorted ludicrously, staggered and fell. Round the hairpin bend—and far, far below, another car was visible racing along the ribbon of road. For a moment Benny stopped chewing.

But back in the city two men had come for Lucy Lalange. Flashing badges beneath their coat lapels, they pushed her into a car and drove away. Pug-nosed, cauliflower-eared, hard-lipped, squint eyed, they were not the cops Lucy in her sophisticated innocence had taken them for, but gangsters. Out of the car and through a back door they hustled her (a quick cut revealed the front of the building as an exclusive night club), and into a room containing a safe, a settee, and a carpet. In this room a thinly moustached man sat picking his teeth.

Now Benny's jaws were at work again. His long greyhound of a car nosed its way round bends, skidded with two wheels the edges of precipices, ate up the shiny road. Slowly, and then quickly, it gained on the other car, whose occupant, weak and shifty-eyed, looked nervously back at overtaking Nemesis.

170

Shifty turned the car into a side road and scrambled down a hillside, clinging to bushes with one hand, holding in the other a bag. But Benny is after him, now he is on him, he grasps Shifty round the neck. Shifty struggles, however, writhes and writhes, brings up his knee to a vital part. Benny staggers, falls to his knees, drops to the ground, and Shifty draws back his foot for a kick that will send Benny half a mile down the hillside to the rocks below. We see the look of pleasure on Shifty's face, cut to the foot in its heavy steel-tipped boot drawn back to kick, cut back to see dismay replace Shifty's gloating expression. Benny has his teeth sunk deep into Shifty's calf, Benny has him down, Benny gives Shifty's neck one quick backhand butt with the heel of his hand. Shifty's neck is broken, head hangs sideways, tongue drops out. He is no good any more. Benny pitches him down on to the rocks, looks in the bag, nods to show that the bonds or jewels are still there and says reflectively: "Where's my gun?" The audience laughs, Benny finds his gun and starts chewing again.

(Anderson became aware of a pressure against his left leg. Without looking away from the screen he pressed back.)

Back in the gangster's office Lucy Lalange has been tied up. She is required to tell something or do something; it is not clear which. It is abundantly clear, however, that she refuses. Her head shakes from side to side, her great eyes roll about in terror. Pug-nose One, thin lipped, hits her across the face, quickly back and forth. The chief goes on picking his teeth. Pug-nose Two, who lights a gas ring, chuckling. Benny, looking "Aw chief, gimme a chance-why don't you gimme a chance?"

(A hand found Anderson's hand. Pointed nails dug into his palm.)

In police headquarters the superintendent puts down the telephone. A car is out, two cars, three cars, a whole fleet of cars screaming along the road. The gangster chief nods to Pug-nose Two, who lights a gas ring, chuckling. Benny, looking at the loot, has somehow discovered the gang chief's complicity. Jaws moving faster than ever, he is on his way back. Quick cuts show Lucy's rolling eyes, the police cars racing, Pug-nose Two heating curious instruments over the gas flame, Benny racing and chewing, the gangster chief picking his teeth.

(The hand moved up Anderson's arm, nails tearing at the skin. A foot found his foot.)

The gang chief stops picking his teeth, walks over to Lucy, looks at the nails on her hand, sighs and motions to Pug-nose Two. Lucy rolls about like a sick cow, Benny arrives at the back door. The police draw up in the front. Pug-nose Two advances on Lucy, drooling a little.

(A heel dug at the side of Anderson's leg, stripping away—it seemed—the flesh.)

Benny breaks down the back door, rushes up the stairs and into the room. He kicks Pug-nose One in the stomach and jumps on his hand as it reaches for a gun, catches Pug-nose Two round the neck and throws him toward the gang chief, who has drawn his own gun. The gang chief's shots go through Pug-nose Two, who is still holding his instruments of torture. Enraged, Pug-nose Two lurches forward against the gang chief pressing him against the wall, pushing the hot irons into his eyes. The gang chief screams.

(Hand and leg were withdrawn. Anderson felt his wrist tenderly.)

And then the formalities: the police, congratulations, bag handed over, Pug-nose One confessing, Pug-nose Two dead, the gang chief blinded. Another close-up of the dark head and the fair. Benny pushes his gun to the side of his cheek and winks. Lucy, her eyes cast down in a maidenly manner, looks up suddenly and winks, too. Curtain.

The lights went up. Anderson turned to his left. There he saw, with a shock of surprise almost equal to that given him by the sight of a bowler hat and an overcoat in the Stag, a small suburban woman in her late forties. She wore hornrimmed glasses and had on no lipstick and very little powder. Her dark brown coat was dowdy. As Anderson stared at her unbelievingly she turned to him full face for a moment and bestowed upon him a mild, dull gaze. This failure of correspondence between the visible and the imagined struck Anderson most unpleasantly. He got up hurriedly and went out.

As he was crossing the rubber floor of the foyer he heard his name called: "Andy." An obscure connection with the incident in the cinema made him walk on faster. "Andy, Andy." He recognized the voice, and turned.

Elaine Fletchley advanced towards him, swinging a little umbrella in one hand, the other resting lightly on the arm of a young and fierce looking Guards officer. "At last, Andy. Wherever did you get to at lunch?"

"I had an international lunch in several Chinese restaurants. They told me to look for you there in El Vino's."

"Not Chinese, darling—Turkish. Bonzo was with me, and we waited and waited. He didn't like it." She patted the stiff Guard's arm. "This is Bonzo. He's a good dog." Bonzo growled unintelligibly. "Andy, I've got to talk to you. Bonzo darling, you must go." The guardsman growled again. "Now, don't be silly. Andy and I have got some business to do, that's all. Oh, I haven't introduced you. Bonzo, meet Andy. Andy, meet Bonzo. Now you're friends."

Anderson's hand felt as though it had passed under a steam roller. Elaine Fletchley pinched her lip. "Bonzo, go home and collect the baggage. I'll meet you at the station in half an hour. If you've been a good dog I'll give you a biscuit." The guardsman growled again, but the growl was hesitant. Under the great peaked cap his face was round, pink and immature. She swung the umbrella lightly against his buttocks. "Go on, go on, don't be foolish, Bonzo." The guardsman growled again. "I shall be all right. I've known Andy for years." The guardsman raised a hand to the peaked cap in a half-salute, about-turned and strode away, moving with the mechanical precision of a toy. Elaine watched admiringly until he had turned the corner. "What do you think?" she said. "Not very intelligent, but he has such beautiful shoulders."

"We were going to talk."

"My God yes, we must talk. I've wanted to find you all week, Andy. Where have you been hiding yourself? And where shall we go? Let's go to the Corner House; it's handy and I've got to be quick. Did you like the film?"

"Not much."

"It gets you where you live, I think. At least, it got Bonzo. He was mad about it. We're going to get married."

"Married!" Anderson said incredulously.

"I'm not married to Fletch, you know. We never got that far. That's why he's so madly jealous, jealous of you even. That's half of the trouble, I think."

"Jealous of me. But he hadn't any cause."

"Since when do you need a cause to be jealous?"

"What do you mean half of the trouble?"

"I'll tell you when we sit down." Elaine trotted along with neat, accurate steps. She was a small woman of thirty-five who looked as if she were made of brass. Bright yellow hair was curled in great coils about her ears, her coat was richly yellow, and brass buckles gleamed on her shoes. These were hard, bright and shining. They attained a gloss that might be mistaken for wit, as her face achieved through cosmetics a freshness that might be taken for youth.

They sat with coffees at a check-clothed table. She stirred with a spoon and said: "I hate that policeman. He frightens me." Quite irrelevantly she added: "Bonzo comes of good family you know. He's the Honourable Roderick Manly. And he suspects because of Fletch. He's a swine, that man. He knows about Bonzo and he couldn't get back at him, so he got back at you. It's not my fault, Andy, honest to God I had nothing to do with it."

"To do with what?"

Elaine rarely listened to what other people were saying. "So now that policeman suspects."

"Suspects what?" Anderson asked with extraordinary patience. "What does he suspect, Elaine?"

"He suspects you." Anderson moved. "Don't tell me, Andy, I don't want to know anything about it. I don't want to be mixed up. I've done the best I can," she added absently: "He came to see me."

"Who?"

"The policeman, of course. He came to the office and told me about it."

"He came to the office," Anderson repeated dully. "And told you. Told you what?"

"About the letters, the anonymous letters. Fletch sent them to the police."

" Fletch sent them." He gasped. Why had he not realized it before? Why had he not understood Fletchley's own hints and the Inspector's questions about an enemy? " But why?"

" Don't ask me why. He's not sane, that man. I tell you, he's crazy with jealousy. He admitted sending them as soon as they asked him. But that's not all. He told them about the switch."

" What about the switch?"

Elaine Fletchley was busy stirring her coffee. This, the revelation, Anderson thought; when she has told me what she knows all my questions will be answered. " You told them," she said slowly, " about the switch being fused. So that Val fell downstairs."

" Yes."

" That was at a quarter to eight."

" Yes."

" Fletch told them he went into the cellar at half past seven and the light was working all right then. Fletch said he hadn't offered the evidence at the inquest because he hadn't realized it was important. So then they came and asked me."

" Asked you?" Anderson found himself simply unable to grasp the meaning of all this. " Asked you what?"

" If we were having an affair. I told them no, we'd never had an affair." Flatly she said: " I don't think they believed me."

Suddenly she said: " What's the matter with your face? It looks funny."

His face was certainly taut with strain and tension. But his questions were not yet answered. " Elaine, you were Val's best friend, weren't you?"

" Well?"

" You'll know then—you must know."

She looked at her gold wrist watch. " I must be going."

" No, no, you can't go yet. There's something I must know." But it was difficult to ask the question, the final and decisive question. He moved uneasily on his seat. " Then you should have told me."

The voice was now altogether brass. " Told you what?"

" Elaine, look here; you were her best friend, she trusted you." Somewhere in Anderson's mind was a terror of what

175

he was going to hear. Among the checked tablecloths, the suburban families and the respectable clerks, some final sentence was to be pronounced. "You can tell me the name," he said with difficulty.

"What name?"

"The name of her lover."

At the next table the waitress dropped knives and forks with a clatter. Elaine leaned a little toward him. "What did you say?"

Anderson put his hand to his throat. He felt as if he were choking. "Her lover."

The smoothness of her ageing forehead stayed uncreased, but her bright eyes stared at him with an unfathomable gaze. "Her lover?"

The waitress was apologizing to the young couple at the next table. "I'm ever so sorry," she said. "It's my nerves. It's a dream I had last night. I've got a little boy and I dreamed I saw him in a coffin. Been upset ever since, I have." The young couple looked at her doubtfully.

"You know who it was," Anderson said. The checked tablecloth, Elaine's wasp-yellow coat, and her intense stare—he sought for some kind of meaning in these things, and did not find it.

"But——" she said, and then looked again at her wrist watch. "I've got to go. I simply must fly."

"No." He pushed away the coffee cup, leaned over and caught hold of her wrist. "Not until you've told me."

"For heaven's sake." She wrenched her wrist away. "You're barking up the wrong tree, Andy." The young couple picked at their food watching.

"What do you mean, the wrong tree? You know the name, I can see you know it. Tell me."

"Andy, I don't know what you're talking about." She was not convincing; she was trying to shield somebody; she did not know of the irrefutable evidence in his pocket. He tried to tell her of it, to speak calmly, logically, but the phrases tumbled out in the wrong order or in no order at all. He heard his own voice, pitched too high. Somebody in his office, it was saying, the letter on his desk, in Val's writing, how could

176

she explain the letter? But of course she couldn't explain—
nonsense to pretend, to shield people—who was it? The
young couple put down the forks with which they had been
picking at their food and looked at it distrustfully.

Elaine had been opening and shutting the clasp of her black
bag. Now she stood up, small neat and determined. "I've
got to go."

But the letter, the letter, Anderson heard the voice say
whiningly—how can you explain? Look, here it is, here, here.

"Now, Andy," Elaine said loudly and clearly and slowly,
"You're not well, Andy. Listen to me. You should go home
and straight to bed and have somebody see to your face."

The fingers dragged out the blue paper, and held it up. She
glanced and snorted angrily. "That's a bill. Now look, Andy,
go home and see a doctor."

He stared at the piece of paper unbelievingly. It was a
tailor's bill. Then the letter—the fingers fumbled again, but
she was still talking. "I knew Val better than anyone, and
I tell you you're all wrong." Anderson stretched out his hands
imploringly. The young couple at the next table looked at one
another, pushed away their food and got up.

Now the voice was saying it could find the letter, and was
crying out over and over again *Tell me the name, please tell
me the name.* And the blow fell, the blow he had expected and
feared. She turned on him, the bag snapped tightly, finally, as
tight and final as the look on her face "You're crazy, Andy.
I didn't want to say it, but you've made me." She paused—the
young couple and the waitress waited eagerly, expectantly—and
spoke the irrevocable words: "Val was sold on you from the
day she met you. She never had a lover. You've invented
him." She walked with hard, firm steps on her high heels,
past the cash desk and out of the restaurant.

9

He stepped out of the small, safe box of the taxi, into a
world full of enemies. It would be unwise, no doubt, to let
the driver know where he lived. He got out at the Demon,
tipping the man half a crown, watching carefully to see if

177

he betrayed any extravagant reaction. But the driver merely tested the coin with his teeth, said " Thanks, guv," and put in his clutch. Anderson leaned forward confidentially and made a gesture with his thumb at the Demon behind him. " I don't live here."

." You don't, eh?" The driver laughed, showing projecting teeth. " I wish I did. 'Night, guv." And he was away, leaving Anderson standing shivering in his raincoat, on the pavement. The rain, thin and slanting, damped his face and his uncovered head. His uncovered head; he remembered now that he had taken off his Homburg—his second-best Homburg—in the taxi cab and put it by his side. Would the man bring it back? How extraordinary it was that he should forget his hat after, last night, forgetting his hat and taking the wrong coat. The wrong coat, the lost hats—they had a meaning, he knew, but what was it? He recognized a meaning, also, in the words Elaine Fletchley had spoken; although its precise significance still eluded him, although for that matter he could not remember exactly what she had said, he knew that he had ground for being deeply upset. But that was all too tangled, too difficult: and besides, it distracted his attention from the immediate problem. Was his home being watched? He walked to the entrance of the Demon, paused as though about to go in, and then moved quickly into the shadow by the side of the pub. In his shadow, not impenetrable but deep, he tiptoed to the corner, and stared into the darkness of Joseph Street. The house *was* being watched. In the front portico a figure lounged, unidentifiable, just out of range of the street light. Anderson drew back. His whole body was trembling.

The clumsy fools had stationed somebody outside the front door. He could have laughed aloud. But this was not a matter, after all, for laughter. It meant that the instinct which had warned him not to return here—the distasteful and even terrifying images that had arisen in his mind at thought of the disordered rooms, the empty drawer of the desk, the broken picture, and, yes, the cellar, the uninvestigated cellar—that instinct had been right. It would be falling into the trap, the trap for which that motionless and weary figure was acting as bait, if he turned the corner and walked across the road.

Is that what I believe, then? Anderson asked himself. Must I turn round and go back? Let me be logical. And now a whole set of completely different arguments came into his mind. Was it really likely that they would be as clumsy as that? Was there not an obvious motive for stationing a man just where he would be seen? Wouldn't Anderson, in fact, be playing into their hands by running away like a scared child, failing to remark that a double trap had been laid for him? Anderson began to laugh. He said aloud: "Come on now, give them credit for a bit of subtlety. They're not fools—we all know that." But beneath these uttered words, or above or behind them or anyhow existing in some relation to them, were the things Elaine had said, the things he had forgotten and could not now try to remember. He spoke again, without knowing the meaning of the words "The letter," he said, and turned the corner. With rain blowing directly into his face he stepped firmly into the roadway. The figure in the door straightened up, moved slowly to the gate, tucked a newspaper under one arm and then ran to meet him. They met in the middle of the road. It was Molly O'Rourke. "Andy," she cried, "Andy, are you all right?" He said nothing, but stood looking at her considering. "What's happened to you, Andy? Why are you looking at me like that?"

In a voice so consciously soft and low that he could not recognize it as his own, Anderson said: "Who sent you?"

"What do you mean? I heard about it this afternoon."

Distracted for a moment, he said: "About what?"

"That dirty devil Reverton—he's been wanting to get you out for a long time. When you're not well, too."

What was she talking about? But the last phrase caught in his mind and was linked with other things that had been said recently. "What do you mean not well? Who told you I was not well?"

"Andy, we can't stand here in the rain. Let's go and talk." Quite passively he allowed himself to be led to the curb, and then broke free of the hand she had placed on his arm. He said, again with that conscious gentleness: "Who told you I was not well?"

"Anybody can see for themselves. You're shivering. And—what's the matter with your face?"

"You don't care to give me the name of your informant?" he said politely

"Oh, don't be silly." Now they were at the front door. "Give me the key." He handed the key to her obediently, but as she turned it in the lock he moved swiftly. He was inside the front door, and had snatched the key from the lock. He held the door open a little, facing her and laughing. "My dear girl, you must be very simple to think I should fall for *that*."

"For what, Andy? I don't know what you mean."

He laughed again. How easy it had been to outwit her. "I'm afraid you'll have to go back to them and report failure. Suggest that they should try something subtler next time."

"Let me in." She took a step forward.

"Ah ha," he said, and laughed again. "No nearer." But now she darted forward, with a suddenness that took him by surprise, and they were struggling together in the doorway. He had been overconfident, he had relaxed his guard, and the result was a fight to expel this creature who was all hair and claws, who sobbed even as she tried to push past him. She had come out now, however, thank goodness, in her true colours; there was no subtlety about it; she was simply trying to come in where she was not wanted, and as they swayed together he felt the exhilaration of one whose dubieties had been lost in the satisfaction of righteous action. He heard a voice crying out something of this, but he was unable to listen closely, because his energy was given to the struggle with the enemy. Her approach might have been clumsy, but she fought cleverly, eel-like, eluding his grip, trying to get past him. But he was filled with the strength of ten; he caught her by the throat and when she tore his hands away brought up his knee as Shifty had done to Benny Baily. She cried out, and sprawled on the ground with her skirt up, showing a patch of thigh. Somehow the evening paper that had been in her hand was inside the door, as though it had been delivered by a newsboy. He picked it up, slammed the door shut, and burst out laughing.

180

But that, after all, was not the end of her. She got up, kept her finger on the doorbell, which chimed most musically, and cried to be let in. What stupidity! And what effrontery! Did she take him for a fool? He was suddenly very angry and, standing on the other side of the door, shouted at her a mixture of insults and obscenities—rather shameful words, perhaps, and he waited for Fletchley to come down. But Fletchley did not come down; Fletchley was out somewhere. *Go away*, Anderson heard a voice screaming. *Go away*. And at last she went away, walking slowly and dejectedly, dabbing at her face with a handkerchief. He opened the door of his own flat, tiptoed into the sitting room and looked out through a window (the curtain edge lifted the merest fraction) until she had turned the corner. He had won the first round. Now to sit back and take stock of the situation.

But the kind of stocktaking he had promised himself—the rational working out of his own position, the plans for his own defence—proved impossible, after all. For when, hesitantly, he had pressed the switch and the fluorescent light, cold, even and blue, shone out into the room, it illuminated also the fact that only yesterday the enemy had been here, poking and snuffling, opening doors and sniffing out secrets. How ridiculous to have made that prodigious struggle to keep the woman out tonight when yesterday she or her friends had invaded his privacy and discovered the mysterious things they wanted to know. Looking round at the room, catching sight of the dirty whisky glasses, he felt utter hopelessness. And beneath the hopelessness, fear.

He sat in the chromium-armed chair and put his hand in his pocket. And now the first thing he pulled out was the letter from Val, creased and crumpled but unmistakably in her hand. Another dip—and here was the anonymous letter that had strayed mysteriously into Greatorex's overcoat. Why had he been unable to find these things when he talked to Elaine? He stared at them, spread out upon his knees. But the words were blurred in front of his eyes, and he quickly lost interest in the letters and let them drop to the floor.

Groping on the carpet for these dropped letters, he found

the evening paper that had been dropped so neatly and, i
now appeared, cunningly inside the door. They had had i
purpose in leaving the paper, for they had a purpose in every
thing. Was it to try to scare him with a paper dated Februar
the Fourth? He looked at the type, but it danced away fron
him. It danced away—and yet after a moment the date wa
clear, although everything else wavered up and down. Th
date upon the newspaper sneered at him in letters and numeral
that grew larger until they exploded in his brain. The date wa
the thirty-first of February. And at that moment, when clea
warning was given him—but warning of what?—he noticed th
smell.

Head raised, nostrils sniffing apart, he was able to separat
from the faint odor of dust another smell equally familiar: th
smell of a particular scent. Lovely Evening, that Val used
And the smell, pungent now in his nostrils (how could he hav
failed to notice it before?), came from the bedroom. Now h
knew that the struggle and victory outside had been an illusion
On the thirty-first of February the last fight must be fough
and won before he could rest.

How many seconds, how many minutes, how many hour:
were used up while he switched off the light at the door
moved silently to the door of the bedroom, and then with on
decisive gesture flung it back. The darkness within was almos
complete, but still his eyes recognized, deceptively motionles
upon the bed, the faithless woman he had married. This, then
was the struggle for which the events of these last days ha
prepared him; and shouting like a battle cry, *The Thirty-firs
of February*, he flung himself upon the bed.

But this woman was a hundred times more cunning an
skilful than the one in the street. She slipped into his clutche
and out again; is was impossible to get a grip on her; sh
fought silently and at times invisibly. His throat was con
stricted and, gasping, he pulled at the invisible hands, breakin,
their grip, tearing at collar and tie as he rolled to the floo
The Thirty-first of February, he cried again and, strugglin
wildly with her, felt his face cut by pieces of glass, the bloo
running down it warmly. He kicked out, but she brough
down something heavy which struck him in the stomach. H

moved his head, and something else was shattered just where his head had been. He brushed a hand across his eyes and pursued her again, unable to see clearly where she was, blundering round the room, catching and losing her.

The light came on, and he stood still. If she had brought in reinforcements there was little hope. Panting, he turned slowly to face the door. There, solid as a bowler-hatted bulldog, with legs apart and face graven into sad lines, stood her chief ally, and behind him faces that he had known in a past life, the woman at the door, a young fresh face that was unrecognizable, men in blue. Would they be too much for him? It was with the consciousness of defeat that he cried for the third time *The Thirty-first of February*, and was among them, fighting with the strength of virtue, knocking off the bulldog's—2017—The Thirty-first of February—Fifty-three—BJ—198 hat and getting the snarling beast down to the floor, squeezing the corded throat. Then he felt a dull pain in his head, spreading all over it, his hands became strengthless, he slipped down, down, down into defeat, into permanent and shameful defeat.

The two men walked up the gravel drive toward the large grey building. They walked in step, without speaking. Neither of them noticed the brightness of the blue sky, or the geometrically neat gardens on either side. At the door of the building the younger of the two, a fair-haired inconspicuous figure in a brown suit, paused and said: "What are you trying to prove?"

His companion was taller and bulkier, and—looked even larger than he was because on this April day he wore a thick, dark overcoat. He lifted his bowler hat, wiped his forehead, replaced the hat and said, "What?"

"What are you trying to prove? Isn't it enough for you to have driven an innocent man mad?"

"*Innocent*," the other said with a bursting, incredulous impatience. "You think like the Commissioner. I've been asked to resign." He sneered. "My handling of the case is not approved. Unorthodox methods."

"That's a polite name for burgling a suspect's flat and frightening him out of his wits."

The other turned on him savagely. "I suppose you think the responsibility worries me, do you? You were careful not to say anything at the time."

"I carried out your orders. But I haven't hated a job more than the one of harrying that poor wretch since I became a policeman ten years ago." Greatorex added with deceptive mildness: "It's the first time I've ever driven an innocent man mad, you see. You're used to it."

"What do you mean?"

"You like to watch them squirm, Cresse. You like to pull off their wings and see them crawl over the table under your omniscient eye. You're a sadist." The big man made a noise. "What about Mrs. Lowson, that woman who strangled her baby because she thought it was growing up to be a mental defective? She committed suicide after some friendly chats with you. What about Makepeace, that forger who'd gone straight for years until you picked him up. You framed him, didn't you?"

Cresse said violently: " He was a criminal. Habitual. Filth. Scum."

" A sadist, Cresse, you're a sadist. You like to play God."

" A policeman," Inspector Cresse said, " is God—or God's earthly substitute." The strong shape of his body was firmly outlined against the grey building. " Justice should be intelligent. If we are obstructed by the forms of legality in reaching the ends of justice, the forms of legality must be ignored." His flat white face was eager, his voice persuasive. " And what did we do that would distress an innocent man? A few hints were dropped here and there. We telephoned Sir Malcolm Buntz and arranged that you should be installed in the firm as his nephew. Nobody else was told. You changed the date on his calendar. His flat was searched. What was there in that to upset an innocent man?"

" The letter," Greatorex said. He seemed during this recital to have shrunk inside his suit, and in spite of the warmth of the day he was almost shivering.

" The letter," said the Inspector blandly. " A tribute to your skill as an amateur forger, although of course it would never have deceived a handwriting expert. And, after all, what was the effect of the letter?"

Still shrinking inside his brown suit, Greatorex said: " It helped to send him off his head."

" Not at all. At the most it tipped the scale for a man who was obviously guilty. But take it for a moment that you're right. What was there in the letter to frighten an innocent man? Why didn't he tell me he was being persecuted? Why didn't he say his journal had been stolen? Because he was afraid of the truth. My God, man," Cresse said with the first approach he had shown to loss of self-control, " even the Commissioner didn't dare to suggest outright that he was innocent. He didn't deny that my methods worked. He simply said that he couldn't possibly approve of them, and that he'd warned me before, etcetera, etcetera." The graven lines were deep on the Inspector's face as he looked up at the sky. "They don't want people who get results."

Almost sulkily, Greatorex repeated: "He was innocent. I believe he was innocent."

"*You're* innocent," the Inspector sneered. He ticked off points on his fingers. "Think of the case against him. One, the money. Five thousand pounds is not to be sneezed at when you're slipping in your job. Two, he hated his wife. You remember that journal? 'I can't see why I didn't push her down the stairs long ago.' Do you want anything clearer than that?"

"That doesn't prove anything. It's the kind of thing any man might write who didn't get on with his wife."

"Didn't get on with his wife," Cresse echoed mockingly. "And he'd been playing around with Elaine Fletchley."

"She denied it."

"What would you expect her to do—give it to us on a plate? He blew a fuse on that cellar staircase deliberatly. Or how was it that Fletchley a few minutes earlier found the light still working? Then he hit his wife on the head and fractured her skull, she fell down the stairs and broke her neck."

"You don't know that Fletchley told the truth."

"Why should he lie? And what about the matches? What can you say about the matches?" The man in the brown suit said nothing about the matches. "Where did those matches come from that lay by her body? She left the kitchen to go to the cellar—Anderson said she had no matches in her hand. She had no pockets in her dress. She walked along a passage where there was no ledge on which matches could have rested. She switched on the cellar light and found it didn't work. She started down the stairs—where could she have got hold of the matches? There's only one explanation for them being by her body. Anderson put them there after he'd killed her. What other explanation can you offer, can anyone offer?"

"I don't know," the other said. "Perhaps she was holding a box of matches in her hand and he didn't notice them. Perhaps someone had left a box at the head of the cellar stairs." He said weakly: "Funny things happen."

"But not as funny as that." The Inspector chuckled softly.

The sound was not pleasant. "We scared him, didn't we, with our letters and the little tricks we played, the calendar and the messages. It was fun."

"And events helped us—if you can call it helping," the younger man said. "All the trouble at the office—the mess he got into over Kiddy Modes, Reverton trying to get rid of him, the Hey Presto business." He shuddered. "I shall never forget his face that night all puffed and red with that poisonous stuff, and bloody where he'd cut himself fighting with a ghost."

"And by the way," the Inspector said, still moved by his internal amusement, "I understand they're not putting that stuff on the market. It's back in the experimental stage. One person in ten had a skin allergic to it." There was a silence. "No use hanging about any longer." He turned to in. Greatorex caught his arm.

"I can't go in there."

The Inspector turned to look at him. "Don't be a fool."

"What do you expect to prove?" Greatorex repeated insistently. "What do you expect him to tell you?"

"If he's able to recognize me," the Inspector said slowly, "if this madness of his isn't all a stunt—if I can get a written confession to put before the Commissioner—*then* we'll see what he has to say about orthodox methods and resignation."

"I don't want to see it," Greatorex said. He shuddered. "I don't want to see you with him."

The Inspector stared at him. Then he began to laugh. The laughter grew until it filled his whole hard body, until he took off his hard hat and revealed the great shining bald head. Between gusts of laughter he said: "You know, Greatorex, I'm not sure you shouldn't be in this place." He was still laughing when he entered the grey building.

Inside the asylum he was received deferentially, but perhaps a little ambiguously. "You must be prepared for a change in him," the doctor said. "He has grown a beard. He has a horror of shaving."

"I've seen worse things than a man with a beard," the Inspector said. "Can he talk sensibly?"

"That depends," said the doctor. He had a fresh face and a shock of white hair. "What do you want to talk about?"

" I want to ask a few questions about the murder of his wife. Can it do any harm to discuss it?"

" I don't think," the doctor said, " that anything can do him harm."

" You mean he's incurably mad."

" That's hardly a clinical way of putting it," the doctor murmured. " But he will certainly never stand trial, if you have that in mind. Shall we go?" The Inspector nodded and the doctor pressed the bell. To the burly white-coated man who came in he said: " How is Anderson?"

" Quiet. He's writing."

" Writing," the Inspector said. " That may be important."

" We shall see," the doctor said.

Inspector Cresse was not an impressionable man, but he felt a little strange when the door of the room was opened and he saw what appeared to be a complete stranger bent at a table, writing. " Is this——"

" This is Anderson," the doctor said. " Here is a visitor for you, Anderson."

The man at the table hurriedly closed the book in which he had been writing and pushed it into a drawer of the table. Then he looked at his visitors. The lower part of his face was hidden by a straggling beard of a dull brown colour, but the features themselves had changed curiously in shape and texture. The whole face was fatter and somehow blunted, and had lost its look of intelligence. The eyes, which had in the Inspector's memory looked watchful and hunted, were now like dull buttons.

" Well, Mr. Anderson," the Inspector said, " so we meet again. You remember me, don't you?" He held out his hand, but Anderson did not take it.

" Certainly I remember you. Your name is Rex."

" Cresse."

" Rex Imperator, son of the Almighty." Anderson stood up and made a mocking bow. " Where is your companion?"

" My companion?"

" The greater Rex, your drinking friend, advertising manager to God. An amiable youngster, but deceitful. He told me God fathered him on Sir Malcolm Buntz."

188

The Inspector said to the doctor: "Are you sure this isn't all put on? I believe he knows quite well who I am."

"We shall see," the doctor said. "What have you been writing, Anderson?"

The blunt features twisted into an unpleasant expression of cunning. Anderson shook his head.

"About *her*?"

Anderson nodded.

"May we see it?"

With a look of alarm Anderson shook his head again.

"Let us see it, Anderson," the doctor said pleasantly. "I will keep her away." He said to the Inspector: "He thinks his wife comes to torment him, and that writing in the book is the only thing that stops her."

"You can't keep her away," Anderson said. He took the book out of the drawer, and held it close to him.

"I shall put a spell on her."

"She knows all your spells," Anderson said. "She came last night, tearing and scratching. She knew the date."

"What date?" The doctor glanced at the Inspector.

"The thirty-first of February," Anderson said. He began to cry out in a high voice, over and over again: "The thirty-first of February, the thirty-first of February." He stood up in the middle of the room and flapped his arms like wings. "Here she is," he screamed. The book dropped to the ground. The doctor picked it up.

The room was square, with no furniture in it except the table and a bed, both bolted to the ground. Anderson ran from side to side of the room, holding his hands to his head, uttering shrill unintelligible noises, like an animal in pain. He blundered into the three men standing there as if they were statues. Then, still with those inhuman cries coming from his mouth, he began to knock his head against the wall. The man in the white coat locked Anderson's arms behind his back and threw him on the bed. There he lay quietly, with his face turned away from them.

The doctor opened the book. Each page was covered with thousands of fine lines of incoherent scribbling written across, up, and down the page. A few disconnected words could be

189

made out in various pages: *London, God, wife, scheme.* The doctor looked at the Inspector. The Inspector shrugged his shoulders.

Outside in the April sunlight Greatorex was waiting. The Inspector said nothing, but clapped his bowler hat on his head.

"What happened?"

"Nothing happened. He's mad."

"He made no confession."

"No."

"Then we shall never know," Greatorex said. "We shall never know whether he was guilty."

"He was guilty," the Inspector said. "But he is mad. There will be no confession."

"Your resignation stands?"

"My resignation stands," the Inspector said. He took out a pipe, looked at it, filled it, and felt in his pockets. "I thought I had a box of matches, but I must have left it——"

Greatorex said in an odd voice: "There's a box by your feet."

For a moment the Inspector looked almost disturbed. Then his face cleared. "There is a hole in my pocket. They must have dropped through it."

"A hole in your pocket."

Very slowly the Inspector bent and picked up the matches, struck one and lighted his pipe. "A hole in my pocket," he said. "And what of it?"

Smoke rose from the Inspector's pipe. The two men stood looking at each other.

THE END

190

FINE MYSTERY AND SUSPENSE
TITLES FROM CARROLL & GRAF

- [ ] Brand, Christianna/FOG OF DOUBT $3.50
- [ ] Browne, Howard/THIN AIR $3.50
- [ ] Browne, Howard/THIN AIR $3.50
- [ ] Boucher, Anthony/THE CASE OF THE BAKER STREET IRREGULARS $3.95
- [ ] Boucher, Anthony (ed.)/FOUR AND TWENTY BLOODHOUNDS $3.95
- [ ] Buell, John/THE SHREWSDALE EXIT $3.50
- [ ] Burnett, W.R./LITTLE CAESAR $3.50
- [ ] Carr, John Dickson/THE EMPEROR'S SNUFF-BOX $3.50
- [ ] Carr, John Dickson/THE BRIDE OF NEWGATE $3.95
- [ ] Carr, John Dickson/LOST GALLOWS $3.50
- [ ] Carr, John Dickson/NINE WRONG ANSWERS $3.50
- [ ] Chesterton, G.K./THE MAN WHO WAS THURSDAY $3.50
- [ ] Crofts, Freeman Wills/THE CASK $3.95
- [ ] Coles, Manning/NIGHT TRAIN TO PARIS $3.50
- [ ] Coles, Manning/NO ENTRY $3.50
- [ ] Dewey, Thomas B./THE BRAVE, BAD GIRLS $3.50
- [ ] Dewey, Thomas B./DEADLINE $3.50
- [ ] Dewey, Thomas B./THE MEAN STREETS $3.50
- [ ] Dickson, Carter/THE CURSE OF THE BRONZE LAMP $3.50
- [ ] Douglass, Donald M./REBECCA'S PRIDE $3.50
- [ ] Fennelly, Tony/THE GLORY HOLE MURDERS   Cloth $14.95
- [ ] Freeman, R. Austin/THE RED THUMB MARK $3.50
- [ ] Hughes, Dorothy/IN A LONELY PLACE $3.50
- [ ] Innes, Hammond/ATLANTIC FURY $3.50
- [ ] Innes, Hammond/THE LAND GOD GAVE TO CAIN $3.50

- [ ] Innes, Hammond/THE WRECK OF THE MARY DEARE $3.50
- [ ] L'Amour, Louis/THE HILLS OF HOMOCIDE 2.95
- [ ] Leroux, Gaston/THE PHANTOM OF THE OPERA $3.95
- [ ] Lewis, Norman/THE MAN IN THE MIDDLE $3.50
- [ ] MacDonald, John D./TWO $2.50
- [ ] MacDonald, Philip/THE RASP $3.50
- [ ] Mason, A.E.W./AT THE VILLA ROSE $3.50
- [ ] Mason, A.E.W./THE HOUSE IN LORDSHIP LANE $3.50
- [ ] Mason, A.E.W./THE HOUSE OF THE ARROW $3.50
- [ ] Miller, Geoffrey/THE BLACK GLOVE $3.50
- [ ] Priestley, J.B./SALT IS LEAVING $3.50
- [ ] Rinehart, Mary Rogers/THE CIRCULAR STAIRCASE $3.50
- [ ] Rogers, Joel T./THE RED RIGHT HAND $3.50
- [ ] Royce, Kenneth/CHANNEL ASSAULT $3.50
- [ ] Royce, Kenneth/THE THIRD ARM $3.50
- [ ] Siodmak, Curt/DONOVAN'S BRAIN $3.50
- [ ] Woolrich, Cornell/BLIND DATE WITH DEATH $3.50
- [ ] Woolrich, Cornell/VAMPIRE'S HONEYMOON $3.50

Available from fine bookstores everywhere or use this coupon for ordering:

Caroll & Graf Publishers, Inc., 260 Fifth Avenue, N.Y., N.Y. 10001

Please send me the books I have checked above. I am enclosing $_____ (please add 1.75 per title to cover postage and handling.) Send check or money order— no cash or C.O.D.'s please. N.Y. residents please add 8¼% sales tax.

Mr/Mrs/Miss _____

Address _____

City _____ State/Zip _____

Please allow four to six weeks for delivery.